JANICE PRESTON

—

The Cinderella Heiress

HARLEQUIN®
HISTORICAL™

PLEASE RECYCLE

THIS PRODUCT IS RECYCLABLE

Recycling programs
for this product may
not exist in your area.

ISBN-13: 978-1-335-50626-9

The Cinderella Heiress

Janice Preston grew up in Wembley, North London, with a love of reading, writing stories and animals. In the past she has worked as a farmer, a police call handler and a university administrator. She now lives in the West Midlands with her husband and two cats and has a part-time job with a weight-management counselor—vainly trying to control her own weight despite her love of chocolate!

Visit the Author Profile page
at Harlequin.com for more titles.

To Dad

Reunited with Mum

Rest in peace together

Chapter One

January 1816

Miss Beatrice Fothergill sucked in a long, silent breath as she eased open the front door and slipped outside. She held that breath as she quietly closed the door behind her. It released as a white plume as she hurried down the driveway, away from Pilcombe Grange, dreading the entire time a shout that would summon her back. For she knew she would obey that summons, despite her desperation to discover the meaning of the letter she had received two days ago from Messrs Henshaw and Dent, solicitors, of Bristol. She would have no choice but to return, because the hint in that letter of something that would change her life might be nothing more than a cruel joke, and if she burned her bridges with her half-brother, Percy—and with his wife, Fenella, who frequently threatened to turn Beatrice out—what *would* she have? Where would she go? As Percy and Fenella never hesitated to remind her, on a daily basis, she was utterly dependent upon them for the roof over her head and the food she ate.

But the letter… She cradled the hope that letter had sparked deep inside her as she reached the road, where the stone pillars that marked the entrance to the Grange would hide her from view. Her hope was for a miracle. For something...*anything*...that would change her life.

It had been sheer luck she had met the postman as he delivered the post on Monday while she walked Fenella's obnoxious, pampered pug, Gertrude, around the garden in the rain. And there, among the letters for Percy, had been one addressed to Miss Beatrice Fothergill. For her to receive a letter was unheard of, for she knew no one who would write to her. No one at all, in the entire world. She had hidden it under her cloak and then, shaking with excitement—and with nerves, lest she was caught—had opened it in the privacy of her bedchamber.

The letter had been from Mr Arthur Henshaw, solicitor, and it had summoned her—for it was more of an order than a request—to his office in Bristol for a meeting at noon on Wednesday the thirty-first of January 1816, when she would learn something to her advantage. A post-chaise would be sent, at no expense to herself, to collect her from Pilcombe Grange at ten o'clock. It would convey her both to the meeting and home again afterwards. And, Mr Henshaw had written, should Miss Fothergill choose *not* to attend the meeting, then she would miss out on the opportunity of a lifetime.

Beatrice had resolved there and then that neither Percy nor Fenella should know about that meeting because she knew Percy would insist upon accompanying her and her instinct was to keep this to herself, because he would somehow contrive to spoil things for her.

Beatrice peered anxiously along the road, praying the post-chaise would be on time and Fenella would not notice she was gone before she was safely on her way. She would doubtless pay the price for disappearing without a word, even though she had left a note in her bedchamber promising to be home before darkness fell, but that price would be worth it, for this one adventure. The idea of an adventure made her laugh. Her! Beatrice Fothergill—the least adventurous person in the world—eager for an adventure. But, since Father had died five years ago, and Percy had inherited the baronetcy and the Grange and *she* had been left with nothing but Percy's charity to rely upon, Beatrice had—ever more frequently—looked ahead at the life that stretched before her and she had seen a future of nothing but drudgery and loneliness.

She peered along the road as the thud of hooves and the rattle of wheels penetrated her thoughts. A bright yellow post-chaise, drawn by four horses controlled by two postilions, headed towards her at pace. She stepped away from the shelter of the pillar, and the vehicle slowed before halting next to her.

'Miss Fothergill?' The lead postilion touched his tall hat.

'Yes. I am Miss Fothergill.'

The postilion leapt down from his horse. He opened the chaise door, and Beatrice, her heart pitter-pattering, climbed inside.

'Two hours should be plenty of time to get you to Bristol for your appointment, miss.'

'Thank you.'

Beatrice sank back into the squabs as the post-chaise jerked into motion. She opened her reticule and withdrew the letter to read it for the umpteenth time.

The journey took longer than anticipated when the post-chaise was held up behind a heavily laden farm cart, its driver deaf to the postilions' yells and insults. The road was too narrow to overtake at first but, finally, they managed to pass the lumbering wagon—its driver waving cheerfully, grinning toothlessly, seemingly still oblivious to the curses hurled in his direction—and Beatrice found herself bouncing around as the team were urged faster to make up time.

They pulled up before a house in the middle of a terraced row of similar houses and the door was opened by the same postilion as before.

'Here you are, miss. All safe and sound, in the nick of time,' he said, grinning up at her.

He handed Beatrice down the steps. 'We've orders to pick you up in an hour, miss, so we'll see you then.'

'Thank you.'

Beatrice gazed at the building before her, her heart quailing as she realised she had accomplished the easy bit. What would she learn inside there? How would she know what to say…how to behave? Percy was right—she was stupid. Why did she ever think she could cope with something like this on her own?

The door in front of her opened, to reveal a young man with slicked-back brown hair and stooped shoulders. He stared at her, his eyebrows raised.

'I received a letter from Mr Henshaw. I have an appointment. I am Miss Fothergill.'

'Follow me, Miss Fothergill. Mr Henshaw is waiting for you.'

As Beatrice followed the man, presumably a clerk, up a steep, narrow flight of stairs, a clock somewhere above them chimed the hour and Beatrice counted as she climbed. Noon. At the top of the stairs, the clerk crossed the landing to a door and knocked.

'Enter.'

The clerk opened the door. 'Miss Fothergill, sir.' He stepped aside for Beatrice, who was quaking inside but desperately trying to hide it.

The brightness of Mr Henshaw's office reassured

Beatrice after the dinginess of the stairs and landing. Her gaze swept the room, taking in the bookshelves lining the walls and the massive mahogany desk with a high-backed chair on one side and three ordinary chairs lined up opposite. In the middle of those sat a woman dressed in a royal blue gown and a matching bonnet who did not even glance around when Mr Henshaw—a balding, middle-aged man with eyeglasses and pursed lips that gave him an air of disapproval—bowed to Beatrice and said, 'Thank you for attending this meeting, Miss Fothergill. Please, may I take your cloak?'

He hung it on a coat stand in the corner of his office. 'If you would care to take a seat, Miss Fothergill?'

He indicated the row of three chairs and Beatrice sat to the right of the woman in blue, shivering a little as she did so. A sidelong glance at the woman next to her revealed she was tall and slim, with an incongruous-looking smattering of freckles across her beautifully sculpted cheekbones and aristocratic nose. A strand or two of hair at her temple revealed hair of rich, fiery red. She did not as much as glance in Beatrice's direction and gave the impression of being the epitome of reserve and restraint. Beatrice said nothing, not quite daring to attract her attention in case... Her thoughts stuttered to a halt and shame curled through her as she understood she did not dare in case the other woman became angry with her.

Is that really what I have become? So unsure of myself that I dare not say boo to a goose?

She smiled then at the mental image that popped into her mind—a white goose seated next to her and dressed in a blue velvet gown and bonnet, but she soon bit back that smile. She would be mortified if the other woman thought she was laughing at her. To divert her thoughts, she scanned the surface of the desk, hoping for some clue as to why she had been summoned, but it was bare apart from a pile of documents, an inkstand and a wax jack.

Mr Henshaw made no attempt to introduce the two women but remained behind the chairs, out of sight. The silence—unbroken apart from the tick of a clock on the mantelshelf and the occasional sigh and an impatient tap of his foot from Mr Henshaw—did nothing to reassure Beatrice. She nibbled her lower lip, her thoughts turning to what Percy would say when she got home. What punishment would he deem fitting for what he would label disobedience on her part? Her vision blurred as she stared down at her hands, twisting together in her lap. She wished someone would say something to break the tension and, more importantly, to keep her thoughts from her horrid brother and his even more horrid wife.

A knock at the door made her jump.

'Miss Croome, sir.'

Beatrice couldn't help herself. She twisted to look over her shoulder at the newcomer as Mr Henshaw relieved her of her coat and told her to sit down.

The poor thing. That was her instant reaction as she took in Miss Croome's general air of poverty—a shabby dove-grey gown that hung on her frame and that particular large-eyed, hollow-cheeked, dull-skinned appearance of the hungry. She was pretty, though, despite her gaunt appearance. Then she shot a look at Beatrice, who felt an immediate jolt of energy run through her. She whipped her head back around to face the front, feeling herself grow red. Did she know Miss Croome? Had they met before? She seemed familiar somehow but, more than that, it felt as though the room had suddenly come to life with the newcomer's arrival. The lady in blue, she noticed, did not as much as glance at Miss Croome, even as she sat in the third chair.

Mr Henshaw returned to his chair. 'Allow me to make the introductions,' he said. 'Miss Aurelia Croome.'

Beatrice leaned forward to smile a greeting. Miss Croome's hair was hidden under her chip straw bonnet, but the eyebrows that framed her blue eyes—those eyes that so reminded Beatrice of...who? She still could not place her—were fair, suggesting her hair would also be fair.

'Miss Leah Thame.' Mr Henshaw indicated the woman in the middle, who acknowledged the other two with a cool nod.

'And Miss Beatrice Fothergill.'

Beatrice felt her cheeks glow, but she managed a smile. Miss Croome frowned for an instant as their eyes met, but soon turned her attention to Mr Henshaw, staring at him with a look of irritation.

'Well. This is quite unprecedented.'

Beatrice waited for the solicitor to elaborate, but he removed his spectacles to stare at each woman in turn before removing a handkerchief from his pocket and wiping his brow. Very slowly, it seemed, he replaced his handkerchief.

'Yes. *Quite* unprecedented, not to mention perplexing. You ladies must appreciate it has given me a real dilemma as to how best to proceed.'

His expression turned even more disapproving.

'Perhaps if you enlightened us as to the purpose of this meeting, Mr Henshaw, we might shed some light on your...er...dilemma,' said Miss Croome.

Her speech was more refined than Beatrice had expected.

'Yes. Well...' This time the pause was to allow Mr Henshaw to polish his eyeglasses—again, moving with frustrating slowness—with that same handkerchief. 'Yes... the terms of the will are quite clear, of course. I just...

I simply…' Again he paused, his high forehead wrinkling in puzzlement. 'Lord Tregowan—the *current* Lord Tregowan—will be unhappy, you may be sure of that. I have written to him again, to clarify matters. Bad tidings for him, but *I* did not draw up *this* will, you understand. I thought I had her latest will and testament—drawn up by me and signed and witnessed three years ago in this very office.'

Tregowan? Mama had been companion to Lady Tregowan, before she married Father—and, of course, before Beatrice had been born. But…a will? Could it be that Lady Tregowan had remembered Mama? But Mama had died ten years ago, when Beatrice was twelve. How did that explain why Beatrice had been summoned? But that hope for a miracle still glimmered deep inside… What if *this* was the miracle she had been praying for?

'This…' The solicitor picked up a document, dangling it by its corner as though it were distasteful. '*This* arrived last week. And yet I cannot refute its authenticity. I'd recognise Her Ladyship's signature anywhere and it is witnessed by the partners of a legal firm in Bath, although quite why she went to them I have no notion. No. I am afraid it is authentic. There can be no doubt of it.'

The lady in blue… Miss Thame…straightened, her chin lifting. '*Mr* Henshaw. *If* you would be good enough to proceed…?'

'Patience, Miss Thame. Patience.'

Beatrice could almost feel the other woman's indignation as the solicitor eyed her patronisingly.

'The three of us have been sitting in this office for twelve minutes now,' Miss Thame continued, enunciating very precisely, 'and, in my case, considerably longer, and all we have learned is that the reason for this meeting—which *you* arranged, requiring the presence, I presume, of all three of us—meets with your disapproval. I have taken leave from my post to attend here today and I should appreciate your expedition of the matter in order that I may return to my duties as soon as possible.'

Inside, Beatrice cheered Miss Thame for her courage in speaking so to the solicitor.

'*Miss* Thame—'

But Miss Croome interrupted as he began to remonstrate with Miss Thame.

'You spoke of a will, Mr Henshaw?'

The solicitor settled back in his chair. 'Indeed, Miss Croome. The will of Lady Tregowan, late of Falconfield Hall, near Keynsham in the County of Somersetshire.'

Silence reigned in the office. Beatrice leaned forward to glance at the two other women. They looked like she felt—utterly dumbfounded. Both of them had spoken out and she forced herself to find her own courage and say *something*.

'My...my mother worked at Falconfield Hall. She was companion to Lady Tregowan. Before I was born.'

'Quite. Your mothers each had a connection with Falconfield. And with Lord Tregowan.' Mr Henshaw's expression was close to a sneer as his gaze travelled over the three women and Beatrice's courage fizzled away.

'*My* mother did not work there,' said Miss Thame. 'She and her parents were neighbours of the Earl and the Countess.'

Beatrice immediately felt chastened and wished she had neither spoken out nor confessed her mother's connection to the Tregowans and Falconfield Hall, even though she was aware Miss Thame was putting the solicitor in his place rather than belittling her contribution. But it was hard to dismiss years of being reminded by Percy that her mother had been a nobody.

Miss Croome spoke then. 'I know of no connection between my mother and Falconfield Hall,' she said, 'but Lady Tregowan did once visit my mother's milliner's shop in Bath.'

Beatrice felt better on hearing that Miss Croome's mother had been a milliner. And, come to think of it, Miss Thame had spoken of her post, so she was really no better than either Beatrice or Miss Croome.

Mr Henshaw checked the will. '"Miss Aurelia Croome, born October the fourth 1792 to Mr Augustus Croome and Mrs Amelia Croome"?'

'Yes.'

'Then there is no mistake. I am convinced it is the three of you who are to benefit from Her Ladyship's largesse.'

Excitement stirred. Benefit? Largesse? Could this indeed be the answer to Beatrice's prayers?

'What is the connection between the three of us?' Miss Thame asked. 'It is clearly through our mothers, but how?'

Henshaw appeared to sneer.

'The connection is not through your mother, but through your sire. You are half-sisters.'

Beatrice gasped but, before she more than half-grasped what he had said, Miss Thame blurted out, 'But…that is not possible. Papa…he would never… He was a man of the Church! He would *never*…' Her voice drifted into silence as Mr Henshaw pursed his mouth. Then Beatrice heard her inhale sharply. 'My father,' she said, haughtily, 'would *never* have played my mother false.'

'Well, I would believe almost anything of *my* father.' Miss Croome's blue eyes bored into the solicitor, before flicking a sideways look at Miss Thame. 'And, as for yours, I believe what Mr Henshaw is implying is that

Lord Tregowan fathered each of us—presumably, in your case, before your mother married Mr Thame.'

Her words seemed to jumble inside Beatrice's brain. She heard them all, but she couldn't make sense…couldn't work out what it meant for her… Did it mean Father was not her father? Her head swam and she closed her eyes to stop the sensation that the room was in motion, gripping her hands together on her lap. She could feel the familiar, unwelcome quiver of her legs beneath her gown and she concentrated on taking deep, even breaths.

'That is correct.' Henshaw's voice appeared to come from a distance away. 'It was Lord Tregowan who arranged the marriage of each of your parents, once your mothers'…er…*conditions* were made known to him. And, from what I gather, each marriage was to a gentleman in need of funds and none of your mothers suffered a lowering in their status after their indecorous behaviour.'

Mama was already with child—carrying me—when she wed Father? Lord Tregowan was my father? I am illegitimate? Beatrice's stomach tangled hopelessly into knots as the implications swirled inside her head. *Does this mean Percy is not my brother? Not even my* half-*brother?*

'This…' She sucked in a deep breath, trying in vain to control the wobble in her voice. 'If this is true, it changes everything. I do not know what I shall do.'

Mr Henshaw sent Beatrice a withering look, causing her to shrink back in her seat even as the full implication of his words still battered her. *Percy is* not *my brother.* Resentment bit through her confusion and that fact resounded in her head, bringing a surge of joy in its wake, for—if this were true—then Miss Thame and Miss Croome were her half-sisters! She had family…someone other than Percy and Fenella. And her miracle had already happened.

'You mentioned the *current* Lord Tregowan earlier.' Beatrice tried to quash her own conjectures in order to concentrate on what Miss Croome was saying. 'Does that mean our father is dead?'

'He died eight years ago and the title and the Tregowan estates—which were entailed—passed to his heir. Falconfield and the London house were brought to the marriage by Lady Tregowan and he left them to her. He'd fallen out with the current Lord Tregowan's father years before and so refused to leave his heir any more property than he was forced to under the entail.'

'Have you proof of this?' asked Miss Thame. Leah. Beatrice's *sister*! Joy continued to bubble inside her.

'I have had copies made of Her Ladyship's will, which you may take with you when you leave,' Henshaw said. 'It confirms your paternity.'

'Would you kindly get to the point swiftly, Mr Henshaw?'' said Miss Croome. *Aurelia.* Such a pretty name. 'Clearly you are unhappy, and I, for one, will be pleased to leave this fusty old office behind. You mentioned bequests, so please say why you have summoned us and be done.'

Mr Henshaw glared at her. 'Very well. Lady Tregowan of Falconfield Hall has passed away and it is my duty to advise you that she left the three of you her entire estate, to be divided equally between you subject to certain conditions.'

Beatrice quivered with excitement and anticipation. *I've inherited something? Will it be enough to break away from Percy?*

'How much is it worth?' Aurelia asked.

'It is substantial. It comprises Falconfield Hall and its land, which, as I said, is near to the village of Keynsham on the Bath Road, plus a town house in London, and various funds, the income from which, in the past year, amounted to over fifteen thousand pounds. You are now three very wealthy young ladies.'

Chapter Two

Wealthy?

Beatrice gasped, feeling herself sway. *No! Please! Not here. Not now.* She put her hand to her brow, then felt a bottle pushed into her other hand. She smiled her thanks at Leah—her *half-sister*—before raising the bottle and sniffing the contents. The pungent smell of the *sal volatile* made her cough, but it had the usual effect of clearing her head—why had she not thought of her own bottle of smelling salts, which was in her reticule? Percy's voice crawled into her head.

'You are pathetic. You should be thankful you have me and Fenella to look after you. You would never manage without us.'

She shoved him from her thoughts and handed back the smelling salts, smiling shyly at Leah, who tucked the bottle back inside her reticule before continuing to quiz Mr Henshaw.

'You mentioned conditions?'

Beatrice reined in her imagination hard. It was more important to understand what they—she and her half-sisters—were being told.

'Ah. Yes. They are quite straightforward. For a full

twelve months from today, the three of you will have the joint use of the two properties and your living expenses will be met out of the income from the funds as mentioned. After that year, providing you have met the further conditions of the will, you will inherit your share of Her Ladyship's estate outright.'

'What further conditions?' Aurelia demanded.

'I am getting to that, Miss Croome. The conditions specified in the will are that you will reside in London for the entirety of the coming Season and you will remain under the chaperonage of Mrs Butterby, who was Lady Tregowan's live-in companion, until you marry. After the Season ends you will have the choice of whether to reside in London or at Falconfield Hall, but you must each of you marry within the year.'

'*Marry?* Why?'

Aurelia sounded unhappy, but Beatrice was thrilled. Marriage! The chance to have her own little family!

'As Lady Tregowan failed to consult me in drawing up this final will, I am not privy to her reasoning,' Henshaw snapped. 'I dare say Mrs Butterby will be able to enlighten you.'

It is us against him. We are linked together now, for all time. Family. A team. Friends. At least, I hope we will be.

Beatrice looked across at Leah and at Aurelia. They were looking back at her and at each other, and a happy glow warmed her, right through from the depths of her belly to the tips of her fingers and her toes. Yes. She was right. She could see that same hope she felt reflected in the others' eyes. She had been alone for such a long time... since Mama died, really. Father had only cared about her in terms of what comfort she could provide for him as his health slowly failed and Percy and Fenella did not care for her at all.

'And if we do not marry within the year?' asked Leah.

'If you fail to wed, Miss Thame, you will forfeit the major portion of your share of the inheritance, which will then be divided between the other two sisters. You will be required to return any purchases made during the twelve-month period, other than purely personal items such as clothing. So, jewellery, for instance, or carriages, or even houses, will be forfeit. A cottage on the Falconfield estate will be provided for you to live in and you will receive a lifetime annual allowance of two hundred pounds so you are not left entirely destitute. Plus, there are two final stipulations. If any of you wish to sell your share of Falconfield Hall, the others—or, strictly, their husbands—will get first refusal. And, finally, you must not marry your father's—that is, the late Lord Tregowan's—successor, the current Lord Tregowan, who is a distant cousin.'

'Why?' Leah asked, frowning.

'As I said, Lady Tregowan sought neither my services nor my advice.'

Silence reigned in the room and Beatrice's thoughts again turned inward as she contemplated the idea of marriage—something she had all but given up on when she never met anybody other than their nearest neighbours. She would not expect love—how could any sensible gentleman love a stupid fool like her?—but her inheritance would surely make her more eligible, and a marriage of convenience to a kind gentleman must be her goal. If she remained single, although she would have some money and somewhere to call home, she couldn't help but fear that would somehow leave her under Percy's control. It was all very well feeling excited and relieved, and blessed that she had two half-sisters she had not known existed when she awoke that morning, but they were still females and relatively powerless in this man's world. If she were to marry, though… Percy would have no say in her life ever again. That vision of a Percy-and-Fenella-free future elated her, and her spirit—that part of her that had been bruised and battered into submission by Father and then by Percy—began to unfurl. She had little idea of how rich she would be—the men had always taken care of such matters—but it sounded a great deal of money. Mr Henshaw had *said* she would be wealthy, and he must know.

Mr Henshaw coughed, then handed a document to each woman. 'As I said, I have had copies made of the will—' he extracted three small leather pouches from his desk drawer '—and here is a purse of money for each of you, to offset any interim expenses before you arrive in London. You will no doubt need a little time to prepare for the change in your circumstances and to leave your old lives in good order, but I would urge you to allow time in London for your new wardrobes to be made before the Season proper begins after Eastertide.'

Beatrice carefully put both the document and the purse of money in her reticule, vowing to take extra special care of them because, to her, they spelled freedom from the toil and drudgery of her life.

'All I require is your signatures to this declaration, confirming that you have been advised as to the contents of the will and the conditions attached to your inheritance, and then you may leave,' Henshaw said.

Beatrice dared not make eye contact with either of her half-sisters as she signed the declaration, her hand trembling slightly at the enormity of this change to her life.

'Three post-chaises will be waiting outside to transport you home,' Henshaw continued. 'You must arrive at the London house—the address is in the will—at the very latest on the day after Easter Sunday, that is, by the fifteenth of April, or your share will be forfeit. Mrs Butterby is already in residence and preparations to accommodate you are under way. Do you have any questions before you leave?'

'I do.' Beatrice noticed Aurelia's distress and she fought the urge to take her hand and offer comfort, afraid of rejection. 'Might I...*may* I go to London immediately? Will I be allowed to live in the town house straight away?'

I could go, too. Just go with her. Now. Never return to Percy and Fenella.

'Yes, Miss Croome, you may.' Beatrice stared at the solicitor's unexpectedly sympathetic response as he drew a sheet of paper towards him and wrote on it. 'Here is a note for Mrs Butterby. Shall you need to return to Bath first?' Aurelia shook her head. 'Then I advise you to travel on the mail coach. It leaves the Bush Tavern on Corn Street at four every afternoon. It is not far from here. I shall send my clerk to purchase a ticket on your behalf and instruct him to dismiss your post-chaise.' He looked at Leah and Beatrice. 'Would either of you care to go immediately to London with Miss Croome?'

Here was her chance. She *could* do it...but...what about Spartacus? She could never abandon him and then there were Mama's mementoes... She must return for them or she would never get them back—Percy was vindictive enough to destroy them and he had threatened to kill Spartacus often enough for her to fear for her pet. So, rather than the *Yes* she longed to say, out of her mouth came the words, 'Oh, no! My brother... I will be expected home.'

'No, thank you,' said Leah.

Henshaw opened the door and spoke to someone before retrieving their outer garments from the coat stand in the corner.

'I shall bid you all good day now. Miss Croome, you

may wait downstairs in the general office until my clerk returns with your ticket.'

'Why would Lady Tregowan concern herself with us?' Leah asked, frowning.

Henshaw paused in the act of helping Aurelia with her coat. 'I know nothing more than I have told you, but I dare say Mrs Butterby will provide you with more detail. She was Her Ladyship's companion for the last twenty years or so. I suggest you ask her when you convene at the town house.'

Beatrice followed the other two women down the gloomy staircase and out into the chilly January afternoon. Two post-chaises waited at the kerb, each with a postilion stationed by its door, while a third post-chaise drove away.

Beatrice looked at the other two. Her sisters. And felt unaccountably shy.

'We cannot discuss this here on the pavement,' Aurelia said. 'But... I am happy to meet you both. I always wanted a sister.'

Her smile lit her face and, with a sudden jolt of recognition, Beatrice saw that her eyes were familiar because they so closely resembled her own, albeit they were a brighter blue than Beatrice's more greyish-blue hue.

'As have I,' said Leah.

'And I...' Beatrice swallowed down the emotion that threatened to overcome her '...and now I have two.'

'Well, I hope you will both join me in London very soon and we can get to know one another properly.'

'Ladies?' A postilion interrupted them. 'Transport for Miss Thame? We must be leaving, or we won't get back before dark.'

'Thank you. I will come now.' Leah smiled at Beatrice and Aurelia. 'If you wish to write to me, I live at Dolphin

Court, Westcliff, Somerset. I know where you will be, Aurelia. And you, Beatrice?'

Beatrice shrank back. 'Oh. I am not sure… That is…' Percy would find a way to stop her, to spoil this. He always did. 'My brother…he will disapprove. I *shall* come to London, though, no matter what he—' She bit back the rest of what she had been about to say. It was too long… too complicated…to explain now. 'I shall see you both then.' She scurried to the second post-chaise. 'Is this one for Miss Fothergill?'

The postilion—whom she now recognised—nodded and she stepped up into the vehicle.

'Can you make haste, please?' she begged, low-voiced, ashamed to reveal her pitiful lack of backbone to her new sisters. 'I must get home as soon as possible.'

Not that it would make any difference. Percy and Fenella would be livid whenever she arrived home, furious she had dared to go out at all. As the chaise pulled away from the kerb, she lowered the window, looked out at her two new half-sisters and felt that same warm glow of joy flood through her once more. She waved, and forced a smile even as she wondered how on earth she could hide the truth about what she'd learned today from Percy.

She shut the window of the post-chaise and leaned back against the squabs to ponder what she would say. Definitely not the truth, for Percy would simply take over, as he had done all her life—ordering her around, using the excuse that he was her older brother and therefore in control of her. Beatrice frowned. Did he know Mama had already been with child when their parents had wed? Probably not—he had been seven at the time of the marriage and was now thirty, to her two-and-twenty. Mama had once let slip that Father had only married her to provide a mother for Percy after his mother died giving birth to a second child, but she had never even hinted that Father was not Beatrice's real father.

Beatrice had few memories of her parents together. They had lived quite separate lives. Her parents—but Father wasn't her father, was he? All those years she had devoted to him as his health had failed…all those years believing it was her duty as a daughter to care for him, with rarely a kind word and never any thanks and, in the end, not even a penny left to her in his will, casting her on to Percy and Fenella's charity.

Resentment rumbled through her, scraping at her as she thought about her life till now, and how much she had sacrificed. She recalled Leah's anguish when she had understood that Lord Tregowan had fathered her, but Beatrice could only summon relief that Percy was not her brother. As to what she would tell him…well, she would tell him something close to the truth, but not everything. She would claim that an old friend of Mama's had died and had left Beatrice a small bequest in her will. Mayhap that would prevent him from discovering the whole.

Beatrice pulled open the drawstring of her reticule to extract the leather pouch Mr Henshaw had handed her, tipping the contents into her lap, and removed her gloves to count the coins. Twenty guineas! A fortune to someone like her. But Percy would take it given half the chance and then how would she get to London? She must hide the will, and most of the coins, and hope she could fool Percy. The will was simple enough—she took it from her reticule and tucked it down the front of her bodice. The coins, though. She held the empty pouch, undecided. Where could she hide them?

She started at a sudden shout from outside. The post-chaise swerved violently to one side and then the other, slowing and tilting. As Beatrice tumbled along the seat, she saw the bare brown twigs of a hedge nearing the window, and she ended up pressed hard against the now-steeply-slanted side of the vehicle as it finally halted. The clink and tap of the coins as they slid from her skirt to the floor distracted her from speculation as to what had happened—all that mattered was to retrieve her money, for that was her ticket to freedom.

The pouch was still in her hand as she levered herself away from the side of the chaise and dropped to her knees, propping one against the door and the other on the floor. The angle between floor and door was below her—it was here her coins had gathered, and she reached down to carefully pick them up, one by one, counting them into the pouch. She barely registered the jerk of the post-chaise, or that the door that was now above her head had been flung open, so intent was she on finding every last coin.

'What *are* you up to?'

Beatrice froze at the drawling, amused voice that sounded from behind and above her. She twisted her head to peer up at the now-open door and the figure silhouetted within its frame. She thought it was one of the postilions and opened her mouth to tell him it was none of his business. After all, was she not an heiress now? She did not have to take insults from anyone. But, before she spoke, she registered that the man was a stranger, dressed as a gentleman in greatcoat and beaver hat, and the words would not come.

'I am collecting my belongings.' Years of biting back what she longed to say had sapped her confidence, even when it came to rebuffing a stranger. 'What happened? Was there an accident?'

The stranger removed his hat before climbing awkwardly through the door. He slid down, his boots scraping on the sloping floor, until he was perched next to Beatrice.

She shrank back, feeling intimidated in such a cramped space with this strange man, but a glance at his face from beneath her lashes gave her some reassurance—he was younger than she'd first thought, with thick, ruffled dark blond hair, kind eyes and an easy smile that played at the corners of his mouth. And he smelled divine—of leather and horses and a hint of something spicy, with an underlying musky scent that stirred strange sensations deep inside her.

'Allow me to help.' His deep voice resonated around the stricken vehicle. 'Don't be afraid. My name is Jack. Jack King. What is yours?'

'Beatrice. Miss Beatrice Fothergill.'

Lord Jack Kingswood studied the woman crouched down in the stricken post-chaise in the light from the side and front windows. She reminded him of a mouse confronted by a cat, huddled down in her brown cloak and bonnet, those wide, smoky, blue-grey eyes dominating her pretty, heart-shaped face.

'I am pleased to meet you, Beatrice Fothergill, and, yes, in answer to your question, there was an accident, and your post-chaise ended up in the ditch.'

Jack quashed his natural male interest even before it stirred into being. He might still appreciate a pretty face, but that part of his life was over now. No woman would be interested in a damaged man like him. He focused on the situation instead, scanning the area beneath them.

'What were you searching for...? Ah!'

He propped his left elbow against the edge of the bench seat for stability, pulled his right glove off with his teeth and stuffed it into the pocket of his greatcoat before reaching down to retrieve the coin he had spied. A half-crown. The mouse twitched into action, her hand shooting out to his, and Jack felt his eyebrows climb. He passed the coin to her, trying not to take offence. Even if he *was* to steal her coin—which he would not—a woman who could afford the blunt for a post-chaise and four could surely afford the loss of one measly half-crown. Maybe if she knew his identity she would be less anxious, but he preferred to remain anonymous rather than have people treat him differently simply because he was the twin brother of the Marquess of Quantock. Mr Jack King passed unnoticed in a way Lord Jack Kingswood could not.

'I'm sorry,' she rushed to say, in a breathless voice. 'I did not mean… Please, I did not mean to be rude.'

Anxious eyes searched Jack's. He nodded. 'Apology accepted.'

An uneasy feeling stirred in his gut. He smelled trouble. She was clearly a gentlewoman. Why was she travelling alone in a hired post-chaise? He wrenched his gaze from hers and concentrated instead on searching for further errant coins. He had no desire to get involved in some random woman's troubles, whether or not she had a pretty face and smelled deliciously of lemons. He had enough on his plate, what with learning to live with the loss of his left forearm at Waterloo and with persuading his twin brother, Kit, that he was ready to lead his own life. Left to Kit, Jack would remain at Wheatlands, twiddling his one remaining thumb and being mollycoddled by Kit and the staff for the remainder of his days, under the pretext of helping his brother run the estates even though Kit employed a full-time steward for that purpose.

Jack dashed his own problems from his thoughts as he spied another coin. 'Here's another.' He picked it up, careful to hand it straight to the mouse. 'Is that all of them?'

'Yes. Thank you. I counted them into the purse. Twenty

guineas.' She showed him a small leather drawstring pouch.

Jack whistled. A considerable sum for a young lady to be carrying around, especially without any protection. Again, as his wayward mind speculated about her story, he tamped it down.

'Come, then. Allow me to help you out of here.Then we shall see what can be done about hauling the post-chaise from the ditch. These fellows on these yellow bounders always travel like the hounds of hell are on their heels, don't they? It's no wonder they came off the road.'

'Oh. But *I* asked them to hurry. It is my fault.'

'It is *not* your fault.' That came out a bit harshly. He softened his tone. 'They would have driven at breakneck speed anyway. They always do.'

Her eyes really were beautiful. But haunted. Again, Jack dragged his thoughts from speculation about Beatrice's secrets and on to her current predicament. He cupped her elbow to help her to rise.

'My gloves! They were on my lap.'

She began to sink down, bending her knees. Jack tightened his grip under her elbow to stop her.

'Allow me.' He crouched down to peer into the angle between the floor and the side wall of the post-chaise. 'Could they be right beneath you? I cannot see due to your shadow.'

'Let me…' Beatrice hitched her cloak and skirt up. 'Can you see better now?'

Jack's heart kicked as he inadvertently caught a glimpse of a shapely calf above her half-boot. He jerked his gaze down, to the floor.

'Ah…there they are.'

He scooped up a pair of pale grey kid gloves. As he straightened, her lemony scent filled him and the brush of his fingers against hers as he handed her the gloves sent a pulse of tingling energy up his arm, stirring his slumbering senses to life.

Chapter Three

Once again, Jack Kingswood thrust down his awakening but unwelcome awareness of Beatrice Fothergill as an attractive woman.

'Thank you. I am so sorry to be a nuisance.'

Her smile was shy, revealing two adorable dimples in her cheeks, but she avoided meeting his gaze as she pulled the gloves on to her small, dainty-fingered hands. He didn't want to make the comparison, but she reminded him of himself when he was a boy—the diffidence; the quickness to take the blame; the need to apologise; the fear of causing offence.

He had battled hard to leave that boy behind. Eight years in the army, fighting in the Peninsular Wars and, again, at Waterloo, had toughened him up and he had successfully discarded that shell he had grown to protect himself from his father—a harsh man around whom both his young sons had learned to tread carefully. Now, though, it was a different battle he was fighting. One in which he must accept the cards fate had dealt him and try, somehow, to regain that same spirit that had seen him defy Father to run away and join the army as a Gentleman Volunteer at the age of eighteen.

Jack forced his attention back to the practicalities of helping Beatrice out of the post-chaise. As if to mock him with the reminder of his loss, a sudden pain shot from his stump up his arm, causing a sharp intake of breath. He stilled and, sure enough, the pain subsided. If only he could predict when that agonising, stabbing pain might strike—as he could predict the maddening itch when he got overheated and the throbbing ache when the weather turned cold—but they appeared seemingly at random, no doubt part of the healing process, which the surgeon had warned him would still be going on inside even if the scar appeared healed.

The pain, though, reminded him to think carefully how to assist Beatrice rather than swing into action without a plan. He studied the interior and, in particular, the door above their heads.

'The tilt is not too acute,' he said. 'You should be able to clamber up to the door if I provide you with a foothold. The postilions will help you down the other side.'

He expected her to make a fuss. To claim she couldn't possibly manage. He expected her to play the helpless woman card and to demand he lift her up and out of the door. He braced himself to tell her why he could not, for he knew she hadn't yet noticed his missing arm. He still wasn't hardened to the typical swift second look, followed by the inevitable flash of sympathy when people first noticed it. Nor to the poorly masked distaste of some, especially some ladies. He silently breathed his relief that the inevitable moment of shock was postponed when Beatrice did not object to his plan. Instead, she simply gazed up at the door above them before assessing the inside of the post-chaise. She nodded her head, set her bonnet straight and placed her right foot on the sloping seat cushion of the bench seat. He could not deny a spark of admiration.

'Yes. If you can provide me with some sort of foothold, I think I can do it.'

She reached up to grasp the edges of the door frame and pulled herself up by pushing her foot against the edge of the cushion while Jack crouched down again and gripped the back of her heel to support her. Her other leg swung up and she wedged her left foot against the opposite seat cushion. Without thought, Jack glanced up, catching sight of a sweetly curving stockinged calf, a garter tied above her knee and the tantalising glimpse of glimmering pale skin as her inner thigh disappeared into the deep shadows beyond. He swallowed, and averting his eyes, he pushed his shoulder beneath her other foot, supporting her weight as she managed to hoist herself high enough to clamber out of the door. He heard the postilions assisting her down to the ground as he awkwardly heaved himself up and through the doorway—with much scrabbling of his boots against the cushions—before dropping down on to the road.

He took his time in brushing down his coat and his breeches—taking care to stand at an angle to shield his missing arm from view—partly to allow his natural male response to that enticing glimpse to subside and partly because he was curious to see if Miss Beatrice Fothergill would take charge of the situation or if she would stand back in the hope that Jack would assume control. She was silent for several minutes as she took in the tilt of the post-chaise, with its two offside wheels in the ditch, and eyed the team of four, who were standing quietly at the side of the road, still harnessed to the vehicle. He could almost see her gathering her courage to speak to the postilions.

'How did this happen?'

'A deer, miss. Ruddy huge, it was. Jumped out of the

woods and ran right into our path, it did. Had to swerve to miss it. Naught else we could do.'

'Oh. Of course…but…this is most unfortunate…' Beatrice cast an anxious look at the sky. 'I must get home, you see. Will the horses be able to pull the chaise from the ditch, do you think?'

'Course, miss. We was only waiting till you was safely out first. C'mon, Wilf.' He addressed the second postilion. 'You lead 'em forward, but tek it slowly, mind. I'll give the old girl a push from behind.' He positioned himself behind the post-chaise. 'Ready when you are, Wilf. And *heave*.'

The vehicle lurched forward. 'Whoa! Stop!' Jack shouted to Wilf.

Wilf halted the horses and both postilions looked enquiringly at Jack. 'The front wheel's damaged.' He pointed.

The first postilion blanched, then ran to check the wheel, which had broken spokes and a splintered rim. He looked around wildly, then stared across at Beatrice. 'Sorry, miss. It looks like we'll be stuck here a while until we can get that wheel mended.'

A prudent man would take his leave now and leave them to it. No one was hurt. The wheel would be mended. Miss Beatrice Fothergill might arrive home a little late, but that was not the end of the world. And yet Jack lingered, watching as Beatrice, her reticule clamped to her chest, turned even paler than the postilion.

'Oh, no. But… I must get home.' Her distress was palpable. 'How long will it take? I promised I would be home before dark.'

'Sorry, miss. I can't be sure. An hour? Mebbe two? We'll have to get the wheel off and I'll have to ride back to that village we just passed through to get it mended.'

Jack heaved a silent sigh. Could he really drive away

and leave her here at the roadside? Despite his inner voice clamouring at him not to get involved, he asked, 'Where were you going, Beatrice?'

He ought to call her Miss Fothergill. A gentleman would certainly do so, but Jack felt backed into a corner and was feeling contrary and so he called her Beatrice, provoking her cheeks to bloom pink.

'Pilcombe Grange.' She turned to the postilion. 'How far is it from here?'

'Seven or eight miles, mebbe. Not too far to walk, but it'll be dark well afore you get there.' He jerked his head skyward. 'Besides, 'tisn't wise for a lady to wander about the countryside alone. There's lots of them old soldiers about…rob you as soon as look at you, they would.'

Jack bristled at his words but held his tongue. It appeared to be a universally held view of the men—the *scum of the earth*, as Wellington had dubbed them—who had returned from the Continent to no jobs and who, in order to survive, now travelled the countryside seeking casual work or begging for scraps. It wasn't worth even trying to point out the horrors Britain might now be facing had those men not been prepared to fight for King and country.

'Yes, I suppose you are right.' She tipped her head to one side and said to Jack, 'Are you a soldier, sir?'

She indicated his missing arm, her eyes sympathetic, and Jack swore silently. He'd forgotten and had inadvertently shifted so he faced her, his pinned-up sleeve in full view. He smiled, though. He could not bear people's pity and he'd found the best way to deflect it was to act as though it was a trivial matter.

'Well,' he drawled, 'I was, but no longer. There's not much use for a one-armed cavalryman.'

He fought the compulsion to leave, to get away from these people…these strangers. But he would not turn tail and run. He must learn to withstand the prying eyes and the pitying comments. Somehow.

Beatrice's brows twitched into a fleeting frown before she turned from him, peering up and down the road, as if hoping for a miracle. The only other vehicle in sight was the curricle Jack had been driving. Rodwell, another veteran of Waterloo whom he had taken on as his groom, stood at the horses' heads.

Beatrice's gaze moved to Jack in an unconscious plea and, with another silent sigh—this one of inevitability—Jack accepted his fate. He could not leave a lady stranded by the side of the road.

'Allow me to escort you home, Beatrice. Pilcombe Grange is not so far out of my way.'

It was, as it happened, but she need not know. To get to Wheatlands he should carry straight on at the next junction, whereas the village of Pilcombe, and, presumably, Pilcombe Grange, was off to the right.

'Oh. I could not possibly accept… Why, we are strangers and—'

'Beatrice.' Jack worked to keep any hint of impatience from his voice as her over-anxiousness grated on him, reviving those unhappy and unwelcome boyhood memories. 'You have my word you will be perfectly safe with me. The choice is yours…allow me to drive you home or wait until the wheel is mended.'

'Oh. Oh, yes, of course. Then…yes. Thank you.' She smiled tentatively before an anxious frown creased her brow. 'I did not mean to imply I do not trust you. It was merely that I did not wish to be a nuisance.'

'Of course you did not.' And he believed her—more and more she reminded him of himself as a boy and of his father's tyranny. Memories he had worked hard to suppress. Who, he wondered, was guilty of bullying Miss

Beatrice Fothergill? 'And your thoughtfulness does you credit, but there is no need to be so apologetic. Now, come, let us be on our way. We will have you home before you know it.'

Beatrice passed a coin to the postilions for their trouble and Jack extended his hand to assist her into the curricle. She stopped with one foot on the step.

'This is truly kind of you.'

Her smile reached right inside him, finding its way through his defences, stirring all those feelings he'd long since suppressed. As she finished climbing into the curricle and settled herself on the seat, Jack rounded the vehicle and sprang up into the driver seat. Rodwell released the horses' heads and limped to the rear, where he clambered up on to the back. Beatrice immediately twisted in her seat and smiled at him.

'Good afternoon, Mr...?'

'Rodwell, miss. Just Rodwell'll do.'

Her smile widened. 'Rodwell, then. I am Miss Fothergill.'

She faced forwards again, sitting bolt upright and clutching her reticule to her chest as Jack gave the horses the office to proceed. As soon as the greys settled into a steady trot, Jack said, 'Relax, Beatrice. I might only have one hand, but I am quite capable of driving.' He prayed he wouldn't prove himself wrong and make a fool of himself. Today's outing was an experiment, to see how well he would cope out on the roads with a pair after only having driven around the estate up till now. 'You will not suffer another upset like the post-chaise.'

She shot him a timid smile and lowered her bag to her lap.

'I am sorry. I did not mean to imply... That is...yes. I feel perfectly safe.'

'I am glad to hear it. Do not forget to tell me where to go, will you?'

He glanced sideways at the muffled giggle that reached his ears.

'Well,' he amended, happy he had made her laugh, 'I realise you are too much the lady to tell me where to go, precisely, but you will tell me when I need to make a turn, won't you?'

And he sent up another prayer that he would complete the manoeuvre without showing himself up. A couple of times that afternoon Rodwell had been obliged to help him out, much to Jack's disgust.

'Yes. Of course, Mr King. Jack.'

After several more minutes of silence broken only by the thud of the horses' hooves and the occasional creak of the curricle, Jack said, 'Fothergill? Are you related to Sir Percy Fothergill?'

Her smile was strained this time. No dimple peeping through. 'Yes. He is my brother.'

Jack didn't really know Fothergill, but they had been at Winchester School at the same time, and Fothergill had been one of the seniors the younger boys knew to avoid. Beatrice's reaction suggested his behaviour had not improved and Jack had his answer as to who was guilty of bullying Miss Beatrice Fothergill and why she put him in mind of his younger self.

'Do you live with him?'

She fidgeted with the drawstrings of her reticule. 'Yes. I have lived with him and his wife, Fenella, ever since my father died.'

'You have my sympathy.'

'Thank you, but it was five years ago.'

Jack grinned at her. 'You misunderstand me. Although, of course, I commiserate with you for the loss of your father, I actually expressed my sympathy for the fact you have to live with your brother.'

'You know him?'

'Not really, but I knew of his reputation at school. He was several years above my brother and I at Winchester.'

'He is *not* my brother.'

Jack stared at that seemingly out-of-character outburst.

'Oh! Oh, I am sorry. I hope I have not embarrassed you.'

'Do *not* apologise.' Her surprised gaze flew to his at his growled response. He cocked his head to one side. 'You are entitled to speak your mind. You are when you are with me, anyway.'

'Oh. Yes. It is just… I have only learned the truth today, and I am…' She fell silent as she fiddled again with the drawstrings of her reticule.

'You are…?'

He caught the left rein more securely in the crook of his left elbow so he could use both reins to slow the horses in preparation for the approaching right turn that would take them towards Pilcombe village. He breathed a sigh of relief as they completed the turn without mishap. Beatrice had not responded by the time the greys settled once more into a steady pace. This road was more exposed to the elements and a brisk wind had sprung up. Jack glanced at Beatrice as she pulled her cloak more snugly around her.

'Come on, Beatrice. You can trust me.' He sent her a winning smile. When she did not respond, he added, 'You are shocked, perhaps?'

Although he had no wish to get drawn into anyone else's troubles, it nevertheless felt good to have something to occupy his thoughts other than his own problems and shortcomings.

She bit her lip, her brow furrowing. 'I am unsure. I feel

as though it is all bottled up inside me, ready to burst. I am… Yes, I am shocked, but most of all, I am *angry*.'

She sounded astonished with herself.

'And you are also allowed to be angry, you know. It is a legitimate emotion.'

'But…ladies…women and girls…should do as they are told and not make a fuss. They ought to be quiet and supportive and obedient at all times.'

Jack laughed. 'Is that so, or is that what your brother tells you? Yes, it is what many men would like their womenfolk to believe and how they wish they would behave. In my experience, however, such blindly obedient females are as rare as hen's teeth.'

'But it *is* true a lady ought never to reveal her emotions, especially in front of strangers.'

'Strangers?' Jack pulled a sad face. 'You wound me, Beatrice. Why, we are on first-name terms, are we not? Or are you in the habit of allowing strange men the liberty of calling you by your Christian name?'

She blushed rosily. 'Of course I am not.'

'I am pleased to hear it. So, will you tell me how you learned Fothergill is not truly your brother?'

A sideways glance revealed a frown creasing the skin between her eyebrows as she worried again at her lower lip. Did she have any idea how that simple, unconsciously erotic habit sent his pulse soaring and the blood surging to his groin? Jack shifted in his seat, willing his wayward body under control. He'd been waiting since Waterloo for his libido to return…wondering if it ever would…only for it to manifest itself in wholly inappropriate circumstances with a woman he would probably never meet again.

He couldn't decide whether to feel relief at its return, or disappointment. Life would doubtless be easier, if dull, without sexual desire. Easier because, that way, he need never take the risk of exposing his deformity to anyone else's gaze. It was all very well for Kit to remind him it was still early days—Waterloo was less than eight months ago—but it was not Kit who must face people's pity or, worse, their revulsion.

'I cannot tell you the whole,' she said, finally. 'But I shall tell you some of it. After all, for all your teasing, we *are* strangers. But we will probably never meet again and I feel such a need to speak of this and to try to make some sense of it.

'Percy is my half-brother. Or that is what I believed. His father was widowed and he married my mother. And I was born. But today I have learned that my father was *not* my father. Mama...she was...' She hauled in a deep breath. 'She did not cuckold him,' she said, in such an earnest voice that Jack smiled. 'She was w-w-with child before they were married. And he knew—it is the *reason* he married her. He was paid money to do so.'

'And you are angry rather than upset? Why is that?'

She shook her head and her bonnet slipped back on her head, revealing soft golden-brown curls at her forehead. She settled the bonnet more securely on her head and tied the ribbons in a bow beneath her ear. At first, he thought she would not answer him. When she did, it was in a low voice he had to strain to hear.

'My father was a strict man. My mama died when I was twelve years old and Father's health was already failing. I was told—it was drummed into me by Father and by Percy—that it was a daughter's duty.' Her face twisted. 'And now I find I was not his daughter and I am not Percy's half-sister. At last I understand why Father left me nothing in his will and made no provision for a dowry. He left me reliant on Percy's charity and I have been paying for that ever since.'

'You had no chance to wed after your father died?'

'No. I was seventeen. Percy and Fenella had just married. Father died, Percy became Sir Percy, and I... *I* became the poor relation. Someone they could order about at will in return for a roof over my head.'

Her voice throbbed with anger; her gloved hands clenched into fists. Her cheeks were still flushed and her eyes flashed, sending another rush of heat through Jack.

'I sacrificed my happiness for a familial duty that was a lie. And I feel cheated. Because, heaven forgive me, it was not for love that I sacrificed my future. That man never showed me love in my entire life.'

Her words were spat out and Jack enjoyed her defiance—proof, perhaps, that she wasn't such a country mouse after all.

'But here—' Beatrice rattled the pouch '—*here* is my salvation.'

Chapter Four

'Salvation? Beatrice... I hate to disappoint you—' and Jack felt a rotten killjoy for saying it '—but twenty guineas will not get you far.'

'Oh! Yes. I do know. But I do have somewhere to escape to and this money will help.'

Escape? Such an evocative word. Could she not just leave? And where did she plan to go? Did she have a beau, perhaps? But he dismissed the idea as soon as it occurred. Any man worthy of the name would surely not leave her to *escape* on her own—he would surely march into Fothergill's house and rescue her.

He asked none of those questions, still reluctant to get drawn further into a stranger's troubles, even if this stranger did possess seductively rounded calves and an adorable smile.

'I must...' Beatrice paused, before rushing on. 'Please excuse me a moment, while I think...'

From the corner of his eye, Jack saw Beatrice tip the contents of the pouch on to her lap. She glanced his way, catching him watching her, and although she tucked her lips between her teeth, her cheeks dimpled, hinting at her hidden smile.

'I *do* trust you, do you see, not to tip your curricle over or I would not risk losing my coins in a roadside ditch.'

'What is it you plan to do?' Jack could not quite work her out. 'I shan't ask for payment, so what reason have you to risk spilling your money again?'

'I have told you I trust your skill as a driver, so I take no risk.' She flashed him a smile. 'But... I *know* Percy, do you see? He will search my reticule when I get home, and when he finds this pouch with, say, five guineas inside, he will think he has discovered it all. But I shall still have the remaining fifteen—which I shall hide somewhere outside—and *they* are vital for my future plans.'

She took out her handkerchief and spread it across her palm and counted most of the coins on to it before knotting it around them. The remainder were put back in the pouch and tucked into her reticule, but she kept tight hold of the bundle of coins in the handkerchief. She then sat back with a sigh and her teeth worried yet again at her lower lip.

Jack hated to think of her facing that brother of hers on her own, but he was still wary of getting involved. So instead of asking Beatrice if there was any way he could help, he set out to distract her with observations about the countryside, trying everything he could to make her laugh. He failed dismally and eventually he began to irritate himself, let alone her, so he, too, lapsed into silence until they were approaching Pilcombe village.

'I presume it is not far now,' he said, 'but you will have to guide me, as I do not know where the Grange is.'

She started at his words, as though she had been lost in thought. 'Are we here already? I am so sorry... I—I am aware I have not repaid your kindness with much in the way of good company, but I have been thinking about what I shall say when I arrive home. Here! Turn right here.' She pointed out a turning just before they entered the village. 'It is only a mile or so along this lane. I can walk from here. I shall be in no danger.'

'I would not dream of allowing you to walk.' Jack slowed the horses and carefully steered the curricle into the lane before urging the greys into an extended trot. 'I shall drive you right up to the front door and that way I shall know you have arrived safely.'

'No! You must not. P-Percy will be furious if I arrive home unchaperoned with a gentleman. Please. Take me as far as the entrance, if you must, but you *cannot* drive up to the house.'

Jack had no desire to face an enraged brother, who might—he realised with a shiver of alarm—accuse him of compromising his sister and insist on reparation for supposedly ruining her reputation. Reparation such as marriage. And marriage was an impossibility for him. He might possess a modest income, derived from funds left to him by his maternal grandfather, but it was barely sufficient to support a wife and family. Besides, no woman would want to be saddled with half a man.

'Very well. If that is your wish.'

'Here! Stop here, please.'

Jack reined the horses to a halt. From the curricle he could see over the wall to a stone-built, Jacobean manor house about fifty yards from the road. The entrance, flanked by two granite pillars, lay behind them—he'd been so lost in thought, he hadn't even noticed driving past the gateway.

'If you carry on up here and turn right, and right again, it will bring you back to the road we turned off.' Beatrice's lips widened into a smile, but her dimples did not appear, and her huge eyes were as anxious as ever. 'Thank you so much, Mr... Jack.' Her cheeks coloured as she ducked her head to check her reticule and her knotted handkerchief. 'I am more grateful than you can know.'

Pure impulse prompted Jack to touch her arm and the words came out before he could censor them. 'Are you sure you do not want me to come with you and help you to explain?'

She shook her head vehemently. 'Oh, no! Please…it is best if Percy believes I came home by post-chaise.'

Rodwell was already at the greys' heads. More than a little relieved at Beatrice's further refusal, Jack jumped down to the ground and rounded the curricle, ready to hand her down. But with her hands full of her belongings, Beatrice hesitated, clearly at a loss, but equally clearly not prepared to let go of her 'salvation'. Without stopping to think about the wisdom of it, Jack moved closer and reached up. He put his right hand on the side of her waist and then pressed the side of what remained of his left forearm to the opposite side and swung her down to the lane.

He quickly moved his stump from her waist, not wishing to disgust her, but his right hand lingered of its own volition. She felt so good. She barely reached his chin, and though her cheeks were plump, her waistline was shapely, narrowing enticingly from her ribcage and then flaring into very feminine hips. A wave of lust coursed from his fingertips, up his arm and through his body, straight to his groin. Their eyes met and fused, and they both stilled.

Beatrice's gaze seemed to reach deep inside him as her breathing hitched and her cheeks washed a delicate pink. Her lips were slightly apart and, unbidden, Jack's face lowered to hers. At the very last moment, however, he retained enough presence of mind to turn his head so his lips brushed her cheek and not that soft, inviting mouth.

'Oh.' Her gasp whispered across his skin and his pulse

leapt anew even as he desperately wrestled his confused emotions into submission.

'It was a pleasure to meet you, Miss Beatrice Fothergill.' He forced his hand from her waist and stepped back. 'I wish you luck with those plans of yours.'

'Th-thank you. Wh-where do you…? That is…do you have far to go?'

'Not too far. Seven or eight miles.' He resisted the urge to be honest with her. It would achieve nothing and lead to too many questions. He raised his hat and sketched a bow. 'Goodbye.'

'Goodbye. And thank you again. And goodbye to you, too, Mr Rodwell.'

She turned and hurried back along the road to the gates, where she stopped and crouched down by one of the pillars, pulling at the weeds at its base, presumably to hide her money.

Jack climbed back on to the curricle and watched over the wall as Beatrice hurried up the carriageway towards the house. Before she was halfway, the front door flew open and a large man, both in height and girth, stalked out of the house, closely followed by a tall woman. The light was dimming, but their jerky gestures even before they reached Beatrice made it clear they were furious. Beatrice had halted and, from her cowed posture, Jack guessed she was being shouted at, although the wind was in the wrong direction to actually hear anything. He fought the urge to fly to her defence.

'Poor lass.' Rodwell had climbed up next to Jack and, like him, now watched the scenario unfolding in the grounds of Pilcombe Grange. 'Is that the brother she talked about?'

'Yes. And his wife, presumably.'

'Are you going to let them get away with it?'

'She said it'll make matters worse for her if they know I drove her home. I have to trust her to know best.'

'Aye?'

Jack clenched his jaw. It felt wrong to drive away, yet Beatrice had been clear she didn't want her brother to know a stranger had driven her home. Besides, it would be way past dark by the time he arrived at Wheatlands and they already faced a slow and cautious journey if they were to avoid ending up in a ditch like the post-chaise.

Nevertheless, guilt snaked through him as he drove away.

'Wicked, *wicked* girl!' Fenella shrieked as she and Percy reached Beatrice. 'I have had to manage *all day* without you. My nerves are shattered to pieces—up and down stairs all day long, not to mention in and out of the garden with my Gertie.'

'Fenella. That's enough.' Percy's growl shook Beatrice more than Fenella's complaints ever could. She was hardened to her sister-in-law's resentment of her presence at Pilcombe Grange. Percy, though, had a vicious streak and a way of looking at her sometimes that made her shiver. 'Where have you been?' He gripped her upper arm, tightening his fingers painfully. 'How dare you treat us like this when you owe us everything you have? Even the clothes on your back and the cloak you wear.'

Before Beatrice realised his intent, he ripped her cloak from her and flung it to the ground. The wind bit into her, penetrating the thin wool of her gown—a cast-off of Fenella's. Percy then bent and grabbed her foot, almost causing her to topple. 'Even the shoes on your feet.' He ripped off her half-boot, wrenching her ankle viciously as he did so, then put her stockinged foot down and snatched her other foot up to repeat his action. The sharp gravel of the driveway bit into the sole of her foot and her ankle flared with pain, but Beatrice squeezed her eyes shut and gritted her teeth, knowing from experience that it would be over sooner if she simply endured. Percy slammed her other foot to the ground and surged to his feet.

Beatrice bent to gather her belongings.

'Leave them! Get indoors. Don't you think this is the end of it, you ingrate. I'll expect a full explanation inside. And I will take that, too.' He snatched Beatrice's reticule from her unresisting grasp. 'Come, cherub…' he took Fenella's arm '…let us go indoors. It is too cold for you to be out here, risking a chill because of that selfish wench.'

Percy and Fenella strutted towards the house, leaving Beatrice to hobble in their wake, her arms wrapped around her waist in a vain attempt to combat the sharp wind. Resolutely, she banished the worry of the punishment to come, instead conjuring up an image of Jack King and his smiley eyes and ready smile. He was so handsome. She wondered where he lived and if she might ever see him again… He had made her feel like a normal woman even though the force of his personality had, at times, been a touch overwhelming. He had made her feel attractive, and that moment when their eyes fused and time had appeared—at least for her—to stand still spread a shiver of delight across her skin. He had kissed her cheek! Her heart gave a funny little somersault at the memory.

She halted outside the front door and gazed up at it. She would be gone soon, she vowed. And she would not miss this place at all. It had ceased to be home for her when Mama died. She lifted each foot in turn and brushed any dirt from her soles before she stepped inside the richly gleaming, highly polished oak-panelled entrance hall. The heat hit her immediately and, for once, she welcomed the stifling temperature at which Fenella insisted the house was maintained, with generous fires in every room. Percy stood at his study door, his arms folded across the straining buttons of his waistcoat, a scowl on his face. Fenella, thankfully, was nowhere in sight, which probably meant Beatrice would be spared a beating. Humiliation crawled over her. What twenty-two-year-old woman submitted so meekly to such treatment from her own sister-in-law? She'd wager neither of her half-sisters would allow themselves to be so ill used.

'In.' Percy stood aside and Beatrice crept past him into the study. 'No. Don't sit,' he barked, even though she'd made no move towards a chair. 'There.' He pointed at his desk, which was bare apart from Beatrice's reticule, carefully placed in one corner. Beatrice's heart stuttered, and her stomach dropped. *No. Please.*

'Bend over and raise your skirts.'

'Wh-wh-where's Fenella?' Percy never beat her himself—Fenella enjoyed administering the switch too much to relinquish that role.

'She clearly doesn't beat you hard enough. So, this time, you have me. And I shall make sure you learn obedience.' His hand landed between Beatrice's shoulder blades. He shoved her forward until her nose pressed against the hard surface of the desk and the edge cut into the soft flesh of her stomach.

'Skirts up.'

Beatrice's stomach roiled. This man wasn't even her brother! He was no relation at all. On that thought, she squirmed violently and, taking him by surprise, managed to free herself. She backed away from him, the agony of her ankle a distant backdrop to her current fear as he glared at her, clearly astonished by her defiance. If she distracted him, maybe he would forget. Or Fenella would come. Or something…*anything* rather than submit to a man who wasn't even related to her.

'You have not even asked where I've been.'

His top lip curled. 'Don't think I shall forget the lesson you need to be taught, you ungrateful brat. But, by all means… I confess I am curious, so let us delay the inevitable while you tell me precisely what you mean by disappearing like that.'

He rounded the desk to plonk his bulk into his chair and reached for her reticule. He wrenched it open, tipping the contents on to the desk—her comb, a spare hatpin, her own purse, containing the few coins she had taken with her, her smelling salts, Mr Henshaw's letter and the leather pouch. Percy's eyes narrowed in suspicion as he picked up the pouch and shook it before pulling it open. The five guineas Beatrice had counted into the pouch spilled onto the desk, the remaining fifteen having been carefully hidden in the undergrowth close to the base of one of the entrance pillars, ready for her to retrieve when the time came for her to go to London.

'Where did you get such a sum of money?' Percy glared at her. 'If I find you have been acting immorally—'

Beatrice pictured Leah's reaction if someone were to accuse her of such behaviour and it gave her the courage to speak up for herself. 'I have done no such thing! You may see for yourself—' Beatrice indicated the letter '—a friend of Mama's died. She left me five guineas in her will.'

Percy scanned the letter. 'A friend of your slut of a mother? She didn't have any friends. Who was it?'

Beatrice tilted her chin. 'Lady Tregowan.'

'Hah! Not precisely a friend, was she? Your mother was merely her paid companion, before she bettered herself by wedding my father.'

So, it seemed Percy had not known Beatrice's mother

was with child at the time of their marriage after all. That made his treatment of Beatrice even worse—imagine caring so little for your own flesh and blood that you would intentionally make their life little better than that of a drudge. Although, to be fair, he had learned that attitude towards both Mama and Beatrice from his father, who had, of course, always known the truth.

'Well, I shall keep these.' Percy scooped up the coins and replaced them in the pouch. 'They will help reimburse us for the expense of keeping you.' He scowled then. 'And what was your reason for not showing me this letter immediately?'

'I was afraid you would stop me going to the meeting,' Beatrice said. 'The letter did not say anything about an inheritance, but I was curious and I wanted to find out what it was about.'

'Hmmm. Very well. But don't think you will get such an opportunity again. I have ordered Bulstrode to confiscate all your outdoor clothing and footwear. Not even you are stupid enough to venture out in winter without adequate protection. Now go. Get out of my sight. Ask if there is anything Fenella wants you to do, and as soon as you've carried out any tasks for her, you will go to your room and stay there until I say you may come out.'

Beatrice's heart sank. Bulstrode, the butler, was no friend of hers. In fact, none of the servants was—they were all overworked and much too afraid of Percy to flout his rule.

'Yes, Percy.'

'And if I find you have deviated one inch from my instructions, then the beating I shall give you will be twice as hard as the one I have spared you now. Is that clear?'

'Yes, Percy.'

Beatrice, her heart hammering, limped from his study,

shards of pain shooting through her ankle with every step. The hall was empty and she laid her hand against her midriff, feeling the reassuring shape of the copy of Lady Tregowan's will tucked inside her bodice. Did she dare go to her bedchamber first, before going to Fenella? The heavy tread of footsteps from within Percy's study decided her. She could not risk it, even though she must hide the will as soon as she possibly could.

But Fenella was so distressed by Beatrice's ingratitude and disobedience that she was resting in her bedchamber with strict instructions not to be disturbed and Beatrice hobbled gratefully to her own bedchamber and bolted the door behind her.

Her first action was to hide Lady Tregowan's will at the bottom of her wicker mending hamper, beneath her sewing box, which she stored in there, and the pile of mending awaiting her attention. No one but her ever looked in there. Next, she looked in her wardrobe. Not only had her pelisse and her next-best cloak—her warmest—disappeared, but also the warmer gowns she owned. Not even her Sunday shoes remained. The only footwear were light slippers—utterly unsuitable for going outside. Although, as pain again sliced through her ankle, she realised she would not be able to leave yet even if she did have her boots and cloak.

How long would Percy's edict last? Knowing him and Fenella, she guessed it would be rescinded as soon as Beatrice's confinement in the house had an impact on either of them or on their comfort. Her best ally, therefore, would be Gertrude, Fenella's pampered pug. As Fenella never ceased to remind Beatrice, the servants had enough to do and so Beatrice was required to help ease their load—and that included walking Gertrude outside several times a day.

A scratch at her door grabbed her attention. Spartacus! She'd forgotten all about him. She hoped he'd already caught a mouse to eat tonight because she wouldn't be allowed into the kitchen to find any scraps for him, even if she could face the agony of the stairs again. She hobbled to the door, tears of pain smarting her eyes, and opened it to see her only friend in this house sitting outside patiently: Spartacus, a big black tomcat she had found as a kitten several years before and, for some reason, had been allowed to keep. Spartacus entered the room, rubbed around her ankles, then hopped on to the bed and curled into a ball, purring loudly. Beatrice sat next to him and stroked his somewhat moth-eaten coat and his ragged ears. He opened his eyes and pushed his head up into her hand, and every time she stopped stroking him, he licked her hand until she started again. Her stomach rumbled loudly, but she knew she would get no supper tonight, so she pushed her hunger to the back of her mind.

All I need to do is sit this out. Be obedient. Lull them into believing I am contrite and that I will never rebel in such a way ever again.

Chapter Five

Guilt continued to plague Jack throughout the slow, careful drive back home to Wheatlands. He should have insisted on taking Beatrice to her front door despite her refusal of his help. He could at least have attempted to explain what happened and to placate her brother. He wondered uneasily what would happen to her now and what her plan for her future was. She had seemed quite confident—unusually so when in many other respects she was as timid as that country mouse he had pictured when he had first seen her, shrinking from him in the confines of the tilted post-chaise. Again, he wondered if she had a beau tucked away somewhere. Her features materialised in his mind's eye—her bluey-grey eyes, almost smoky in their hue, and innocently trusting. Her delicate nose. Those sweet cheeks that dimpled when she smiled. Her quickness to blush. That lush, pink mouth he had so nearly kissed.

'Still frettin' about the lass?' Rodwell interrupted Jack's musings as he drove through the dark along the main drive to Wheatlands, lights glimmering intermittently through the trees that bordered the way.

'What? No. Thinking about my brother.'

'Aye.' Rodwell was sitting upright next to Jack, one hand on each knee. After another minute, he said, ''Appen 'e'll come round to your way of thinking. Given time.'

'I hope so.'

He hated being at odds with Kit, who was dead set against Jack's plan to leave Wheatlands. He was determined to find a new purpose to his life, even though the thought of branching out on his own racked his nerves.

I've done it before. I can do it again.

He had been just as determined to make a success of the army as his chosen career, if only to prove himself to his father, who had wanted Jack to enter the Church and had flatly refused to buy him a commission. Jack could still hear his scornful laugh. *'The army? You haven't the balls to be a soldier, boy!'*

So Jack had run off and volunteered, and he'd successfully worked his way up to Captain in the First King's Dragoon Guards before his injury at Waterloo.

But I had two arms and two hands back then. It was different.

They rounded the final curve of the carriageway, and the house—ablaze with lanterns lighting the frontage—came into full view. Jack stared at his boyhood home, conscious of that same old apprehension lurking deep in his belly even though it was ridiculous. Father had died three years ago… There was nothing to fear any more and, besides, Jack was a man now—a seasoned soldier who could no longer be bullied, even if Father *were* still alive. But he was also aware of a shameful sense of relief that the old tyrant was no longer alive to mock the sorry excuse for a man his younger son had become.

What use will I be to anyone now?

Jack thrust aside his self-doubt as he jumped down from the carriage and the huge oaken front door opened and that lingering echo of boyhood fear vanished as Kit appeared.

'Did you think we'd got lost?'

Kit's smile was strained. 'I was worried. You did not warn me you would be gone so long.'

Jack bit back his instinctive retort before he snapped it out. Kit had, understandably, slipped into the role of protector during Jack's convalescence and, at first, Jack had been content—even relieved—to allow his twin to take charge. Now, though, Kit's concern irritated Jack... When would his twin accept that he was capable of looking after himself, even if one of his arms *was* missing? Jack might harbour his own doubts about his abilities, but not for the world would he ever reveal them, even to Kit. They were for him to deal with.

'That is because I had no idea I would be back so late. I trust I haven't inconvenienced you too much by delaying the dinner hour?'

'Not me, no. But you may need to make your peace with Mrs Rendell.'

Mrs Rendell had been their family cook for as long as Jack could remember. She was married to their butler and the Rendells had been more like parents to him and Kit than their own father had ever been. They had never known their mother. Jack headed for the kitchen first, sniffing appreciatively at the wonderful, mouth-watering smells emanating from the range, apologised to Mrs Rendell with a hug and a kiss to her cheek, then climbed the stairs to his bedchamber, which had remained unchanged since his boyhood. As ever, the years slipped away as he ran his fingers across the familiar surfaces. Notwithstanding the bad times, there were plenty of good memories of Wheatlands, too, and he tried hard to focus on those and banish the rest.

He quickly washed and changed his clothes—with the help of his former batman, Carrick—before joining Kit five minutes before dinner was announced.

'So why were you delayed?' Kit asked after the food and wine were served and the servants left the dining room. 'You must have known I would be worried, thinking the worst.'

Again, Jack bit back his resentment at Kit's over-protectiveness, which had grown out of all proportion since Jack had mooted the idea of him moving to London. How could he ever convince himself he still had worth as a man when his own brother believed him incapable?

'I have told you there's no need to worry about me. How do you think I managed all those years in the cavalry without you to watch over me?' Jack paused, breathing deeply to calm himself. 'I had to make an unexpected detour, that's all.'

'Oh?'

Jack told him the tale of coming across the stricken post-chaise.

'Fothergill?' Kit sipped his wine. 'He's not well liked in the county... Do you remember him from school? He hasn't changed. Is the sister the same? I'm surprised you put yourself out for her—I would have left her there. They'd have soon got that wheel repaired, you know. No need for you to feel obligated to her.'

'She isn't like Fothergill. And she's not his sister by blood. Only by upbringing.'

'Still partial to a pretty face, eh, Jack? Did she flutter her eyelashes and play the maiden in distress?'

Jack frowned. It wasn't like Kit to be so cynical. Or, at least, it hadn't been like the Kit he'd grown up with. But they'd been apart for eight years until Jack's return last year, and both of them had changed. This wasn't the first time Jack had seen signs in his brother of a distrust of females in general but, until recently, he had been too distracted by his own woes to take much notice of the changes in Kit. Since then, however, all Jack's attempts to coax his twin into revealing more of himself—of his hopes and his dreams—met with a polite but unyielding resistance. The fun-loving young man who never missed a London Season, and who had encouraged Jack to follow his dream of joining the army against their father's wishes, was now quiet and brooding...a man who clearly valued his privacy and who now rarely socialised. Jack could only wonder what had happened to bring about that transformation because Kit was not letting on. Jack missed the easy camaraderie they had enjoyed as boys and the fun they had shared.

'You are mistaken to accuse Miss Fothergill of using coquetry, Kit. She was distressed. I felt sorry for her. That's all.'

'So...no plans to call upon her?'

'I may call on her, in a week or so.' Until the words left his lips, he'd had no intention of seeing her again. But now the idea had arisen, he couldn't deny its appeal. 'Merely to reassure myself that she is safe and well,' he added.

He'd already told Kit about witnessing her brother castigating Beatrice upon her return.

Kit's brows rose. 'And what excuse will you give? How will you explain having met her before?'

'I'll think of something.'

They spent the rest of the evening chatting about the estates and Kit's favourite pastimes of hunting, shooting and fishing—the typical pursuits of a country gentleman—avoiding, seemingly by mutual consent, the contentious issue of Jack's determination to leave Wheatlands in the spring.

* * *

The winds changed early in February, swinging round
to the east and bringing severe frosts. The ground froze
solid and to ride or to drive was to risk damage to the
horses' legs. Jack's injured arm ached abominably as the
weather turned colder, and by the middle of the month
the ground was white with snow that was piled into drifts
by the bitter winds. With temperatures remaining below
freezing until the end of the month, there was no hope of
an early thaw.

Jack thought about Beatrice from time to time at first,
but it was with decreasing frequency as February pro-
gressed. The weather had put a stop to all but essential
journeys, so he'd had no opportunity to call upon her
brother as he intended and, as time passed, she entered his
thoughts less and less, supplanted by his concerns about
his own future and what it might hold.

Beatrice's dejection grew as the days of February and
early March dragged past. Her ankle made excruciatingly
slow progress towards healing and she was still hobbling
around with the aid of a stick. The chore of walking Gertrude had fallen to Perkins, Fenella's maid, who resented
Beatrice and hated anything to do with the outside, and
who now watched Beatrice like a hawk in an attempt to
prove she was fibbing about her injured ankle.

Percy did not return Beatrice's outdoor clothing because, as he rightly said, 'If your ankle pains you too much
to walk Gertrude in the garden, then you can have no reason to set foot outdoors for any other purpose.'

And Beatrice did not argue because she had no desire to
go outside in the increasingly winterish weather. Fenella,
however, made few concessions to Beatrice's injury and
still expected her to fetch and carry for her within the

house. Egged on by Perkins, who was furious at having to walk Gertrude in such severe weather, Fenella was half convinced Beatrice was slacking and that her sprained ankle was a figment of her imagination.

'If you had ever suffered from the number of ailments *I* have endured,' Fenella said, drawing her thick shawl more tightly around her torso, 'then you would not make such a fuss.'

'You could learn a lot from your sister,' added Percy. 'She is a fine example of uncomplaining martyrdom to her poor health. *She* would not make a fuss over a twinge or two in her ankle.'

It was fortunate the February weather was so bad that, even had her ankle been strong enough, Beatrice could not have attempted to flee to London. Harsh, glittering frosts followed by heavily drifting snow made any thought of travel impossible but, even though she understood she could do nothing and must wait until her ankle healed and the weather improved, still she fretted as time passed, the deadline of Eastertide looming large in her mind.

But all that also gave Beatrice plenty of time to think about Jack King. He occupied her daydreams more than was wise, with his ready smile and that roguish twinkle in his eyes. Not to mention his hand on her waist and that sudden stillness and intensity in his expression after he'd swung her to the ground as though she weighed no more than a child, despite his missing arm…well, hand, really, because it seemed as though he still had part of his fore-arm. Her fertile imagination conjured up all sorts of heroic scenarios in which he had been injured, and her tender heart longed to comfort him as she relived that moment when their gazes had fused. Her blood heated at the mere memory of it—her heart pitter-pattering and her breaths growing short.

In her fantasies, he turned up on her doorstep and cast his heart at her feet, and he whisked her away from horrible Percy and spiteful Fenella. It was a harmless daydream about a handsome stranger, but as the days and weeks passed and winter continued to hold Somerset in its grip, Jack invaded Beatrice's thoughts less and less.

Instead, she turned her attention to the problem of how she would get to Bristol to catch a stagecoach to London—or even the mail coach that Mr Henshaw had told Aurelia left the Bush Tavern, Corn Street, at four o'clock every day. Beatrice, who had absolutely no experience of travelling by public coach, had memorised that information, reassured there would be alternatives in Bristol, for the thought of being stranded alone, overnight, in the hurry and scurry of such a big city made her shudder. But at least she need not fear Percy would chase after her and force her to come home, for as long as she managed to leave the house without being noticed, she was convinced they would not concern themselves and would no doubt be overjoyed to be rid of her.

The temperature did not rise above freezing until the very last day of February—the twenty-ninth, as it was a leap year—and Beatrice's ankle finally felt strong enough for her to walk a little outside, so as to build up its strength.

'My ankle is almost better now, Percy,' she said at breakfast the following morning. 'May I please have my cloak and boots back? I think if I take Gertrude out as I used to, a little light exercise will help to strengthen it.'

'About time, too. You have no idea how inconvenient this has been for the entire household—it's about time you shouldered your share of the chores around here—Fenella has been run ragged and Perkins is exhausted while you have been living a life of leisure.'

Beatrice did not retaliate, although his accusation was utterly unfair. She had still done as much as she could and no doubt delayed the healing by not resting enough. But she held her tongue. The return of her clothing was what was important—that and the freedom to actually walk outside in the garden and, maybe, the park.

'I shall instruct Bulstrode to return the items, but be warned, Sister—if I catch you flouting my rules again I might very well take my darling wife's advice and cast you adrift. I'd like to see how you fare then, out in the big, wide world without me to guide you. You are far too stupid to hold down even the lowliest of jobs. You would be earning your living by lying on your back in no time.'

Beatrice stilled, knowing he was working himself up into one of his frequent rages. There was nothing she could do as he surged to his feet and paced the room.

'You really are an ungrateful chit, aren't you? You are all take and no give. You take our charity for granted, as though it were your right. Well, let me tell you…' he paused next to her, looming over her '…your place here hangs by the slenderest of threads. One wrong move…one impertinent remark…one insolent look from you and you will be thrown out. Is that clear?'

She nodded. She had been threatened like that so many times she knew his words were empty—both Percy and Fenella were too concerned with their images as upright and charitable citizens to ever actually cast Beatrice out. Fenella, especially, enjoyed acting the lady at the local church. This time, however, Beatrice wondered if the threat might work to her advantage. After all, it would suit her purposes to be banished. It was what she wanted.

Later that morning—having completed the tasks demanded by Fenella—she donned her cloak and pulled on her half-boots, wincing a little as her ankle protested, and headed out into the garden—pockets of snow still evident—to enjoy her first breath of fresh air in over a month.

Beatrice's first thought was of her hidden coins, but she dared not approach the entrance in case she was spotted from the windows. Instead, she followed the garden paths with the snuffling, grunting Gertrude at her heels. Spartacus shadowed them, teasing Gertrude by crouching behind bushes and pouncing on the portly pug, causing her to yelp, twist and snap. But Spartacus was too quick—streaking away as Gertrude waddled in his wake, yapping indignantly, giving Beatrice something to smile about for the first time in weeks. Finally, spots of rain began to fall, forcing them indoors.

No sooner had Beatrice entered the house than she heard Fenella's shrill tones calling her name. Heart sinking, she shrugged off her cloak and pulled off her half-boots before heading for the parlour, where Fenella usually reclined on the sofa in the afternoon.

'I am here. What is it, Fenella?'

'This!' Fenella held up her arm to reveal a section of lace edging on her sleeve that had come away. 'It is typical of your shoddy needlework… This is *your* stitching. See how it has fallen off—practically the first time I've worn this gown since you repaired it. That's your trouble, Beatrice. You think you can get away with sloppy work and we just have to suffer for it.'

'I mended that lace trim over a year ago.' *I do not have to put up with being treated like a servant now. I am wealthy. Mr Henshaw said so. And Leah and Aurelia would never stand for this.* 'You have worn the gown several times since then.'

'Oh! You *insolent* creature! How *dare* you speak to me

like that?' Fenella swung her legs to the floor and sat up. 'Your brother told me all about your impertinence this morning. How do you imagine you would fare if you didn't have us to cater to your every whim, you wicked, ungrateful hussy? Do you think coal grows on trees? Do you think the food you eat appears out of the ground by magic? It is time you learned some humility. This…' Fenella grabbed the edging and tugged at it. It gave a loud rip as the sleeve itself tore. '*Now* see what you have made me do. You will mend it. Now.'

Fenella stalked across the room and tugged at the bell pull. Beatrice waited. Did she dare defy Fenella? But what if they took her coat and boots again, rather than throwing her out? She couldn't risk it, so she remained silent. When Bulstrode answered the summons, Fenella ordered him to send Perkins for Beatrice's mending hamper and to bring it to Fenella's bedchamber.

'Come with me,' she said to Beatrice.

Perkins emerged from Beatrice's bedchamber carrying the hamper as Beatrice reached the top of the stairs. Spartacus, who had followed them up the stairs, streaked across the landing and through the open door.

'Perkins, give that hamper to Miss Fothergill and then come and help me change my gown. You—' she turned to Beatrice '—will get no supper until you have mended every last one of those items, starting with this gown.'

Which meant Beatrice would not eat that night—there was too much work to be completed by midnight, let alone the dinner hour. But that hardly worried her, for her appetite had deserted her over the past weeks—so much so that her gowns now hung from her shoulders instead of fitting snugly across her bosom.

Perkins, her eyes gleaming with spiteful malevolence, strutted towards Beatrice, who saw, with a lurch of her stomach, that the catch on the lid was unfastened. Perkins made no attempt to even try to make her stumble appear genuine. Beatrice leapt forward to try to catch the hamper as it toppled out of Perkins's unresisting grasp, but was too late. She could only watch in horror as the pile of assorted sheets, shirts, stockings and handkerchiefs tumbled across the landing and down the stairs. And, last of all, Beatrice's copy of Lady Tregowan's will fell from the hamper, landing on top of one of Percy's shirts.

Chapter Six

Beatrice's breath seized in her lungs and her knees trembled as Fenella's gaze swept over the scattered linens and clothing.

Please don't see it. Please don't see it. She grabbed on to the balustrade, her heart racing.

'Your Ladyship.'

Despair washed through Beatrice as she saw the direction the maid was pointing.

'What is it, Perkins?'

'What is that, Your Ladyship?'

Perkins bent to pick up the will and passed it to Fenella. Beatrice closed her eyes, gripping the rail tighter.

'"The last will and testament of…"' Fenella's voice trailed off and the only sound on the landing was her nasally breathing. Beatrice didn't dare to look. 'Oh! You—' She shoved Beatrice away from the balustrade, causing her to stumble. 'Get in your room. Perkins—you are to stay outside this door and make sure Miss Fothergill does not leave this room.'

As her bedchamber door slammed behind her, Beatrice could hear Fenella yelling for Percy. She slumped on to her bed, picking up Spartacus, who nudged his nose beneath her chin, purring loudly.

What on earth will happen now? She could barely think straight.

Half an hour later, there was a knock on the door. It opened to reveal Percy.

'Now then. Beatrice, my dear sister, please come with me to the drawing room. Fenella and I wish to talk to you.'

Rather than be reassured by his pleasant tone, it made Beatrice even more nervous.

He will spoil everything. I know he will. He'll find a way.

Nevertheless, she rose and followed Percy downstairs, panic welling in her throat. Fenella was waiting in the drawing room, a tea tray set in front of her, and the sight calmed Beatrice as her brain began to work again. They might know about her inheritance, but they could do nothing to claim it without her. *She* had the upper hand. Didn't she?

Percy ushered Beatrice to a chair by the fire while Fenella poured three cups of tea and handed one each to Beatrice and Percy, her lips thin with disapproval.

'Why didn't you tell us of your good fortune, you silly girl?' Percy shook his head. 'Did you think we wouldn't be happy for you? Why, you will get a Season in London, all paid for, and a house of your own—Falconfield Hall is a fine place indeed. It almost seems a travesty to bestow it on the daughter of a mere companion. Did you find out why Lady Tregowan bequeathed you such a fortune?'

Beatrice sipped her tea while she assembled her thoughts. She coughed, clearing her throat. 'It won't all be mine. There are three of us. And none of it will be mine until I marry.'

And you cannot get your hands on it.

'It will belong to your husband then, of course.'

Fenella shot a knowing look at Percy. *They are planning something. I can feel it.* Beatrice felt trapped, but less panicky than she had earlier. Her ankle was still not strong enough to risk walking any distance—especially as she would have to carry both Spartacus and a bag. It was a blow, this happening now when in a week's time her ankle would be so much stronger, but it was not a complete disaster.

'Who are these other two women named as beneficiaries?' Percy held up the copy will. 'Leah Thame and Aurelia Croome—what were they to Lady Tregowan? Were they her companions, like your dear mama?'

'I believe so.' The less Percy and Fenella knew about Beatrice's half-sisters—or about why Lady Tregowan had left them her estate—the safer she would feel.

'That clause about marriage seems a bit harsh for two spinsters.' Fenella's eyes gleamed. 'With any luck, you will end up with half the inheritance, or even the entire amount.'

'Although,' said Percy, 'there will always be men willing to overlook a multitude of failings in a woman if she is wealthy enough. I do not think we can count on them failing to wed, unfortunately. And those sorts of men will pose a risk to you, too, my dearest sister, for you won't have the nous to sort the wheat from the chaff. There'll be men galore who only want you for your money—telling you all sorts of lies to get what they want. But at least you have me to look out for you, eh? *I'll* make sure you're all right.'

Beatrice closed her eyes and continued to sip her tea. Let them both believe she would go along with them and that Leah and Aurelia were vastly older than her, rather than just a few years. She saw no reason to set them straight about anything, for this was her business and nothing to do with either of them.

Percy and Fenella were almost sickeningly attentive towards Beatrice after their discovery, excitedly making plans for the three of them to go to London before the deadline. Beatrice wondered nervously what else they planned—for she could tell there was something they were not telling her. She was rarely left alone for more than half an hour and it felt as though suspicious eyes tracked her every move. No longer could she rely on Percy not chasing after her if she ran away and she worried incessantly about how she would manage to escape their vigilance.

By the end of the first full week of March, Beatrice's ankle finally felt strong enough to risk her escape. Even though she knew Percy and Fenella would never let her miss the London deadline, she loathed the idea of arriving with them in tow. She didn't want Percy contaminating her new life and she desperately wanted to prove to her sisters—and to herself—that she could do this without help. She couldn't bear Leah and Aurelia to see her as weak and in need of rescuing.

And so, gradually, she formed her plan. Although there was a stagecoach that travelled through Pilcombe village and into Bristol every Friday, she soon realised that route would be Percy's first thought if she were to escape and he was bound to come after her now he knew about her inheritance. So, she would leave Pilcombe Grange next Friday—somehow—but she would head west, away from the village, using a footpath that crossed Percy's land rather than a road where she would be more likely to be seen. The footpath was around two miles long and it eventually emerged on to the mail road from Axbridge to Bristol, right next to a posting inn. If there was no coach due, mayhap she could hire a post-chaise to take her into Bristol, where there would be plenty of opportunities to get to London.

She hoped.

'I have a proposition for you,' Kit said over their post-dinner port one evening towards the middle of March. Jack's heart sank, suspecting what was coming and knowing his refusal would spark an argument.

'Go on.' Jack sipped his port.

'Go to London if you must—I will pay you an allowance and the town house might as well get *some* use—but then come back here and help me run the estate.'

Jack sighed. 'We have had this conversation before, Kit. You don't need me. You have Wright and he does a sterling job stewarding the estate. Or do you propose letting him go, knowing he has a family to support?'

'No. I would not do that.'

'Then you have no need of me and I cannot spend the rest of my life in your shadow.'

I need to find some purpose to my life.

And that was at the heart of his need to push himself into re-entering the world and socialising once again, even though the prospect worried him more than he cared to admit. He felt emasculated. No use to anyone. It would be so easy to stay at Wheatlands, hidden away, living an easy life, but that would not help restore his self-esteem. He said none of that to Kit, however.

'What about when you marry?' he said instead. 'I will be utterly *de trop*. I thank you, but no.'

'I have no plans to wed. I doubt I ever shall.'

Jack stared at Kit's brusque reply. What *had* happened

to turn Kit into a near-recluse? He still refused to confide in Jack. Fair enough, he supposed. They both had
their secrets.

'But you will need an heir.'

Kit played with his port glass, tilting it this way and
that to catch the candlelight. 'I have an heir. You.' He did
not meet Jack's eyes.

Jack frowned. 'Why are you so against the idea of marriage?'

Kit shrugged. 'I don't wish to discuss it, Jack. I'm not
interested in a wife or a family. If I ever wed, it will be a
marriage of convenience purely for the purpose of siring
an heir. But I should be happier to remain single. So, my
offer to you is this. Make your home here. Marry. And
produce heirs for the title and the estate. I know you would
struggle to afford a family on your income. This way you
will want for nothing.'

Jack emptied his glass, his stomach tightening. So, he
was to be entirely beholden to Kit…become his depen-
dant, in effect. And marry, when he had cast all thought
or hope of such a thing from his heart, for what woman
would choose a one-armed man unless, of course, she had
additional incentives such as a title for her eldest son and
a wealthy lifestyle? But what kind of woman could respect a man who could not even afford to support his own
family and who instead meekly became his twin brother's
pensioner? His pride bruised and battered, Jack reached
for the bottle, pouring out a measure of the amber liquid,
anguish narrowing his throat.

'Would you like a refill?'

Kit pushed his glass towards Jack. 'Thank you,' he said
as Jack poured. 'Well? What do you say?'

Jack replaced the bottle, ran his hand through his hair

and scratched the back of his head. 'Thank you, but no. You know my feelings on making my own way in this life.'

'I cannot decide whether to admire your stiff-necked pride or lament it, Jack. I *want* to help you. Allow me to help. Please.'

Jack tamped down the anger that curled in his gut. He didn't need Kit's pity. 'Kit... I was a soldier for eight years. A captain, in command of a company of men. I am my own man and I have no intention of reverting to your trusty second-in-command simply to fill a gap in your life.' He might still feel like only half a man, but it was time to drag himself out of that belief. And he could not do that here at Wheatlands under Kit's thumb. 'You ought to rethink that decision not to wed—mayhap you would not then be so eager to meddle in my life.'

Dismay flashed in Kit's eyes, gone in a second, and his real motive for wanting Jack to remain at Wheatlands hit Jack squarely in the gut. Kit was lonely. Protecting Jack was only part of it—how had he not seen it before? Jack did not reveal his sudden insight, but he did vow to help his brother to break out of his self-imposed cage, just as Jack now intended to break out of his. It would help neither of them to continue to wallow in isolation with just one another for company.

'I promise I shall visit Wheatlands often, but I cannot accept your proposition. I need to make my own way. Not spend my life as your right-hand man,' Jack added, with a wry smile.

Kit huffed a laugh. 'This is not about your...erm... injury.'

'My lack of a left hand? You can speak about it, Kit. It is a fact and you skirting around it does not change anything. We both must come to terms with my life as it is now.'

'Am I allowed to feel guilty about it, though?' Kit asked quietly. 'If I had not encouraged you to follow your dream and join the army—'

He fell silent as Jack slammed his hand on the table. 'Enough! It was *my* dream…*my* decision. I'd have gone with or without your encouragement.' He hauled in a deep breath. 'You must know that, Kit. I would have gone anyway. And now… I need some direction in my life now I am no longer in the cavalry, which is why I need to go to London. To find my way.' Jack drained his port glass and stood up. 'Kit…why do you not come to London with me?'

The idea had only just occurred to him. That Kit was lonely was no surprise, really—he had just not thought through what he had seen with his own eyes over the past months. Kit never socialised in local society and the hunt appeared to be the only activity he shared with his neighbours. He rarely even attended church, claiming to be too busy. If he could but entice Kit to London, perhaps he could help his twin rediscover his own lust for life.

'I've no interest in balls and all that Season nonsense,' Kit said with a curl of his lip. 'When will you go?'

Jack argued no further. For the moment. But he would try again. After all, he was hardly suited to dancing at balls either, but he was sure the change would do them both the world of good. The irony of the situation made him smile—he, who had every reason to shun society, having to coax Kit, a wealthy marquess, to become more sociable.

'Monday.'

That would give him a few more days to change Kit's mind, not to mention time to mentally prepare himself for the ordeal of attending society events with all those eyes on him. With his departure from Somerset now imminent, however, Jack remembered he still had not called upon Beatrice Fothergill to check all was well. February, of course, had proved too difficult for travelling more than the shortest distances, but March was now nearly half over and he was ashamed to admit she had barely registered in his thoughts. Now he *had* remembered her, however, his sense of responsibility was fully awakened. Even though they had only met for the briefest of times, she might need help. He could not rest now, not until he knew for sure she was all right, even if he had left his concern late in the day.

Her image arose in his mind's eye, but he pushed away the unbidden thought that he would simply *like* to meet her again. On the day they met, there was no doubt she had aroused responses within him he had believed long dead, and he was curious to discover if they had been a fluke. Even if they weren't, however, he was still a one-armed man on a strictly limited income and with no purpose to his life. A man with precisely nothing to offer any woman, not even a country mouse.

'I've decided to call upon Sir Percy Fothergill tomorrow,' he said to Kit. 'I wish to satisfy myself that his sister is safe and well before I return to London.'

Kit frowned. 'I thought you'd forgotten all about that chit. Did you actually promise to call on her?'

'No, but I shall do so out of common courtesy.'

Kit shrugged. 'Well, I would not waste my time if I were you.'

'You are not me, though, and I am curious to see if her brother is as awful to her as she implied.' Jack eyed Kit. 'Come with me, Kit,' he urged. 'We can ride over and you can distract Fothergill while I try to snatch a private word with Beatrice.'

'Beatrice, is it?' Kit's blue eyes gleamed. 'Yes. I rather think I *shall* accompany you, Brother, if only to keep you out of trouble. If the sister is anything like her brother, she'll have her eye on you as a way to elevate herself in society. Did you think of what excuse you will give him for calling on him?'

Jack raised his left arm. 'I am raising funds for soldiers maimed in the war, don't you know, and Fothergill has been recommended as a possible donor to the cause.'

Kit's grin turned impish, in an echo of the boy Jack remembered. 'As good an incentive to accompany you as any. I shall take great pleasure in helping you to loosen Fothergill's purse strings.'

I will be gone from here tomorrow. Gone for ever.

Beatrice's stomach churned as she bent over her embroidery and concentrated on her stitches as she sat in the drawing room with Fenella one Thursday afternoon in the middle of March. She could barely think of anything else but her escape. Her plans were all made—she had found a wicker basket with a lid and a handle to carry Spartacus, and a small cloak bag in which she had already packed the barest minimum of clothing and the few mementoes she had of her mother: her few pieces of jewellery, her fan, an embroidered handkerchief and a tortoiseshell miniature writing set. After a moment's thought, she had filled the ink and pounce bottles of the latter, checked that all the disassembled parts of the pen were present and put half a dozen sheets of writing paper at the bottom of her cloak bag. Who knew what she might need on her journey? She tried not to worry about how she would manage to carry both her cat and her bag the two miles to the mail road—there was no alternative to walking the distance.

I should just wait until Percy takes me to London. That will be safest. Percy's right. I am too stupid to manage on my own. I'll get lost or something.

But every time that defeatist voice whispered temptation inside her head, her pride knocked it back down again. She had to prove herself not only to Leah and Aurelia, who must surely have thought her a complete ninny after her performance at the solicitor's office, but also to herself.

Perversely, Beatrice felt braver now Percy and Fenella knew her secret, her courage boosted by their seeming belief that she would comply unquestioningly with their plans. Just knowing she no longer need rely on them for her very existence had increased her confidence. No longer would she cower before them—they could do nothing to her. Never would they risk her forfeiting her inheritance, not while they had hopes of somehow benefitting from it themselves. But Beatrice was determined that would never happen.

They are not my family. Leah and Aurelia are my family.

The door flew open, jerking her from her thoughts, and Percy lumbered into the room.

'Visitors,' he gasped. 'Two gentlemen, on horseback.'

Unexpected visitors were a rarity at the Grange. Percy was followed by Brown, the housemaid, and Beatrice watched her as she scurried around straightening ornaments and chairs, before refuelling the fire and running out again.

'Who? Oh, who?' Fenella's hands flew to her hair, tidying it around the edges of her lace cap. Then she pinched her cheeks and bit her lips to bring some colour to them. 'Is it...? Could it be...?'

'Hush. No. You know that is next week.'

Beatrice frowned, her suspicion aroused by the look that passed between Percy and Fenella.

What is next week?

She had no time for further conjecture, however, as

Bulstrode came in, carrying a silver salver bearing two calling cards.

'The Marquess of Quantock and Lord Jack Kingswood,' said Percy in an awed voice.

Jack...? Beatrice's heart gave an odd little flip in her chest. *But...no. Kingswood. Not King.*

Percy straightened, clearing his throat. 'They asked for me, I collect?'

'They enquired for both you *and* Lady Fothergill, sir.'

'Show them up, Bulstrode.' Percy positioned himself in front of the fire, his chest puffed out and his chin high. 'Well, my cherub. To be recognised by the highest-ranking nobleman in Somerset is a fine thing indeed. I was at Winchester with Quantock and his brother. They are twins, you know.'

'Ooh, Percy! No, I did not know. Just fancy, a marquess in *our* home.'

'Shh! They're coming,' Percy hissed.

Fenella folded her hands in her lap, fixed a serene smile on her face and cast her eyes down. Beatrice, however, unable to completely dismiss that glimmer of hope, could not tear her eyes from the door, waiting breathlessly for her first glimpse of their visitors.

Chapter Seven

Jack! It is *Jack...*

And yet, it was not. The gentleman who entered looked like Jack, yet something was not quite right, other than the fact he had two hands. But then the second man entered and Beatrice's breath seized in her lungs. It *was* Jack—so similar to the first man—his twin, Percy had said—and yet broader, blonder and that easy smile that she remembered, and which was lacking from the other man's more sombre visage.

She barely heard the greetings exchanged. She stood and curtsied as Percy introduced her. The Marquess acknowledged her with a curt nod and a narrow-eyed, assessing stare that unnerved her. Jack gave no sign of recognition and she took that as her cue, keeping her eyes downcast although she could not resist several peeks through her eyelashes. She was afraid if she looked directly at him...if their eyes met...she might give away that they had met before and so she concentrated on remaining outwardly calm.

'Such an honour to welcome you to our humble home, my lords,' Fenella gushed as she bade them sit. 'Bulstrode!

Madeira for the gentlemen and ratafia for myself and Miss Fothergill. And cake.'

Beatrice sat back down on the sofa. Quantock sat in a chair close to Percy and Fenella while Jack, after the slightest of hesitations, sat on the sofa next to Beatrice, earning her another searching stare from the Marquess. But she soon forgot about him as Jack's scent—horses, leather, fresh air and spicy—reached her and her stomach did a strange flip, sending a tingly sensation speeding through her veins. Was this merely a courtesy call or could it mean more? But the second that thought entered her head, she dismissed it. What nonsense. He was the brother of a marquess—he would never be interested in a boring, stupid woman like her.

'I apologise for the intrusion,' Jack said, after Bulstrode served the drinks, 'but—as one of the most prominent landowners in the Pilcombe area—I wish to seek your support for a cause close to the hearts of both myself and my brother.'

See? It's nothing to do with you. Stupid to even think it might be. Beatrice swallowed and stared straight ahead.

'A cause?' Percy glanced at Fenella, and Beatrice knew exactly what that glance meant. Percy could sense this might cost him money. He sat down on the chair next to Quantock's. 'What is this about? Money for the poor, is it? I already pay the poor tax and give alms when I have to…that is, regularly. I—'

'Perhaps—' Fenella cut across Percy's excuses '—we should listen to His Lordship's request first, my dear?'

For Fenella, the feather in her cap from entertaining a marquess would be worth any amount of money for a cause.

'Yes. Yes. Quite. Do go on, my lord.'

Beatrice's uneasiness at this odd situation faded into

the background as she listened to Jack's description of the plight of maimed soldiers who had lost the ability to earn their living and were reduced to begging in the streets if they had no family to support them.

'I am fortunate. I am from a wealthy family and will never find myself without a roof over my head, whatever life throws at me. But too many men, having given their all for King and country, have returned to find they have nothing. I am sure you will agree with me, sir, that they deserve better?'

Jack grew in Beatrice's estimation. She'd recognised his self-consciousness about his injury when they'd met, even though he'd tried to mask it behind his smile, but to put his own distress aside and to care so deeply about the plight of others that he would take action to help them— that was truly admirable.

Percy inhaled and had begun to shake his head even before Jack finished speaking. Before he actually refused, however, Quantock spoke.

'It goes without saying that my brother has my full support, Sir Percy. And, if you were to donate, it would not only set a good example in local society, but also it would enhance your reputation. I am sure you and your good lady can see the benefits of gaining your neighbours' recognition and admiration of your philanthropy?'

'To be sure.' Fenella leaned towards the Marquess, fluttering her eyelashes. 'It is without doubt an admirable cause, my lord. As old schoolfriends of my dear Fothergill, you do right to seek his support, for he does indeed possess considerable influence in the local area.'

'Schoolfriends?' For the first time, Beatrice saw the glimmer of a smile on the Marquess's face. 'Your husband was several years our senior, ma'am—I doubt he was aware of our existence.'

'Oh, no. You are mistaken, my lord. Why, he told me himself that you were at Winchester together. And my darling brother was there, too. Perhaps you recall him? Walter Belling. Now *Sir* Walter, of course, since our dear father's death. As it happens, he visits us next week. *Such* a pity you have missed him. You *must* come again—he will be delighted to renew his acquaintance with you both.'

'Walter is coming here?'

Beatrice blurted the question out before she could stop herself. The hairs on the back of her neck stirred uneasily. Worshipped by Fenella and insufferably arrogant and intolerant, Walter Belling descended upon Pilcombe Grange every summer for an extended stay, regaling them with stories about London life, where, according to Walter, he was a widely acclaimed pink of the *ton*.

'And why should he not, miss?'

Beatrice wilted under Fenella's glare, wrapping her arms around her torso. 'B-but Walter never visits this early in the year. The Season is about to start. He never misses it.'

'He is coming to visit his family.' Fenella simpered at Quantock. 'He is *such* a devoted brother, my lord. Walter is inordinately fond of me…of *all* of us. In fact, he now hopes to make Somerset his permanent home.'

Beatrice's breath grew short and the sensation of something crawling under her too-tight skin caused her arms and legs to quake. Further conversation washed over her as she mentally added another characteristic to Walter. Unmarried. Her stomach clenched and she swallowed back the bile that scalded her throat. *Now* she understood their plan.

Jack heard a tiny sound of distress escape Beatrice. A swift sidelong look showed her gripping her upper arms while the colour had drained from her face, leaving it the colour of whey. The Fothergills were busily toadying up to Kit, hanging on to his every word, and Jack took advantage of their distraction.

'What is it?' He kept his voice low.

The tension emanated from Beatrice in waves. 'Nothing.'

'Nonsense. You're as white as your gown.'

Her eyes drifted shut. The quiver of her skirts suggested her legs were shaking and the faint sheen of perspiration gleamed on her upper lip. It was stiflingly hot in the room and his stump had started to itch maddeningly, but he doubted it was simply the temperature that had overset Beatrice.

'Why are you still here?' He glanced again at the others, but still they paid no attention to him and Beatrice. 'I thought for certain you would have left by now.'

Her chest moved in and out, both too shallow and too fast.

'Beatrice. If you do not answer me, so help me, I shall—'

Her eyes snapped open and he saw her effort to pull herself together.

'I am sorry.' She rushed into speech. 'I did not mean to—'

'Stop it,' he hissed. 'Stop apologising and tell me what is wrong.'

'They found out,' she said in a choking voice. 'They found out about... I inherited some money, do you see. An income. And a house. And they want it. They mean me to marry Walter. But I won't.'

Jack frowned, but kept his gaze on the others in the room as though he were listening avidly to their conversation even as he muttered, 'I saw your face when your sister-in-law spoke of him. You were unaware of his visit?'

'I was. But...now... I see their plan...' She inhaled shakily. 'I will be all right, though. It was just the shock. I am leaving tomorrow. My plans are made.' Her voice lacked conviction. 'I would have gone before, but my ankle was injured and I had to wait until it healed.'

'Where will you go?'

'London.'

'How will you get there?'

'On the stagecoach.'

Jack frowned. She seemed so small, vulnerable and alone, sitting there, her face devoid of colour while she pretended to be brave. 'You cannot travel alone to London.'

'I must.'

Jack caught sight of Percy watching them, his eyes narrowed in suspicion. 'Keep a smile on your face,' he muttered, before saying, loudly, 'Yes, Miss Fothergill. Those men have fought for their country only to find themselves abandoned when they return to British soil. It is scandalous, in my opinion, and I feel it is my duty to help as many of them as I possibly can.'

Percy was distracted by something Kit said and Jack lowered his voice again. 'Your brother is watching us, so try to hide your distress. Where will you catch the stagecoach? In the village?'

'No. That is the first place Percy will look when they realise I've gone.' She quickly told Jack her plan and he listened with growing incredulity.

'You will come a cropper,' he said bluntly. 'There are too many unknowns...far too many places where luck needs to play its part. For instance, even supposing you get as far as Bristol, how will you manage if there are no seats available on the London stagecoach?'

'I shall have to stay in a hotel.'

'You really do have no idea, do you?' She visibly shrank at his words, but he had to warn her of the pitfalls to her plan. 'No decent establishment will allow entry to an un-accompanied female and you would not be safe in the sort of place that would admit a woman without even a maid to accompany her. Do you understand me?'

He expected her to dwindle further but, instead, her mouth set in a stubborn line and her spine straightened. 'Why are you so convinced I will fail? Who's to say there won't be a single seat available on either the mail coach or a stagecoach?'

'That is a risk you are willing to take, is it?' Jack sighed. 'Besides, you will be lucky to get as far as Bristol, in my opinion. What times do the coaches call at this inn you will walk to?' Her cheeks grew pink, giving him his answer. She had no idea. 'And how far is it from here, again? Two miles? Carrying all your belongings? What if it rains? What if Percy works out what you've done when they tell him you never went near the stagecoach that stops in Pilcombe? What if he works it out and follows you and drags you back here? What then?'

Her eyes sheened with tears, filling Jack with guilt for being so hard on her. But, really, she needed to understand her plan was doomed to failure.

'You think I'm stupid, too.' Her hands gripped together in her lap. 'You're as bad as Percy. He thinks I'm too stupid to manage without him to guide me. But I shall and I must. I have no other choice.' Her eyes darted to Fother-gill, who was still hanging on Kit's every word. 'I do not trust them. I have to get free of them.'

'I do not think you're stupid. I do, however, think you

are inexperienced in the ways of the world. You are going to London, but do you have a place to stay? Other than a hotel, that is.'

'Of course I do. The house…and my friends will be there. And there is a chaperon there, too.'

At least she had somewhere safe to go once she arrived in London. The urge to help her…to protect her—and the knowledge there was somewhere safe to deliver her—combined to drive all the very good reasons why he should not get involved from Jack's head.

'Look… I am going to London on Monday. If you wait until then, you may come with me. Be ready at nine.'

'Nine?' Her horror was evident. 'You cannot drive up to the door and expect them to allow me to leave. You do not know them. Th-the servants already watch me like hawks… They are all on Percy's side.'

Jack noticed Lady Fothergill watching them now, suspicion in her eyes.

'Keep smiling,' Jack muttered. 'We're attracting attention.' He smiled at Beatrice's sister-in-law and raised his voice to ask, 'What day is your brother due to arrive, ma'am?'

'On Monday, my lord. Fothergill, we must invite Their Lordships to dinner while dearest Walter is here.' She turned eagerly to Kit. 'Oh, do say you will honour us with an acceptance, Lord Quantock.'

'I shall have to check my availability,' Kit said gravely and Jack bit back a laugh, knowing Kit eschewed all evening engagements. But he frowned, too, as Kit's comment reinforced how reclusive his twin had become.

'Can you not come earlier than nine?' Beatrice whispered, now all the attention was back on Kit. Jack was pleased to see her smiling. No one, looking at them, would guess the strange content of their discussion as she raised her hand to her hair and tidied away a honey-coloured tendril that had escaped its pin. 'Before dawn? I can sneak out.'

'Dawn?' Jack smiled back at her, keeping his voice low. 'This is not an elopement and you are of age. Surely there is no need for such melodrama? They cannot stop you leaving if you wish to.'

'They will. They will find a way.'

He ought to refuse but, instead, he found himself agreeing, unable to resist the plea in her smoky blue eyes. It would be awkward, but not impossible.

'Six, then. And, no, before you ask, I cannot make it any earlier.'

She appeared to shrink into herself. 'I'm sorry. I'm being a nuisance. If you just help me get to Bristol—'

'No. I said I would take you to London and I shall do so. Be at the gates at six.' He glanced at her again—the curve of her cheek, the delicate profile of her nose, the fullness of her pink mouth—and felt that same tug of attraction he had experienced before. 'And, for pity's sake,' he added, in an attempt to deny his response, 'do *stop* being so sorry for everything!'

It was time to leave. Jack caught Kit's eye and rose to his feet.

'So, Sir Percy—are you persuaded to support my charity? Your commitment to an annual subscription would be warmly welcomed,' he added, improvising with gay abandon, relishing the increasingly haunted look on Fothergill's fleshy countenance.

Kit joined the fun. 'Yes, indeed. An annual subscription would be greatly appreciated.' His eyes glinted with mischief. 'It is a cause exceedingly close to my heart, you understand, in view of my twin's experience of wartime injury.'

'Ah. Yes. Of course. Gladly.' Sir Percy cast a desperate look at his wife.

'I shall send you an invitation to dine next week,' Lady Fothergill said, smoothly. 'We can discuss the details over dinner.'

Jack bowed, conceding defeat on that front. He would be in London by then and he knew Kit would rather cut off his own hand than dine with the Fothergills, but he might as well get something from them now. 'In the meantime, a small advance donation would be *most* appreciated.'

'Ah. Yes. Of course. I shall write you a note on my bank.' Sir Percy heaved himself to his feet. 'I'll be back shortly.'

'So…' Lady Fothergill said as the door closed behind her husband, her gaze fixed on Jack, a hint of suspicion still lingering on her countenance. 'What have you and dear Beatrice been discussing so avidly?'

'We have been debating the plight of injured soldiers.'

Jack placed his left arm, with its pinned sleeve, ostentatiously across his chest. Lady Fothergill averted her gaze, her mouth thinning. Her reaction stung, even though Jack had deliberately provoked it in order to distract her.

Sir Percy returned, and in short order, Jack and Kit were riding away from Pilcombe Grange.

'What did the old skinflint give you?'

'Ten pounds, which is more than I expected, given his reluctance to commit. I shall have to find some worthy cause to give it to. Did you like my idea of an annual subscription? That made old porky squirm, did it not? I'm almost sorry I won't be here to accept his dinner invitation and part him from some more of his cash.' Jack grinned at Kit. 'Of course, *you* could always accept and go on your own.'

Kit snorted. 'Not likely! If I never see any of 'em again,

it'll be too soon. Or you could, of course, delay your departure for London.'

'No. I leave on Monday.'

After a lengthy silence, Kit said, 'What is this? No more trying to persuade me to go with you? Brother, you disappoint me. I thought you had more tenacity than that.'

Jack shrugged, reluctant to admit his arrangement with Beatrice. Now that he was out of the house and he could no longer see her attempts at bravado, serious doubts emerged. What was he thinking? It would be a full two-day drive to London, or maybe even longer, depending on the quality of the horses he could hire at the coaching inns. What was he to do with her? They would have to stop overnight. He had pointed out the pitfalls in Beatrice's plans, but he now had to admit there were more than enough pitfalls—deep and very dark—in Jack's plan, too.

'Jack? What is it?' Kit scanned Jack's face. 'You're worried—is it that sister of Fothergill's? I didn't see any reason to worry about her—she looked perfectly well to me. What *were* you talking about, by the by? You looked very cosy together. Was it all about your imaginary charity?'

Jack told Kit about Beatrice's inheritance and her fear she would be forced into marrying Sir Walter Belling.

'And you believe her?'

'Why would she lie? I already knew she'd inherited some money, but I didn't know how much.'

'You still don't,' Kit pointed out.

'It must be substantial if the Fothergills mean to force her into marrying Belling.'

'You have no proof of any of this, Jack. The Fothergills made no mention of any inheritance, only of the imminent visit of Lady Fothergill's brother. It sounds to me as though your Miss Fothergill is possessed of a lurid imagination.'

Jack reined his horse to a halt and stared at his brother.

'Why would you suspect her of making up something like that? That is what you are implying, is it not?'

Kit shrugged. 'It is a ridiculously Gothic scenario, is it not? The evil guardian intent on forcing the poor, helpless heroine into marriage with a dastardly villain? Just the sort of tale guaranteed to garner the sympathy of a bona fide, injured war hero such as yourself. Jack… I have more experience than you. Women can be deadly devious… All I ask is you open your mind to the other reasons Miss Fothergill might be eager to engage your interest. Some people will do anything to climb the ladder in society. I saw the way she smiled at you, fluttering her eyelashes.'

'What rot! Beatrice isn't like that, which you would soon find out if you knew her. You're talking through your arse, Kit.' Jack nudged his horse into motion.

'Well, if her inheritance story is true,' came Kit's voice from behind, 'at least you no longer need to worry about her welfare.'

Jack clenched his jaw, determined not to continue the argument. But a few paces further on, he could not stop himself. 'If *anything*, she is in worse straits than I realised—she plans to run away to London.'

'Run away? Can she not just leave if she wishes to? And why London?' Kit kicked his horse level with Jack's. His eyes narrowed. 'Does she know you are going to London next week?'

Jack ignored that last question. 'She is scared they will stop her going. The servants watch her like a hawk and she *is* terrified her brother intends to force her to marry Walter Belling. You did not see her reaction when she learned of his visit.'

'Good God, Jack. You've swallowed her bait hook, line and sinker, haven't you?'

They rode on in silence until Kit reached across and grabbed Jack's rein, bringing both horses to a halt.

'What's going on, Jack? I know you...' He searched Jack's face, his expression turning grimmer by the minute. 'You're up to something. Tell me you haven't made arrangements to meet her in London.'

Jack removed Kit's hand from his rein and nudged his horse into movement again. There was no point in telling Kit the truth; it would only cause further argument. 'I've made no such arrangement. You can rest easy.'

'Do you know,' said Kit slowly after a few more minutes' silence, 'I believe I shall take you up on your offer to go with you to London on Monday after all.'

Jack stared at him, aghast. Kit shrugged.

'Call it a whim,' he said.

Jack knew when he was defeated. He had no choice but to tell Kit now. 'Then you may as well know that I promised to escort Beatrice to London. On Monday.'

'You did *what*?' Jack winced at Kit's shout. 'Have you run mad? Why would you get involved with a family like that? Mark my words...she fed you a sob story when you rescued her in the hope you would call upon her. She and her brother and that wife of his are all in this together—just think of the benefits to them in allying their name to ours. All that about her inheritance... Where is your proof she has inherited anything at all? What will your answer be when the brother catches up with you on the road and demands you make an honest woman of dear little butter-wouldn't-melt-in-her-mouth Beatrice?'

'What good would that do them? *I* don't have any money.'

'*They* don't know that, do they? They see the brother of a wealthy marquess, ripe for the picking. And don't forget you are currently my heir. It's no secret in the district that I don't intend to marry. I never thought to say this, Jack, but you are a naive fool if you believe anything that comes out of that girl's mouth.'

The fact that Jack was halfway to believing Kit was right did not help his mood. But he had given his word to Beatrice. And her reaction when she'd learned about Belling's visit—no one could act that convincingly. Could they?

'You can complain all you like, Kit. The fact remains I shall pick her up on Monday.'

Kit sighed. 'Very well. I know when I am beaten. We will take my carriage as well as yours. She can travel with a maid in one, and you and I will travel in the other. And we must pray no one recognises us. Or her.'

Jack shook his head, hardly believing that Kit would be coming with him to London after all.

'If we travel as brothers and sister—Messrs and Miss King—who will know any different?' Kit continued.

'Thank you, Kit,' Jack said, swallowing his grin.

Kit grunted. Then sighed. 'Someone has to protect you from yourself.'

Chapter Eight

Jack is on my side.

She had a friend. Beatrice hugged her secret to herself over the next couple of days. The knowledge bolstered her belief that she would succeed. She would go to London and live with Leah and Aurelia, and find herself a nice husband—not Walter Belling—and she would have a family and live a happy and fulfilled life. All dreams that, even while she had planned her escape, she had never been fully confident were within her grasp.

She battled against the sneering voice inside her head that continued to taunt her, undermining her newfound confidence: *You still couldn't manage your escape without help, could you? You're useless! Worthless! Jack is only helping you because he knows about your inheritance. You're stupid if you think otherwise.*

It's not true. That's the sort of thing Percy would say. I don't have to listen. My inheritance would mean nothing to a nobleman's son. And I could have managed without Jack, but wouldn't it be more foolish to turn down his help than to accept it?

The days crawled by. It was only three days from Jack's visit to their early Monday morning rendezvous, but it felt more like three weeks. As the time passed, however, and Percy and Fenella neither challenged her, nor seemed to suspect she had anything planned, Beatrice felt more secure.

'I make no doubt you will be happy Walter will be here tomorrow, Beatrice,' Fenella said as they dined on Sunday evening.

Beatrice—who had just placed a forkful of mutton in her mouth—chewed as she fought to hide her dismay. Even though she would be gone by the time of Walter's arrival, it still felt too close for comfort. She swallowed her mouthful and laid her cutlery on her plate.

'I am unsure why you expect me to be either happy or unhappy about it, Fenella. In fact, I am astonished he is leaving London so close to the Season.'

'Oh, you know dear Walter… He could wait no longer to see us all again. Especially a certain someone.'

She eyed Beatrice expectantly. Beatrice said nothing. She sipped her wine, her insides quaking, but her hand rock steady.

'Percy…' Fenella glared at her husband. The man who was *not* Beatrice's brother.

'Er…yes.' Percy's expression was shifty. 'The thing is, Beatrice, we are aware what a trial it will be to a shy little miss like you to be thrust into the hustle and bustle of a London Season with only your brother to protect you, not to mention that deadline to find a suitable husband, and so we have gone to considerable trouble to save you the effort. I mean—why go to all that bother, when you can marry Walter and remain in the bosom of your family, where you are safe and everything is familiar? He will apply for a licence when he arrives tomorrow, and you can be married straight away. Come, dear Beatrice…think of the advantages. A timid little creature like you won't enjoy the marriage mart in London—it is far too hectic. You will find Walter a generous spouse, my dear—'

Generous with my *inheritance!*

'And we shall all enjoy a Season in London together— you owe this to me and Fenella for all the care we have taken of you since our father died. We are family and one must look after family in this world.'

It felt as though every muscle in Beatrice's body turned to stone, but she found her courage by picturing Leah and Aurelia. *They* would not allow themselves to be brow-beaten and, even though she was leaving in the morning and it would achieve nothing, she owed it to her own pride to stand up to Percy.

'I do not wish to marry Walter.'

Fenella's knife rattled on her plate as she threw it down. 'What? Why ever not? Do you think him not good enough for you? Let me tell you, he is far superior to any other man you could ever hope to attract, you selfish lit-tle madam.'

'The decision is made,' said Percy. 'You owe this to your family.'

Beatrice bit back the words she longed to scream at him. He was *not* her family. None of them was. They never had been. Instead, she concentrated on the plan they had finally revealed and the wording of the will.

'That will not work, though, will it?'

'Why ever not?' Fenella raised a haughty brow.

'You are focused only on the condition that I must wed within a year.' Beatrice fought to steady the wobble in her voice. 'The terms of the will also state that I must remain under the chaperonage of Mrs Butterby until I marry. If I turn up in London already married, I might forfeit my share of the inheritance.'

Percy and Fenella stared at each other. 'It does not say you may not marry beforehand,' said Percy.

'No. It does not. But neither does it say I may…and I am not willing to risk losing a fortune if that is what was meant.' She stared at each of them in turn, brows raised. 'Would you if you were me?'

Percy reddened, his brows beetling over the bridge of his nose. 'If you put it like that, no. But…' and he brightened '…it makes no difference. You can wed in London. We can all stay in your house—'

He fell silent as Beatrice shook her head. She could feel sweat trickling down her back between her shoulder blades and her head swam as she concentrated with every ounce of her being. It was imperative she kept one step ahead of Percy. If he thought that *she* thought she had won, and that she believed she would have a chance to escape their plans in London, then, she reasoned, they were likely to be that much less vigilant watching over her while they were still at the Grange.

'The terms of the will are crystal clear. I must reside in our house in South Street, together with Miss Thame and Miss Croome and under the chaperonage of Mrs Butterby until I marry. And Mr Henshaw mentioned there are but four bedchambers in the house, meaning there will be no room for you to stay. If you wish to accompany me to London, you may, but you will have to make your own living arrangements.'

Beatrice pushed back her chair and rose to her feet. Her knees felt weak and, for one horrified moment, she thought she might collapse, but she hauled in a deep breath, squared her shoulders and said, 'If you will excuse me? I am weary and wish to retire.'

Percy nodded and Beatrice walked steadily from the room and up the stairs to her bedchamber. Once the door was shut, however, she stumbled to the bed and fell on to it, her entire body shaking.

Half past five the following morning found Beatrice, her heartbeat thunderous in her ears, creeping down the main staircase, her reticule swinging from her arm, her packed cloak bag in one hand and the basket, lined with an old woollen shawl, containing Spartacus—and horribly awkward to carry as the cat moved around inside—in the other. At this early hour the servants would already be up and about, but they would be working at the back of the house—in the kitchen readying breakfast and laying the morning room fire. Rather than unbolt the front door, Beatrice hurried into the drawing room and quietly opened the window. She lowered her luggage out over the low sill, then climbed over and jumped down on to the path below. She reached up to push the window shut behind her.

She had dressed in a lilac kerseymere gown over which she wore her felted wool blue cloak. Her smartest bonnet and her best kid gloves completed her outfit. She stood still, pressing back against the wall by the window, her stomach a mass of writhing snakes. She had pictured herself doing this so many times but, now the time had arrived...her chest felt hollow, her throat full, and her head swam. There were so many things that could still go wrong, but at least Jack would be here soon. He would make sure she was all right. Percy was right—she was too stupid to manage without someone to look after her.

Spartacus growled a complaint from inside the basket, shaking Beatrice from her panic. The riskiest part would be as she walked to the entrance gates in the half-light of the early morning. She forced herself into motion, aware that the longer she lingered within sight of the house, the more likely it was the alarm would be raised. She reached the lane without incident. Spartacus let out a furious yowl as she put her luggage down and crouched down by the spot where she had concealed her coins. They were still there, thank goodness. She unwrapped them and put them in her reticule.

Then she waited.

'They were hiding something, Jack. You take care this isn't a trap—after all, what do you truly know about Miss Fothergill? It could all be a clever ploy on their part. All three of them.'

Kit's parting words echoed in Jack's ears as he drove the curricle, Rodwell perched on the back, to Pilcombe Grange to pick up Beatrice. He didn't want to believe it. He thought he was a better judge of people than to be so completely taken in by Beatrice. Being a cavalry officer had certainly taught him to be a good judge of men. But was it because of her sex that he could not believe Beatrice capable of trickery and deceit? Her misty-blue, wide-eyed, innocent gaze materialised in his mind's eye. He didn't want to believe her guilty of anything, that was the truth. If that made him a greenhead, so be it.

He steadied the horses and guided them around the corner into the road that led to the Grange, more confident now in his ability to drive them. Soon enough, the granite pillars that flanked the entrance came into view—the morning sky was lightening by the second—and a cloaked figure stepped forward. Jack reined to a halt, dismissing the kick of his pulse at the sight of Beatrice. It was merely apprehension that Fothergill would suddenly appear... nothing to do with seeing her again. Was it?

Rodwell climbed down and went to stand at the horses' heads.

'Good morning, Beatrice.' Jack tipped his beaver hat. He'd forgotten how enchanting her heart-shaped face was and he felt his heart shift in his chest at the trust in her smiling eyes. He averted his gaze and eyed the bag and the basket on the ground behind her. He jumped down. 'Is that all your luggage?' He picked up the basket and swung it, in preparation for tossing it on the back of the curricle, where it could be strapped in place beneath the groom's perch.

'No! I mean, yes. It is all, but...please... I shall hold that one on my knee.'

Jack belatedly registered that not only was the basket heavier than anticipated, but also that the contents were shifting wildly about inside it. He frowned and set it down on the ground, where it rocked from side to side. An unearthly yowl emanated from it.

'What the devil...?'

Beatrice picked it up. 'I shall explain but...oh, please, can we make haste? What if we should be seen?' She cast a frantic look in the direction of the house. 'The bag can go on the back, but not the basket. Please, J-J—my lord.'

'Jack will do. Very well.'

He was keen to get going, too; he did not relish the idea of facing up to a belligerent so-called brother this early in the day. He placed the cloak bag beneath the groom's seat at the back and then handed Beatrice up into the curricle. He passed her the basket, from which a steady growl now arose, but he curbed his curiosity. Once he was settled in the driver's seat, Rodwell released the horses. Jack waited until he clambered on to the back before setting the vehicle into motion. Beatrice twisted in her seat.

'Good morning, Mr Rodwell. Have you hurt your leg?'

Rodwell laughed. 'Bless 'ee, miss.' Jack knew without looking that Rodwell was rapping his wooden leg. 'I lost m'leg at Waterloo, but His Lordship gave me a job when no one else would.'

'Oh, that is admirable!' Jack gritted his teeth under Beatrice's scrutiny. 'Is it men like Mr Rodwell here that your charity will help?'

'It is.'

'I should like to know more about it. Will you tell me?'

'There's nothing more to tell, other than what you learned the other day.'

Jack felt shame at his brusque reply, but Kit's doubts had fuelled his suspicions about her motives and he couldn't help but hear a false note in her praise and her interest. They had reached the pike road and Jack urged the horses to a faster pace. The sooner she was inside one carriage and he and Kit were settled in the other, the better.

'Are we going all the way to London in this?'

'Not all the way. We will travel in two carriages which are already en route. Once we catch up with them on the Bath Road, you will travel in one with Mabel, who is one of Kit's housemaids, my man, Carrick, and Taylor, Kit's valet. Kit and I will travel in the other.'

'Oh. I was not aware your brother would be coming with us.'

Was that disappointment? Those unwelcome and un-wanted suspicions again swirled despite his efforts to dismiss them.

'Is that a cat in your basket?'

She coloured. 'Yes. Spartacus.' She patted the lid. 'I could not leave him behind. He is my friend.'

'Your friend?' Jack laughed, then sobered when she turned an indignant look on him. 'My apologies. But, after all, he *is* just a cat, Beatrice.'

'He is still my friend. I *could* not leave him behind.

Percy would turn him out at the very least. He might even kill him. I owe him a happier life.'

'In London?'

She ducked her head. 'Yes. In London. For the time being.'

'For the time being? How long do you plan to stay there?' He frowned, racking his brains to remember exactly what she had told him about this mysterious inheritance of hers.

'I am unsure. I shall have to see. It depends...'

'It depends on what?'

She shrugged. A glance at her profile revealed tight lips.

'Beatrice...you *are* certain you have a safe place to stay once we reach London, aren't you?' She was hiding something from him—but what? And why? 'For I will be unable to help you once we are in London. You will be on your own.'

'Yes. My friends are expecting me at our house in South Street.'

Jack whistled. 'South Street? For some reason I thought it would be in a less select area of town. In that case, it is imperative you are seen as little as possible as we travel, for it would ruin your reputation if it became known you were travelling with two men who are not members of your family.'

'Will we get there tonight?'

Jack laughed. 'No. It is too far for one day's journey. But we plan to do it in two days—if we change the horses frequently, we should manage it. We will have to stay overnight at an inn. That is why we brought Mabel with us.'

'What will happen to this?' Beatrice indicated the curricle and pair.

'One of Kit's grooms will return it to Wheatlands.'

'I see.'

Beatrice lapsed into silence and Jack concentrated on his driving, a hollow feeling growing inside him as the realisation hit him that he would soon be in London and would have to face all those people and suffer the pitying stares of strangers. He had successfully suppressed his fear of that ordeal until now, distracting himself with planning the details of picking up Beatrice and their forthcoming journey.

'There is a great deal I do not know, is there not?' Beatrice said in a small voice, a while later. 'I have never stayed at an inn. I have never travelled further than Bristol. I do not even know if my si—friends will allow me to keep Spartacus, or if he will be safe in London.'

Her defeated tone tugged at his conscience, dragging him from his own concerns and bringing shame that he had not been exactly friendly since picking her up. He studied her profile. Her woebegone expression tugged on his heartstrings.

'We all have to learn these things, Beatrice.'

He smiled reassuringly and was rewarded by a shy smile in return even though her fingers still clutched the handle of the basket as though her life depended on it. He prayed Kit would be kind to her on the road—he doubted her fragile self-confidence would help her withstand his twin if he made his distrust of her too obvious. And, selfishly, he did not want to get caught between the two of them. He would be honour-bound to protect Beatrice, but he was also keen to avoid an argument with Kit, who, like Jack, was uneasy about going to London, but was also trying hard to hide it.

'Ah! Good.' Jack recognised the two coaches ahead of them on the Bath Road. 'There are our carriages.'

He hailed them. Both carriages stopped and Jack pulled in behind. He helped Beatrice down from the curricle and then carried the basket containing the cat—a *cat*, for God's sake—to the carriage in which Beatrice would travel with the servants. Kit jumped down from the foremost carriage and stood between the two, watching unsmilingly. Jack's heart sank. He might have known his twin wouldn't dissemble for politeness's sake. His disapproval couldn't be more obvious and it was the main reason why Jack had decreed Beatrice should travel in the second carriage. It would be a long two days.

'Good morning, Lord Quantock.' Beatrice bobbed a curtsy.

Kit glowered at her. 'You made it, then, Miss Fothergill. It is to be hoped we don't all live to rue this escapade.'

Beatrice hung her head, her cheeks flaming. 'I am extremely sorry to put you all to so much trouble.'

Jack glared at Kit as he assisted Beatrice into the second carriage, giving her hand a surreptitious squeeze of support as he did so. Beatrice flicked a smile at him, but her eyes were troubled as she settled on to the seat next to Mabel.

Jack leaned into the carriage. 'Miss Fothergill, may I introduce Mabel—your maid for the duration of our journey—Carrick and Taylor.'

'Good morning to you all.'

The smile Beatrice bestowed upon her travelling companions was accompanied by her charming dimples, completely unlike the smile she had bestowed upon him, and Jack vowed to make it up to her tonight over dinner. Kit's suspicions *had* infected him but, examining his conscience, Jack realised part of his grumpiness was due to his own worries about being in London and meeting new people and old acquaintances. And his insecurities were not Beatrice's fault. There was nothing he could say in front of the servants, however—he must hope Kit would be on his best behaviour over dinner.

'I hope your journey is comfortable.' Jack passed Beatrice the cat's basket and then shut the door while Rodwell—who would share the driving with Gibbons, one of Kit's men—stowed her cloak bag beneath the box seat.

Kit strode back to his own carriage, where his coachman, Murray, waited on the box along with Peters to share the driving. Another groom hurried to the curricle, which he would drive back to Wheatlands. Everyone was in place and ready to go. Jack eyed the two carriages, praying they would pass unremarked on their journey to London. He then followed Kit into their carriage, cast his hat on to the seat opposite and ruffled his hand through his hair.

'Why did you make your disapproval so obvious? Would it really hurt you to give the poor girl the benefit of the doubt?'

'It will not hurt Miss Fothergill to know *someone* is watching her. When—*if*—she proves herself trustworthy, I shall apologise. In the meantime, I shall keep a weather eye out for that lick-spittle brother of hers. And when he catches up with us and seeks to force an unwanted marriage upon you—or even me—it will be my turn to demand an apology from you, Jack.'

'Why so cynical, Kit? Do you attribute such devious motives to every member of the female sex? No wonder you are so set against marriage.' Twin flags of red coloured his twin's cheeks. Jack frowned as a piece of the puzzle that was his twin fell into place. 'You have never breathed a word of an attachment to a female but...your attitude… One would almost believe you've had your fingers burned in the past.'

'Don't be absurd, Jack.'

Kit tipped his own hat over his eyes, stretched out his legs, folded his arms across his chest and settled back against the cushioned seat back. Within minutes, his heavy breathing indicated he slept, leaving Jack to fret about the ordeal awaiting him in London.

Chapter Nine

They had journeyed all day and the light had leached from the heavily laden sky by the time they reached the Three Swans at Hungerford, where they were to spend the night. Beatrice climbed stiffly down the carriage steps before turning to accept Spartacus's basket from Mabel, the maid Jack had provided to help protect Beatrice's reputation. Apart from two brief stops to allow the occupants of the carriage—including a subdued Spartacus—to relieve themselves, none of them had left the vehicle. The Marquess—whose hard stare still intimidated Beatrice—had insisted she must remain out of sight while the horses were changed, as they were after every few hours' travel. Beatrice—peeping discreetly out of the carriage window—had been fascinated to watch the hustle and bustle of the coaching inns as they catered for private carriages, mail coaches and post-chaises alike, providing hasty meals for travellers while the teams were exchanged for fresh horses. She'd had no idea travel was so well organised. Their own luncheon had consisted of sandwiches, cheese and fruit eaten on the move.

Beatrice put down the basket, stretched and gazed around with interest, ignoring the squirm of apprehension in her belly. She had no idea what to expect of the evening ahead, but the memory of Lord Quantock's disapproval weighed heavy on her. The very air seemed oppressive and, although she wasn't cold, she shivered. The other carriage had driven on ahead to allow the gentlemen to bespeak accommodation for the party and a private room in which to dine, and just as Beatrice began to wonder if they had stopped at the right inn, Jack emerged from the door. Her heart did a funny little tumble in her chest at the sight of him, even as thunder grumbled in the distance.

'We're in luck,' he said without preamble. 'There are no other guests tonight, so no one will see you. You should come inside straight away—we cannot risk being seen by any passing travellers.'

Beatrice flinched at his abruptness, dreading even more the prospect of facing them both…making *conversation*… across the dining table.

I have faced worse. Nothing can be as bad as living with Percy and Fenella.

With that thought bolstering her courage, she picked up Spartacus's basket without reply.

'I will bring Spartacus, miss,' said Carrick. 'And Mabel has your bag, so you had best go inside as His Lordship suggests.'

She smiled at her travelling companion, grateful for his kindness, and passed him the basket. All three servants had taken to Spartacus, who had been released from his prison for much of the journey and had curled happily on the seat between Beatrice and Mabel.

'Thank you, Carrick. Yes, let us go in.' Beatrice walked past Jack, still without speaking, hurt that he'd not even greeted her. She might be travelling with his servants, but that did not give him the right to speak to her like one.

Jack soon caught up with her. 'Beatrice?'

She stopped. 'Yes, Jack?'

He stared down at her, a crease between his brows, no sign of that smile that habitually played around his mouth.

'I am sorry. I did not mean to be unwelcoming. Kit's worry we might be recognised has rubbed off on me, I'm afraid.' His lips curved then and his blue eyes warmed. 'I trust your journey went well?'

'I enjoyed it. Thank you.' Jack would be understandably torn between keeping his brother happy and fulfilling his obligations to Beatrice. She could either take umbrage and make their journey even more awkward, or she could rise above the Marquess's disapproval of her. She decided on the latter. The Marquess might be content to be rude, but she would not sink to his level.

'We all got along famously,' she went on. 'Carrick and Taylor pointed out places of interest and entertained us with stories about highwaymen and footpads.' She smiled at the memory. 'Mabel can't decide whether to be terrified or thrilled by the prospect of being held up by a nefarious character with pistols.'

Jack laughed. 'It is most unlikely. The road is not nearly as dangerous as it once was, although I would still hesitate to travel certain sections after dark.'

'I am reassured, but I suspect Mabel will be a touch disappointed to be thwarted of the chance to meet a handsome, romantic highwayman.'

She said no more as the three servants joined them, carrying the luggage.

'Now,' said Jack, 'I must impress upon you all…my brother and I have registered here under the name of King, and you will address us both as "sir" for the duration of the journey. As Miss Fothergill is masquerading as our sister, she is henceforth Miss King. Is that clear?'

Beatrice and the three servants all nodded.

'And, Beatrice, please remain in your bedchamber until it is time to eat. You must keep a low profile if we are to pull this off.'

At that moment, the landlord emerged from the rear of the inn and offered to show Miss King to her room, in the corner of which was a truckle bed for her maid to sleep in.

'Ooh, miss,' Mabel said, the minute they were alone. 'This is a rare treat—I've never ever stayed at an inn before.'

'Me neither, Mabel,' Beatrice admitted, gazing around the bedchamber. 'Nor have I ever been on such a journey, nor been to London. This is all as new to me as it is to you.'

'Shall I let Spartacus out now, miss?'

'Yes. No! Not yet. I really must take him outside first, if I can find a barn where he cannot run off.' At a second growl of thunder, she added, 'And I must do it before it rains.'

'His Lordship won't be happy, miss. He said most partic'lar you shouldn't leave this room unless going for your supper.'

'Oh, dear...'

Beatrice paused, thinking. Her instinct was to obey. But she was aware she had been indoctrinated into obedience by the father who was not her father and then by Percy and Fenella. In the long weeks since meeting her half-sisters in Bristol, she had promised herself she would learn to be bolder, in the hope they would like her more, for she could not believe either of those two strong women would take pride in having a ninny such as her as their sister. And now, surely, was the time to begin that change. It was not, however, easy to defy Jack. She wanted him to like her, she wanted to please him and she was grateful for his escort to London, but she *must* start to stand up for herself. After all—she was an heiress now. A wealthy woman. Mr Henshaw had said so.

'Well...what His Lordship doesn't know won't hurt him, will it, Mabel? It'll be our secret—but...will you come with me, please?' Boldness would come gradually; it did not include wandering around outside a strange inn in the dark with a storm threatening and with those stories about highwaymen still in her head. 'We shall find a privy or a shed or similar. No one will even know we have left our bedchamber.'

Mabel's eyes sparkled. 'Ooh, miss. It'll be like a proper adventure, won't it?'

As it happened, it was less an adventure and more a sedate outing. They encountered no one. They released Spartacus inside a ramshackle, earth-floored shed at the rear of the inn's stable yard. They fought a grim, silent battle to shut him back in the basket again, during which Beatrice suffered a long scratch on the back of her hand, and they regained their bedchamber without seeing a soul and without encountering a single drop of rain. Spartacus, released from his prison, shot under the bed and refused to come out again, despite Beatrice's attempts to soothe his ruffled feelings.

A peremptory knock sounded on the door five minutes later.

'You answer it, Mabel.'

Although temporarily forgotten in the novelty of the journey, Beatrice still feared Percy would somehow catch up with her and force her back to the Grange. He would not easily give up his plan to marry her to Walter.

Mabel opened the door a crack and peered out.

'Please ask Miss Foth... *King*...to join us in the private parlour at her convenience.'

Beatrice's heart leapt at the sound of Jack's deep voice

and she felt a rush of excitement at the thought of dining with him. She only hoped she would not say anything to make a fool of herself... She could not bear Jack to view her as stupid, and yet... Her insides seemed to shrivel as Percy's voice echoed through her head, calling her stupid and useless.

'Miss? Are you unwell?'

With an effort, Beatrice shook Percy from her thoughts. He was no longer part of her life. *His* opinion of her no longer mattered.

'Yes, of course. I must hurry. I do not want to be late.'

Beatrice hastily changed her travelling gown for her pale blue sprigged muslin and then sat while Mabel brushed her hair with long, steady strokes. She tried hard to resurrect that sense of excitement at spending more time with Jack, but it proved elusive, overridden by the knowledge the Marquess would be joining them.

'Mabel...do you know why Lord Quantock mistrusts me so?'

'Not really, miss. But I heard him warn Lord Jack about you. I think it's *your* brother he's worried about. About what he'll do if he catches up with us. That's why he's determined no one sees us, miss.'

Beatrice thought that over while she enjoyed the sensation of Mabel brushing her hair.

'Is Lord Quantock so protective of his brother because of his arm?'

She couldn't believe that would sit well with a proud man like Jack—he would hate to be viewed as a man in need of pity or protection, even though she suspected he had still not come to terms with his injury. She had noticed how he angled his body to hide his pinned sleeve and how he deflected attention from his missing hand by the sheer force of his personality. But Waterloo was only nine months ago… It was early days yet.

'I think so, miss. But they've always stood by each other, since they was boys. The old Marquess, he was a harsh man, and my ma—she worked at Wheatlands afore she married Pa—said he was right hard on them both. Oh!' She clapped her hand over her mouth. 'I didn't ought to say that to you, miss. I keeps forgetting you're one of them. I'm just tellin' what I've heard.'

So, they were both bullied as boys, just as I have been bullied? No wonder Jack decided to help me. And no wonder he scolded me for being too apologetic.

She had wondered about his tendency to reproach her almost every time she said sorry. This could explain it and it gave her another incentive to emerge from her shell. To impress Jack and to encourage him to see her as something other than a victim who needed his help. It was harder to summon any sympathy for the Marquess, even though he had been bullied, too. He ought not to blame Beatrice for something Percy might do.

'You've no need to worry I shall repeat anything you say, Mabel.' Beatrice met the maid's eyes in the mirror. 'I'm a little nervous about dining with them both and I want to be sure not to say anything I shouldn't.'

Mabel nodded understandingly as she began to braid Beatrice's hair.

'His Lordship isn't happy about Lord Jack moving to London, miss. He wants him to stay at Wheatlands, but Lord Jack can't abide being fussed over any more, now his arm is healed, Carrick says, and that's why he needs to leave.'

That confirmed what Beatrice had thought—being cosseted by his own brother was bound to grate on a proud man like Jack.

'So when they argue, it isn't your fault, miss. Well,' Mabel added, 'not *all* your fault.'

Beatrice had to laugh. 'Thank you. I think. It is good to know I'm not entirely responsible for Lord Quantock's testiness.'

'Ooh, bless you, miss—he's a good man, really, is His Lordship.' Mabel pinned Beatrice's braids to her crown. 'There, you're all done.' She smiled at Beatrice in the mirror. 'It's not *just* you he mistrusts, miss. It's all ladies, since he was let down by that Lady Newcombe... Carrick says she broke his heart with her treachery.'

'What happened?'

'All I know is she's a widow of a baron, and His Lordship fell in love with her and then found out she only wanted his title and money.' Mabel lowered her voice to a whisper. 'They say he found her in bed with another man, miss.'

Beatrice's heart softened towards Jack's twin. At least she now better understood his suspicions.

'Poor Lord Quantock. Thank you for telling me, Mabel, and do not fear I shall betray your trust.' Beatrice wrapped her rather threadbare shawl around her and pushed her feet into her satin slippers. 'Now, I must go or suffer even more black looks from Lord Quantock if his supper is cold.'

Jack and Quantock were awaiting her in the parlour. Beatrice curtsied, earning herself an immediate reprimand from Quantock. 'Don't curtsy. You are our sister. And you are to call us Kit and Jack. Do not forget.'

Jack scowled at his brother, but his furrowed brow smoothed as he returned Beatrice's tentative smile. Her insides fluttered at that smile. He was so handsome... Well, they both were. And yet Kit did not command her attention the way Jack did, with his powerful grace, his compelling blue eyes and those fascinating lips that always seemed on the edge of a smile. Kit was altogether more intimidating, his thick blond hair combed straight whereas Jack's was habitually tousled, as though he'd just shoved his fingers through it.

'Have you everything you need, Beatrice?'

'I have, thank you.'

The landlady bustled in at that point, followed by two serving maids carrying dishes. By the time the three travellers were seated and drinking their soup, Beatrice had decided to ignore Kit's mistrust of her and, even though her stomach roiled with nerves, force herself to make polite conversation in the hope it would ease the tension between the brothers.

As soon as the door closed behind the servants, she said, 'I hoped you might tell me more about your charity, Jack. It is such a splendid idea—is that why you are going to London?'

Kit snorted a laugh.

'You think a charity to aid disabled soldiers is risible, my… Kit?'

Kit's eyebrows flicked up. 'Will you tell her or shall I, Brother?'

One corner of Jack's mouth tilted in a half-smile. 'It was a ruse, Beatrice. There is no charity. I had to think of a pretext to call on Sir Percy and that was all I could come up with.' His brows drew together, his blue eyes on Beatrice's face. 'You disapprove?'

He was asking her opinion. She could be polite and deny how she felt, or she could actually say what was on her mind. What was in her heart.

'I am more disappointed, I think. It is such an excellent idea and a worthwhile endeavour. I may not be worldly wise, but…the way you described the plight of those men to us last week…you demonstrated your understanding of their circumstances and you sounded as though you really cared what became of them. Surely there is a need for something…*someone*…to help them?'

She noticed the two men exchange a look and she feared she had gone too far. Percy always said females should not be too free with their opinions, as their brains were inferior to men's—although Beatrice had noticed he never expressed such views in Fenella's presence. She was on the brink of blurting out an apology when she remembered Leah and Aurelia. Neither of them, she was sure, would apologise for expressing an opinion and that gave her the courage to stand by hers. So she arched her brows and tilted her head enquiringly as she held Jack's gaze.

'Whether or not it is a good idea, I am hardly the man to take on such a role.' His left arm twitched, drawing Beatrice's attention.

She narrowed her eyes at him. 'Why ever not?'

Jack reached to remove a cover from a dish on the table. 'May I serve you a helping of this sole, Beatrice?'

'Yes, please.'

Jack's involuntary movement as he declared he was not the man for such a role and his failure to answer her raised many questions in Beatrice's mind.

'Why are you so sure you are not the man for the job?' she persisted as Jack handed her a plate of fish with vegetables. 'I should have thought you were eminently suitable. You have already demonstrated your understanding of those men's difficulties.'

'Jack is still recuperating after his own injury,' Kit interjected. 'He ought not to risk setting his recovery back by involving himself in others' troubles.'

Beatrice held her tongue as she noticed Jack grimace down at his plate at Kit's words.

'You are mistaken, Kit,' he growled. 'My recuperation is complete, hence this move to town.' His gaze flicked to Beatrice and then back again to his food. 'I am flattered you think me capable of such a role, Beatrice, but I have yet to make a decision as to my future now I am no longer in the cavalry.'

Kit scowled. Jack raised his wineglass and drained it. Without a word being exchanged, Kit leaned forward and refilled it.

'Thank you.' Jack's voice was gruff.

She had touched a raw nerve and regretted reminding both brothers of their disagreement over Jack's move to London. But she sensed there was more. When she first met Jack, she'd admired his bravery and his bonhomie, marvelling he could be so carefree despite his loss. Now, studying him as he ate his fish and recalling both Mabel's revelations and her own observations, she understood he was not as carefree as he appeared. There were lines of strain around his eyes and, when he was not smiling— which was seldom—there was a tension around his mouth and jaw.

She turned her attention back to her food, pondering this new awareness as she thrust aside the hopeless desire that she could somehow soothe his pain. She couldn't even look after herself, let alone help a brave hero like Jack.

Yet.

She reminded herself of her determination to prove worthy of her sisters and to do that she must battle her way out of her shyness. Mayhap in time there *could* be hope for her with a man like Jack.

She looked across at Kit, steeling herself to face his hard stare.

'Do you attend the Season every year, Kit? I understand many peers are in London at this time of year to attend Parliament?'

As baronets, neither Percy nor Walter were peers and therefore could not sit in the House of Lords, much to both men's chagrin. Every summer they lamented the fact their ancestors had not reaped the rewards others had gained with ease.

'Not for the past two years,' Kit said. 'I ceased to find entertainment in that shallow social whirl.'

Two years. Was it then he discovered the truth about Lady Newcombe?

'You have not attended the House of Lords either in that time?'

'I have not.'

Beatrice bit her lip and Jack flicked her a look of apology. She gave him a rueful smile. At least she had tried to make pleasant conversation.

'So... Miss Fothergill,' said Kit, after several minutes' silence. His narrowed gaze studied Beatrice, and her stomach tightened. 'What is this Jack tells me of your unexpected inheritance?'

I am an heiress. He is not my relation. I need not tolerate rudeness.

She gathered her courage. 'Beatrice, surely.' She smiled sweetly. 'After all, someone may hear you, *Kit*. And, as I have no idea what Jack told you, how can I answer your question?'

Her heart thumped at her own daring and her entire body felt cold and damp at the same time. She laid down her cutlery. She had not finished her fish, but she feared she might be sick if she tried to force any more down.

'How about you begin with the truth? *Is* there any inheritance?'

'Kit!' Jack sounded horrified. 'It is not our business.'

'No, Jack. Please.' Beatrice touched his hand, fleetingly. She couldn't bear to be the cause of further argument between them if they were already at odds about Jack moving to London, as Mabel had said. 'He is entitled to ask. The inheritance is real. It is a one-third share in the house in South Street and another property and some invested funds.'

'So you claim to be a woman of means, now?' It was close to being a sneer.

Beatrice's stomach began to churn as shivers chased across her skin. She felt her insides shrivel, despite her vow to be brave.

'Kit!' Jack slammed his hand on the table. 'You owe Beatrice an apology. She has done nothing to warrant such suspicions.'

'I have claimed nothing,' Beatrice said quietly as soon as Jack finished speaking. 'I have answered your question truthfully, as you requested. And—just to be clear,' she added, her voice quivering despite her effort to speak firmly, 'no, I have no proof because Percy has my copy of the will. But I shall be sure to furnish you with all the evidence you could want once we get to London.'

'My apologies.' The deep colour flooding Kit's face went some way to gratifying her, but she could not wait for the meal to be over.

Jack smiled at her, his eyebrows flicking up. It was a look of approval, one to bask in, and despite the anxiety twisting her stomach, a bud of happiness unfurled inside her. Jack's gaze shifted to her hand and his smile faded. He reached across and touched her hand, sending shivers—this time of delight—chasing up her arm. 'Where did you get that scratch?'

Before Beatrice could answer, Kit—his upper lip curling—said, 'That wretched cat, I make no doubt.'

'He did not mean it. He is not vicious. He did not want to go back in his basket.'

'And who can blame him?' Jack uncovered a dish in the centre of the table. 'Might I serve you a portion of this mutton stew, Beatrice?' He picked up a ladle.

'I have eaten sufficient, thank you.'

Jack frowned at her. 'You should try to eat a little more. You do not wish to be ill—we've a long day of travel planned tomorrow.' He ladled some stew on to a plate, which he placed in front of Beatrice. She admired how deftly he managed, using just one hand. 'We hope to reach London by nightfall.'

Beatrice ate a forkful of the stew. It tasted of nothing, yet the two men were tucking in, clearly relishing it. She ate some more, just to please Jack, who, she could see, was keeping his eye on her. 'What time shall we leave tomorrow?'

'We thought about seven in the morning, to give us sufficient time,' Jack said.

'It's over sixty miles,' Kit added. 'It'll be a push to do it in less than eleven hours, but it's preferable to spending another night on the road. At least the Bath Road is well maintained, and if we change teams often enough, we should make it.'

Beatrice pushed her plate away. 'I shall make sure to be ready by seven,' she said, 'but I'm afraid I cannot eat any more. I am sorry. I shall retire, with your permission?'

It seemed better to leave them now that they were in a better mood with one another, and with her, than risk another argument. As she stood, so did the two men.

'I will see you safely to your room,' said Jack.

Chapter Ten

As they walked side by side towards the stairs, Jack said, 'I am sorry Kit was so ungentlemanly, Beatrice. I can only apologise.'

'There is no need, Jack. It is not your fault.' She sent him a sidelong glance, wondering if he was aware of Lady Newcombe's betrayal of his brother. 'I am used to it. Percy and Fenella were often angry with me.'

'Your generosity does you credit. He does not deserve it—it is me he is angry with, not you. He does not want me to move to London.'

'He will miss you, I dare say.'

'I know. He cannot understand why I will not stay at Wheatlands and help him run the estates.'

'And why is it you do not wish to stay?'

They had reached the top of the stairs, and Jack stopped to face Beatrice, a groove etched between his brows. He thrust his hand through his hair, tousling it even more, so it stuck up on end. Beatrice's fingers itched to reach up and smooth it down again. How thick and soft it looked. How would it feel? She pushed such thoughts away as Jack began to talk.

'I cannot stay. I don't expect you to understand but…it

would be too easy. I would want for nothing. Kit would pay me an allowance. An allowance!' He turned on his heel and took two strides along the landing before returning to her. 'What kind of a man would I be if I settled for being my own twin's pensioner for the rest of my days? No. I have my pride... I need my independence and I need... *want*...to find a purpose to my life.'

'A purpose?' She tipped her head questioningly. 'Could that not be to help those veterans even though it was not, at first, a serious proposal?'

He huffed a somewhat bitter laugh. 'I have an income, but it is barely sufficient to look after myself, let alone enough to provide meaningful help for those men. There are so *many* of them, Bea—I have read the reports in the newspapers and it breaks my heart.'

Bea? Her heart fluttered. He had said it without, seemingly, noticing he did so. Never had anyone other than her mother called her Bea. Emotion, both happy and sad, thickened her throat and she had to cough to clear it in order to speak.

'Then use your influence to raise money, Jack.' The taut lines of his face showed something of the strain he usually took such pains to hide and she felt honoured he felt comfortable enough to reveal it to her. 'You did it with Percy, even though that was a ruse. It proves you can do *something*, does it not?'

Jack stared down at her, his blue eyes serious, his tousled hair giving him a boyish appeal.

'Maybe...'

The doubt in his voice pulled at her heartstrings and, without volition, she brushed the back of her fingers along his lightly stubbled jaw. The memory of the touch of his lips on her cheek flashed through her, flooding her with heat, and aghast at her boldness, she snatched her hand away and rushed into motion, heading towards her bed-chamber. When Jack caught her up, she launched into speech to cover her confusion.

'I still fear Percy will find me. He will not easily give up on his plan to marry me to Walter.'

They paused by unspoken, mutual consent outside her bedchamber door. The passage outside was silent and dim, lit only by a lamp left burning at the head of the stairs, giving a sense of privacy that set Beatrice's nerves fizz-ing, resulting in a strange yearning ache deep inside her.

'You have nothing to fear.'

Jack's deep murmur only increased the sense of inti-macy, and Beatrice's pulse leapt as he raised his hand and pushed a tendril of hair from her face, his eyes following his action. Then they slid to hers and captured her gaze. Her breath caught even as her heart pitter-pattered so hard in her chest she felt sure he must hear it.

'I won't allow Fothergill to harm you in any way. I promise.'

'But what about in London? You will not be there. I—'

'Hush.'

His musky scent filled her as his face lowered to hers. His warm breath caressed her lips and exhilaration spi-ralled through her as his mouth covered hers. His maimed arm, strong and unyielding, wrapped around her waist, pulling her close and holding her safe and secure. His hand cupped her cheek; her eyes drifted shut as her lips opened in response to a touch from his tongue and Bea-trice experienced her first ever kiss. It was what she had wanted but had not dared wish for. It was everything she hoped it would be. Her hands clutched his upper arms, her fingers digging into his sleeve and the rock-hard muscles beneath. Her entire body quivered with excitement…with the need for more. Her lips moulded to his as he explored her mouth with his tongue and that strange aching need intensified as it centred between her thighs. Her hands moved up to his shoulders and then into his hair...every bit as thick and soft as she'd imagined.

The slam of a door from below broke the spell and Jack tore his lips from hers. She beamed up at him, but her smile soon slipped as she saw that he did not appear delighted. Rather, he looked *un*happy.

'I am sorry. I should not have done that.' He released her, stepping back.

'I... I do not understand. Are you cross with me?' Her throat now ached as tears threatened. 'What did I do wrong?'

'Nothing. It is not your fault. It is mine. I am angry at myself for letting that happen. Goodnight, Beatrice. Sleep well. And don't forget...seven o'clock sharp. Let us *try* to keep Kit happy, shall we?'

His grin lacked warmth.

'Of course. Goodnight, Jack.'

Beatrice entered her room with a heavy heart, unable to fathom what had gone wrong. Percy's words came back to her: *'You won't have the nous to sort the wheat from the chaff. There'll be men galore who only want you for your money—telling you all sorts of lies to get what they want.'*

Percy was right about one thing, she thought, as she readied herself for bed. She did not understand men. But if Jack kissed her because he now knew about her inheritance, why did he stop kissing her? And why was he angry?

Mabel was snoring softly in the truckle bed in the corner, Spartacus curled at her feet. The room was cool—they'd opened the top window earlier to help the smoking fire to draw—but Beatrice soon warmed up once she was in bed.

Sleep proved elusive, however. She still couldn't fathom Jack's behaviour, but thoughts…ideas…whirled through her brain. Jack must find her a little bit attractive, or he would not kiss her. And he did seem to enjoy her company, even if she did sometimes irritate him with her apologies. And, heaven only knew, she liked him. He was very handsome. She trusted him. He was kind. And she must needs marry *someone*. That was another thing Percy had been right about. The idea of the Season ahead and of parading in front of all those people—trying to determine who was genuine and who false—intimidated her more than she had yet admitted, even to herself.

She knew she could expect no more than a marriage of convenience, but it must be to a man of her choosing, *not* to the likes of Walter Belling. That thought made her feel physically ill. And she had no doubt Percy, Fenella and Walter still posed a danger—she was certain they would follow her and try to force her to marry Walter.

The only way she would be fully safe would be to marry someone else as soon as possible. So…what if—and the idea was so audacious but so perfect she barely dared to think it…but—why not Jack? He needed money. She had money. What could be better?

She eventually drifted off to sleep, her head full of ideas of how best to encourage Jack to view a silly ninnyhammer like her as a prospective wife.

'Where the devil is she?' Kit paced the parlour the following morning. 'It's close to seven. If we don't leave soon, it'll be dark before we reach London.'

Jack stared at the parlour door, willing it to open and reveal Beatrice before Kit completely lost his temper and found more fuel to fire his unaccountable suspicions of her.

Self-recrimination swirled through Jack's thoughts.

Why the devil had he kissed her last night when he knew damned well he could offer her nothing? Certainly not marriage, which was the natural end to a journey begun with a kiss with an innocent lady such as Beatrice. Try as he might, he could not excuse his behaviour. It had been pure, selfish self-indulgence, with no thought of the consequences for her.

Her inheritance must be substantial if Fothergill was so keen to keep it in the family and the house in South Street supported that view. Although, thinking over what Beatrice had revealed, Jack was aware there were still unexplained holes in her story. Why a one-third share? Who were the other beneficiaries? And who had left money and property to Beatrice Fothergill, who, as far as he knew, had led a totally secluded life?

Whatever the answers to those questions, it would not change the facts. Jack's pride already prevented him from accepting Kit's offer of remaining at Wheatlands. How much worse to marry a wealthy woman, and to know every stitch of clothing he wore, every morsel of food he ate, was paid for by her?

That kiss had prised open a door deep in his soul, however. He'd not had a woman since before Waterloo…before his life had changed for ever with the slash of a cuirassier's sabre. He had not even wanted one. Not thought about it. Until he met Beatrice. After their kiss, he'd lain awake long into the night, reliving every moment—his arms around her warm body as she pressed close; her full breasts squashed against his chest; the soft silk of her cheek, the taste of her on his tongue, her fresh lemon fragrance not entirely masking the scent of a woman aroused. He had savoured the flow of desire around his body and the pooling of lust in his groin.

He had come down to break his fast this morning both

longing to see her and dreading it, because he knew he had behaved badly after that door had slammed last night, jerking him from the sensual haze that had enveloped him. He had felt nothing but disgust for himself and his weakness, and he was aware his brusqueness with Beatrice was prompted by his realisation he was starting to care for her. Too much. And he could not afford to. She would have men clamouring after her as soon as she appeared in society, any one of whom would make her a better husband than he ever could. An impoverished younger son who was not even a whole man was a worse than useless bargain for an heiress such as Beatrice.

He strode for the door. 'I'll hurry her along.'

He and Kit had finished eating over half an hour ago. They had arranged to leave at seven, yet Beatrice had yet to show her face even though Carrick had assured them almost an hour ago that both Beatrice and Mabel were awake. Jack took the stairs two at a time, the fear growing that, somehow, Percy had arrived and spirited her away. He rapped on her bedchamber door. There was no answer. With a muttered curse, he thrust the door wide and scanned the room: the unmade bed, the half-packed cloak bag, the cat's basket, its lid open. He stared at that last, frowning. Then he looked around the room again, more slowly. No sign of Spartacus apart from a dish containing scraps of meat. An untouched dish. A cool breath of air wafted across his face and his attention switched to the wide-open window. He ran across the room and peered out on to the slanting roof of an outbuilding below.

That cursed cat.

Jack spun on his heel and raced back downstairs. Carrick was just entering through a side door, his face red and sheened with sweat. He slammed to a halt and stared guiltily at Jack.

'Where is she?'

'Down by the river. Someone said they saw a black cat down there.'

A black cat... How many soldiers had been superstitious about black cats when they crossed their paths? Jack had never set any store by such gullibility but, at this precise moment, he agreed wholeheartedly. Would that this particular black cat had never crossed *his* path. Or its owner, who, despite his very best intentions and almost without him realising it, had worked her way under his skin. This couldn't have happened at a worse time, just when Kit's suspicions had been somewhat allayed by Beatrice last night—he could already hear his brother's complaints if they were delayed by that damned cat going absent without leave. He would without doubt believe Beatrice had released her pet deliberately to give Fothergill time to catch up with them, and God help him, there was still a tiny niggle of doubt inside Jack's brain too, although he hated himself for it and despite his heart telling him she was exactly what she seemed.

He swore under his breath and turned his steps towards the river and there she was, looking delightfully dishevelled in the stiff breeze, her golden-brown hair streaming loose, her shawl—surely too thin to be outside in this weather—clutched around her. Mabel was also there, further along the bank, poking in some undergrowth with a stick. And there was Murray. And Gibbons and Peters as well, for God's sake. They should be putting the horses to, not messing around out here.

'Beatrice!'

She turned, her bluey-grey eyes misty with tears, and the angry diatribe he had been about to unleash died on his lips. All he wanted was to put his arms around her and make everything right for her.

'Oh, Jack! I'm so sorry. I know it is getting late, but I *must* find Spartacus. I cannot leave him here.'

That urge to comfort her made him brusque. 'How long ago did he get out? Why in Hades was the window open in the first place? Have you no sense?'

He hardened his heart as she gulped, dashing a tear from her cheek.

'I'm sorry. I heard him as he scrambled out, but I was too slow to catch him.' She drew in a shuddering breath. 'I'm so stupid. I didn't think he could get out there. It was only the top window. It wasn't even open very wide.'

Jack's exasperation waned, to be replaced by shame.

'I'm sorry I shouted and you are *not* stupid. Look, it's hardly the end of the world. Why do you not come back to the inn for your breakfast? We'll find him. Cats are not fools. He will come back when he is hungry.'

'But he doesn't know this place.' She grabbed Jack's hand between both of hers. '*Please* don't make me leave him behind, Jack. I know your brother will be angry with me and I am truly sorry for causing you such trouble, but I cannot bear to lose him.'

Jack squeezed her hand. 'I won't even try to persuade you,' he promised. This Beatrice put him more in mind of the Beatrice he had first met on the road. For all her attempts to be brave when she stood up to Kit last night—and Jack had been conscious of the effort it had taken her—it did not take much for her to revert to the downtrodden, apologetic girl of before. That damned Fothergill had a lot to answer for and Jack found himself hoping that he *would* come after her and give Jack the chance to thump him as he deserved.

'Murray?'

'Milord?'

'I assume you and Gibbons have already eaten?'

The coachman nodded.

'Good. Keep searching, will you? I'll be out again shortly.'

'Yes, sir.'

'Mabel. You come and eat now, too, for as soon as the cat is found we must be on our way.'

Back in the parlour, Kit was sitting at the table, drumming his fingers, a black scowl on his face. 'Where have you been?'

'Spartacus escaped,' said Beatrice before Jack could reply. He admired how she did not flinch from Kit's hard gaze and his heart melted as he understood that, although she might reveal her vulnerable side to Jack, she would not crumble before Kit and allow him to browbeat her.

'You have found him now?'

Her chin went up. 'No. The men are still looking for him.'

'Well, they have until you have eaten. If he isn't found by then, we go without him.'

Beatrice's jaw set. 'I will not leave without Spartacus.'

Kit's expression hardened. 'It is hardly for you to dictate terms, Miss Fothergill. The carriage and men are mine and I am paying for the horses. We leave when I say we leave.'

'Beatrice...' Jack steered her to a chair, his hand at the small of her back. 'Please...eat your breakfast. Kit?'

Jack indicated the door with a jerk of his chin. He had given his word to Beatrice they would not abandon her cat and he would keep it. 'I should like a word with you. In private.' He ignored the pleading look Beatrice sent him.

Kit followed him into the passage.

'Outside,' said Jack. It wouldn't do to be overheard, not when the inn staff all believed Beatrice was their sister.

He led the way across the street to an empty alleyway between two buildings.

'Why are you so gullible, Jack?' Kit launched his attack immediately. 'She is playing for time. That brother of hers will—'

'He is *not* her brother, Kit.'

'So she claims.' Kit paced along the alley before returning. He leaned back against the brick wall and folded his arms. 'Have you *seen* this will, let alone read it?'

'You know I have not. Fothergill took it from her.'

'Convenient! She did not show you any document when you rescued her from that damaged post-chaise. In fact, she did not even *mention* an inheritance then, from what I recall, just wittered on about her salvation. Do you not find that suspicious? You mark my words—they concocted this tale between them to snare her a husband who would elevate them all in the eyes of society.' Kit grasped Jack's arm. 'How can you trust her, Jack? You barely know the girl. Have you fallen for her? Is that what this is all about?'

Jack snatched his arm away. 'Don't be ridiculous. She was being bullied, as Father used to bully us, and I felt compelled to help her. *That* is what this is all about.'

'Please.' A tearful voice interrupted him and Jack spun around. 'Do not quarrel over me.' Beatrice was silhouetted in the opening of the alley, her hands clasping and unclasping in front of her. 'I cannot bear to be the cause of arguments... Please. Just leave me here. I have enough money to hire a post-chaise to take me to London after I find Spartacus.'

'No!' Jack took a step towards Beatrice, but she backed away, her hands shooting out as though to fend him off. 'Kit!' He glared at his brother. 'This is not like you. How can you be so uncharitable? You go if you must, but I shall stay. Beatrice can complete the journey with me in *my* carriage.'

'You blasted fool, Jack. You'll be walking straight into their trap! If you think I'll leave you to their tender mercies, you can think again. And you cannot arrive in town with her brazenly sitting beside you. There'll be hell to pay.' He turned to Beatrice. 'Well, madam? Have you broken your fast?'

Her chin tilted up at that. 'My appetite has quite deserted me, my lord.'

'Very well. Then let us go and search for that flea-ridden animal of yours. The sooner we are on the road again, the happier I shall be.'

Kit stalked off, leaving Jack facing Beatrice. 'I am sorry you witnessed that, Beatrice. Kit... I do not know why, but he is convinced you mean to entrap me although he cannot give me a cogent reason why I might be a worthy target for such a scheme. I am not wealthy—I've already told you my income is small, and insufficient to support a family, so I doubt I shall ever wed.' He forced a grin. 'As if any woman would choose a man like me.'

He touched his left arm. A frown flitted across Beatrice's features and Jack realised that not once since they met had she really paid any attention to his disability. She had not even flinched when he touched her last night. It was he who was preoccupied by it. He wondered if she would be unique or if others, too, might just view him as a man. No more. No less. He thrust that thought away, recalling the many sidelong, pitying looks he had been subjected to during his convalescence in Somerset. How much worse would it be in a city like London?

He met Beatrice's gaze, her bluey-grey eyes shining with sincerity, and his throat thickened. How could Kit ever doubt her motives? Look at her. So innocent. So kind. So genuine.

'I would not try to entrap you, Jack. I would not do that to any man, let alone one who has been such a friend to me.'

'Even one so lost to propriety that he kissed you last night?'

She really did blush delightfully, but her eyes became guarded. 'I kissed you, too. But a kiss between friends means nothing, does it?'

Jack ignored the tweak of his heart at her words. He should be delighted she was prepared to pretend their kiss meant nothing to her, not disappointed.

'You are generosity itself. I am sorry I took advantage of you.'

'Let us leave the subject. It meant nothing.'

Again, that twinge of regret. 'Very well. And now, as we are friends again, shall we go and find Spartacus?'

'Yes, please.'

Her smile lit her face, but her dimples were absent, leaving Jack to wonder how deeply Kit's suspicions had stung.

As it happened, it was Kit who found Spartacus, crouching in the inn's feed store, his green eyes fixed unblinkingly on a small, irregular gap in the wall, and the travellers eventually set off three hours behind schedule, with Kit grumbling it would mean staying an extra night at an inn and give Fothergill even more of a chance to catch up with them. Jack paid him little attention, his tension ratcheting higher, notch by notch, the closer they got to London and the inevitable stares and whispers he would face.

Chapter Eleven

Jack's words to Kit rankled Beatrice throughout that day. *How can you be so uncharitable?* Was that how he saw her? A charity case? Someone who needed rescuing? A *victim*? So much for her foolish dreams last night—she just hoped she had succeeded in sounding as unconcerned about that kiss as she intended now she knew Jack's true opinion of her. And, as for Kit, what right did he have to suspect her of such a despicable deception?

'Are you quite well, miss?' Mabel's anxious enquiry penetrated Beatrice's inner turmoil. 'Only you've been terrible quiet all day.'

Beatrice swallowed past the lump of hurt misery that had taken up residence in her throat and tore her gaze from the passing scenery, upon which it had fixed unseeingly ever since they set off. 'I am quite well. Only a little weary of the journey, as are we all.' She stroked Spartacus, who uncurled and stretched out on her lap, his side vibrating beneath her hand although she could not hear his purr above the rumbles and creaks of the carriage.

'I should think we will stop for the night soon,' said Carrick. 'There's no hope of reaching London before the light goes and I know Their Lordships won't wish to cross Hounslow Heath after dark.'

The prospect of another evening of stilted conversation with Jack and Kit did nothing to raise Beatrice's spirits and she wondered if she might eat her dinner in her room, alone, rather than with two men who thought so little of her. But, still, old habits died hard and she did not wish to appear ungrateful. After all, they *had* put themselves out a great deal on her behalf. She could only hope they were no longer arguing over her—it distressed her to think her presence was heightening the tensions between them.

Jack's stiff posture as he flagged down the carriage at the Castle Inn at Salt Hill told her that hope was forlorn. Her stomach tightened and the lump in her throat ached as she identified the undeniable strain behind Jack's easy smile as he greeted her and handed her from the carriage. Kit had emerged from the inn and he nodded unsmilingly at Beatrice before turning to speak to Gibbons.

'Have you been here long?' She forced the question through dry lips, just for something to break the uncomfortable silence.

'Half an hour or so. We're still twenty-one miles from town and this inn has a good reputation, so it seemed unnecessary to push on. We've bespoken dinner for half-past six, if that suits you—it will give you time to settle in your room and change your gown should you wish.'

'Jack…' Beatrice hadn't had a chance to speak to him privately since Spartacus had been found. 'I am so sorry for causing a rift between you and your brother. I had no intention… I wouldn't for the world…'

'Hush! There is no need to apologise. We are brothers and brothers squabble all the time. Kit has nothing against you personally—he is merely concerned about…'

Jack paused, shrugged, then gestured vaguely, encompassing the inn, the carriage and the servants who were unloading the luggage required for an overnight stop, including, of course, Spartacus, who was once more fastened securely inside his basket.

'About me and my intentions.'

She had thought of very little else all day, cringing at those silly plans she had made while lying in bed the night before. Those ridiculous, self-deceiving fantasies. She was pathetic and stupid, viewed by one brother as a scheming hussy and by the other as a burden. Someone unable to look after herself—weak and helpless and in need of a kind friend to rescue her and protect her. Beatrice was exhausted by her day-long avalanche of self-blame and, desperate not to show any hint of distress, her temper roused.

'Well, you may inform your brother that—'

'Why not inform me yourself, miss?'

Beatrice spun around to face Kit. So like Jack and, yet, unlike him as well. No ready smile, no warmth in those blue eyes. But Beatrice was done with allowing him to intimidate her, or with making excuses for him because of Lady Newcombe's betrayal. She gripped her hands in front of her to stop them trembling and swallowed hard.

'Very well. As I told you, I have inherited both property and a regular income. A *substantial* one.' She prayed Mr Henshaw had been correct in labelling her and her half-sisters three very wealthy young women. 'Whether or not you choose to believe me is your prerogative. I cannot go into details yet, but you will discover the truth of it once we reach London and I am in a position to reimburse you for all expenses incurred on my behalf for this journey, including the entire cost of this additional overnight stay.'

'There is no need for that,' Jack said, but Kit merely looked at her, his hard eyes brimming with suspicion.

'There is every need. I am sorry, Jack, but from what

I understand, your brother is the one paying for this journey, not you.' A muscle clenched along Jack's jaw. Beatrice regretted she had insulted him, but they had left her no choice. The situation required blunt speaking. 'I will not remain under any obligation to him one minute longer than necessary. Or to either of you, in fact. So I shall repay him, as soon as I have access to my funds.'

Heavens, I do hope I shall be able to access some money.

Her pride in herself for confronting Kit wavered—she really had no idea how *any* details in her life would work once she was in London. But…she stiffened her resolve. She would be with Leah and Aurelia and she must trust it would work out for the best.

'We had better go inside,' Jack said tightly as a postchaise drawn by a pair of horses clattered past them along the road. 'We are too visible standing here.'

Beatrice watched the vehicle stop to allow its passenger to alight at the Windmill Inn—an impressive redbrick building with a veranda along the frontage situated further along the street, on the opposite side—and then preceded the two men into the Castle. A glance back at the Windmill revealed the post-chaise driving around the back, presumably into the stable yard, and the germ of an idea began to form.

A chambermaid showed Beatrice upstairs to her bedchamber, which, to her delight, boasted a fine view of Windsor Castle, which Carrick had identified for them before they reached Salt Hill. Mabel was already there, setting out Beatrice's gown for dinner and her nightgown for later. The room was small and Mabel's truckle bed had been set up in an antechamber accessed through an adjoining door.

'Where is Spartacus?' There was no sign of his basket in Beatrice's room.

'Rodwell took him, miss. He'll let him out in the stables and then bring him up here later. He'll be quite safe.'

Nevertheless, Beatrice fretted until Spartacus was safely back within her sight, and she checked and double-checked the windows to ensure they were securely fastened before going downstairs to join Jack and Kit for dinner. As she opened her door, however, a furious whispered conversation in the corridor outside reached her ears. She paused, holding the door slightly ajar so her presence wasn't detected, having no wish to encounter the man who sounded so angry. She strained her ears to make out who was speaking and what had enraged him.

'It was them, I tell you, Jack. Fothergill and that wife of his, *and* her brother. *Now* will you believe me?'

Percy and Fenella? And Walter? Here? Beatrice's legs trembled and sick dread churned her insides. She had almost expected it, but it still came as a shock. How had they managed to catch up...? But she knew how. They had caught up in the three hours it had taken to find and catch Spartacus.

My fault. All my fault. No wonder Kit is so suspicious of me.

She wanted to retreat, lock herself in her room and curl up under the bedclothes, but she made herself carry on listening, putting her eye to the opening. She saw Kit outside Jack's door, his hands propped either side of the door frame, every line of his body rigid with rage. Jack remained out of Beatrice's sight, but it was his voice she could hear now—a deep, calming response to Kit's angry, whispered words.

'Well, they have gone now, from what you tell me, so

what is it you expect me to do? If there was any collusion, which I still doubt, Fothergill would be here, searching for Beatrice, would he not?'

'The inn is full. You know that. You mark my words— they will find other accommodation and they will be back. We should have left that damned cat behind. We'd be safe in London by now, and Miss Beatrice Fothergill would have missed her chance to snare the brother of a marquess.'

Humiliation curdled Beatrice's stomach, making her feel sick. Kit really did despise her. And she despised herself for coming between the two brothers like this. Any other person would have shown more backbone... Any decent person would have refused any further help rather than causing such a rift.

Jack's scornful laugh reached Beatrice's ears. She could almost picture him, standing nonchalantly inside his chamber, hearing his brother out with a slightly incredulous look on his face—his brows raised, the corners of his mouth lifting in that attractive way he had when he was trying not to smile, his blue eyes twinkling and teasing.

'Kit...has it occurred to you that, if you are right and Beatrice planned to trap me into marriage to advance the Fothergill family's position in society, you have put yourself—a bigger, richer prize by far—very prominently in their sights? How much more beneficial to catch an actual marquess than his brother!'

She ought not to keep listening, but she could not help herself.

Kit's laugh was bitter. 'Hell will freeze, Brother, before that would happen. I could weather any scandal, and *I* wouldn't care if that little Jezebel's reputation was thoroughly and irretrievably ruined. But you? You and I both know a hero like you would never allow that to happen.'

'Let's not argue, Kit. Time will tell where the truth lies—does the fact that Belling is here not lend truth to Beatrice's story? Let us just agree to be ready for Fothergill if he *should* show his face here. Come. I'm for my dinner. Let us get some food in our bellies. Everything will look better then—you mark my words.' Kit moved back and Jack stepped into view. He slung his right arm around Kit's shoulders. 'By this time tomorrow, we will be in town and you and I will laugh together over this little skirmish. And you, my dear Kit, will be forced to admit you are wrong.'

Neither man as much as glanced back towards Beatrice's door before they turned for the stairs. Beatrice closed her door quietly and leaned back against it, tears burning behind her eyes. Kit thought her a Jezebel. And Jack...he'd barely even attempted to defend her against the insult. Instead, he could not wait to be in town and to forget all about her and this ill-starred journey.

Mabel chose that moment to come out of the adjoining room. 'Oh! I thought you had already gone down to dinner, miss. Is there anything you need?'

Beatrice rubbed her forehead and then, surreptitiously, her eyes. 'No. Thank you, Mabel. It is just... I have the headache, so would you please pass on my apologies to Their Lordships and request that a plate be sent up here for me? I intend to retire early.'

'Of course, miss. I thought you had been too quiet today... It's all that upset over Spartacus this morning. And now look at him, curled up on your bed like an innocent angel.'

Beatrice eyed Spartacus. She loved him unconditionally, but even she would not describe him as an angel. Neither in his appearance nor in his behaviour.

'Shall I come back to eat my dinner here with you, miss?'

'No. No, there is no need. I shan't be very good company, I'm afraid. I shall eat and then I shall sleep, so please be sure to come through my room quietly when you return. And take care not to let Spartacus slip out.'

'I'll take care, miss. Goodnight.'

Beatrice waited until after a serving maid had brought her dinner up to her on a tray before she allowed herself to examine the idea hovering at the edges of her mind. She liked Jack—very much—and she had thought, after that kiss, that he liked her, too. But Percy had always warned her men would take advantage of her innocence. Had Jack merely taken that opportunity to snatch a kiss? And was he really her friend, or had he simply followed his instinct to rescue someone who had revived his memories of being bullied as a child? Whatever his motive, the result was disastrous for his relationship with Kit.

Percy's arrival made her decision easier. His motive in chasing her was because he wanted to keep her inheritance in his family but, no matter what she said, Kit would remain convinced she had designs on Jack. She was safe in her bedchamber tonight, but the thought of weathering his suspicions over breakfast and until they were on the road again made her feel physically sick. And there was the risk that Percy might find them and confront them, and where on earth might that lead?

The idea had first come to her when that post-chaise had halted at the Windmill Inn. Jack had said they would not need to leave until nine in the morning, as they had only twenty-one miles left to go. So...what if she hired a post-chaise for the remainder of the journey? If she arose at six, she could go to the Windmill and hire a post-chaise to take her to London. She had no fear of encountering

Percy, Fenella or Walter that early in the day—none of them was an early riser. In fact, even better, she could send a porter with a letter to the Windmill tonight and bespeak a post-chaise for the earliest possible time in the morning.

She focused with fierce determination on what she must do rather than allow herself to think about Jack, for whenever he edged into her thoughts, doubts erupted, her throat would thicken and her eyes blur. She could not afford to be distracted. So she searched through her cloak bag for her mother's tiny tortoiseshell writing box and blessed her own foresight in filling the ink bottle and packing some paper. She assembled the pen and wrote a note to the landlord of the Windmill, signing it as Aurelia Thame, deeming it safer to avoid both her own name and King, and comforted by the thought she would be reunited with one or both of her sisters on the morrow. She shook the page free of pounce powder, folded it, then crept downstairs to find someone to deliver it.

She was in luck. The first person she saw was a youthful porter she'd not seen on arrival. She pressed a coin into his palm and bade him deliver the missive immediately, to bring the reply to her room and not to reveal his errand to a single soul. She hurried upstairs again and ate her now-cold meal, barely noticing the taste. She jumped at a knock on the door, but opened it anyway, her heart knocking in her chest, but it was only the porter, who handed her a reply, confirming the post-chaise would be ready to leave at six-thirty the following morning. Beatrice handed him another shilling, again warning him to keep her secret.

She packed her cloak bag and tucked it beneath her bed next to the chamber pot, then checked for the umpteenth time that the window was securely fastened, for if Spartacus were to escape again, all would be lost. And she wrote a letter to Jack, to thank him and so he would not worry that Percy had somehow captured her.

When she could make no additional preparations, she lay down in bed, and when Mabel returned, she closed her eyes and feigned sleep.

It was for the best. The sooner she left, the sooner Jack could begin to mend his fractured relationship with Kit.

It was for the best. She would prove to herself—and to Jack, although she tried to deny his opinion mattered—that she could look after herself and had no need of anyone's help.

It was for the best. This way, no one in London could ever link her to Jack and she could begin her new life free of complications.

But it seemed that no matter how much she tried to convince herself it truly was for the best, the thought of leaving Jack behind ripped at her heart as she wondered when they would meet again.

She arose while it was still dark outside. Mabel was snoring quietly in the antechamber and Beatrice tiptoed across the room and gently closed the connecting door. She lit a candle before swiftly dressing, then picked up a sleepy Spartacus, and desperately shushing him, she put him in his much-hated basket and strapped the lid shut. She carried her cloak bag and the basket to her door, set them down and eased the door open to peer along the passage, lit by a lamp—burning low—set on a small table near the head of the stairs. All was quiet. She moved her luggage into the passage and closed her door, then picked up the bag and the basket and tiptoed along the passage. Her step faltered outside Jack's door, but she ruthlessly thrust down her regret that it had come to this and she carried on.

He had never promised her anything other than to see her safely to London. Mayhap he *had* raised her hopes with that kiss, but that was her mistake, not his. She tried to channel her anger rather than her regret, but it proved a struggle.

The front door was already unbolted and noises from the back of the inn suggested that the kitchen staff, at least, had begun their long working day, so there was no time to tarry. There was half an hour yet before her post-chaise would leave, but it was better to leave while she could. She sucked in a deep breath and stepped outside, blinking as rain like needles peppered her face. She grabbed her luggage and scurried over the street and along the pavement to the Windmill Inn. By the time she reached it, her feet were wet and cold, and her shoulders felt chilled and damp, the vicious rain having quickly saturated her cloak.

She hurried to the Windmill's stable yard, where men were busy feeding, grooming and harnessing horses and cleaning out their stalls. Beatrice hovered just inside the entrance, shivering, while the rain hammered down from the sky, uncomfortably aware she had no idea who to speak to about the post-chaise she'd ordered. After a few minutes, a man approached her and touched the dripping brim of his tall hat. He was older up close than he appeared at a distance, and beneath his old coat, she glimpsed the uniform of a postilion.

'Are you Miss Thame?'

Beatrice nodded. 'I am early, I am afraid.'

He looked her up and down, his eyes benevolent. 'If yer don' mind slummin' it, miss, there's coffee on the stove in the harness room. It's warm and dry in there.'

Beatrice smiled. 'Thank you. That would be welcome, if you are certain I will not be in the way?'

The man jerked his chin and headed across the yard

without answering, and Beatrice trotted after him, skirting the puddles as best she could. The harness room was indeed warm and dry and—to her relief—empty.

'Sit down, miss. The men'll be comin' in and out for the gear, but they won't bovver you.'

Beatrice put her luggage down and sat on one of the wooden stools clustered near to the stove.

'I'll let you know when we're ready to go. Coffee?'

He held up a tin mug and, although it looked grimy, Beatrice accepted gratefully. Her shivers had begun to subside and the thought of a hot drink inside her was most welcome.

'Will you be driving me?' Beatrice wrapped her hands around the mug. The heat seeped through her damp gloves and warmed her chilled hands.

'Yes'm. All the way to Lunnon. Bailey's the name.' He bent to pick up her cloak bag and the basket, saying, 'I'll get these loaded— Whoa!' He set the basket down again. 'Whatcha got in there, miss?'

'It's my cat. Is that all right? Can he travel inside with me, please?'

'Course he can, missy. Dontcha take no notice of me— took me by surprise, it did, that's all. I shouldn't let it out in here if I was you—too many comings and goings, an' I reckon you'll not want to risk it escaping?'

'No, indeed. But…' Beatrice cringed inside at what she was about to ask, but she raised her chin and tried to sound matter of fact. 'He does need to…' Her voice tailed away.

Bailey tipped his head to one side, an understanding twinkle in his eyes. 'But he needs to do his business, eh, miss?'

Her face burned as she nodded.

'You leave 'im to me, miss.' Bailey lifted the basket and left the room. Five minutes later he was back. 'There, then. All sorted. My, 'e's a big 'un, ain't 'e? Not the sort of tom I'd expect a lady like you to dote over, but there's no accounting for taste, is there? Now! We're all right and tight, ain't we, miss? Drink your coffee and I'll be back afore you know it.'

He left the room, the door slamming shut behind him. Beatrice closed her eyes and sipped the coffee, which was strong and too bitter for her taste, but it did the job of warming her up, and she felt safe and in control for the first time since Spartacus had gone missing and Kit's bubbling resentment had boiled over.

In no time at all, it seemed, the friendly postilion returned. Beatrice paid the innkeeper for the hire of the post-chaise, who handed her inside; the door slammed shut, and they were off. Beatrice gazed out of the window at the rain bouncing off the pavements, happy she was not out in such weather, feeling sympathy for poor Bailey, on the back of the nearside horse, and much relieved to finally be on her way. They set off along the main street, taking the hill at a steady trot. She happened to glance out as they passed another inn—a smaller, shabbier establishment than either the Castle or the Windmill. A pale shape at one of the upper windows caught her eye and, without volition, she leaned forward for a better look. The shape resolved itself all too clearly and Beatrice gasped, jerking away from the window and pressing back into the squabs as though she could make herself invisible.

Percy! Oh, dear God. Why did I look out?

Any sense of relief flooded out of her, chased by fear. He'd seen her. She'd seen the shock on his face. He'd be after her now and she no longer had Jack, or even Kit, to protect her. Her stomach churned and the bitter taste of bile burned her throat. She longed to knock on the front window of the post-chaise and urge Bailey to whip up the horses, but she doubted he would hear her over the horses' hooves and the wind and the rain. She could only sit tight and wait until the first change of horses to beg him to make haste.

'Don't ye fret, miss. This weather ain't the best for speedy travel...' Bailey gestured at the sky '...but that goes fer whoever might be followin' us, too. I'll ride 'em as hard as I dares. Ain't no private rig-out'll be able to catch us, or my name ain't George Bailey.'

Chapter Twelve

'My lord!'

Jack forced open one eye and quickly closed it again, groaning at the sick thud resounding through his skull after too much brandy last night. The spirit had helped lull his incessant speculation about Beatrice's failure to join them for dinner—was her headache real, or was it an excuse to save her from facing Kit—or even Jack—again? He could hardly blame her, not after she'd overheard their argument yesterday morning when the cat was missing. He had missed her company, though.

'My lord!' A hand landed on his shoulder, shaking him. 'Wake up!'

Jack's eyes flew open this time. Good God, he had been drifting off to sleep again. He rolled on to his back and eyed Carrick balefully.

'Well? What is so urgent you must disturb me? We do not depart until nine at the earliest and it cannot be that late.' He levered himself up on his elbows, suddenly doubting his normally accurate inner clock. 'Is it that late?'

'It's barely past seven. It's Miss Fothergill, sir. She's *gone*. Vanished!'

'Gone? Gone where?' Jack threw aside his bedclothes

and sat on the edge of the bed. His head thumped sickeningly, his belly roiled and his arm throbbed.

That damned brandy must have been off. I'll have a word or two to say to the landlord when I...

He forced his fuddled brain away from the distraction of the brandy and back to the matter in hand as Carrick handed him his dressing gown. Beatrice gone? His stomach lurched again, this time with fear. He'd known Fothergill was in the vicinity and yet he hadn't warned her, believing she would sleep better without that added worry. Had Fothergill somehow discovered her whereabouts and taken her? Fear and panic joined the guilt churning his belly.

'Tell me what you know, Carrick.'

'Mabel woke me, sir.' For the first time, Jack realised Carrick was still clad in his nightshirt and nightcap. The planned late start to the final leg of their journey meant the servants, too, had enjoyed a lie-in. 'She went through to Miss Fothergill's room and the bed was empty. *Cold*, sir. She's weeping fit to fill a firkin. Thinks you'll blame her and turn her off, sir.'

'What about...?' Jack scowled, forcing his thoughts into order despite the pain that spiked his eyes and his tumbling emotions. 'What about her luggage? The cat?'

'All gone, sir.'

Jack scrubbed his hand through his hair. 'That sounds as though she left of her own accord.'

'I thought the same, sir. If it'd been that brother of hers, he'd have just grabbed her.'

Relief flooded Jack, closely followed by anger. What the devil did she think she was about? They were so close to London...she'd only to put up with Kit and his grouchiness for a few more hours, and she'd be safe. As it was... He swallowed, his throat raw. Didn't she even consider anyone else's feelings or how much worry she would cause them all by simply disappearing?

Drat her. And yet…the Beatrice he *thought* he knew would never do that. She would hate to be the cause of unnecessary worry.

'Did she not leave a note of some sort?'

'Not that Mabel said, but she wasn't making much sense.'

'Let us go and look. I can't believe she left without a word to anyone.'

The door to Beatrice's chamber was wide open and the first thing Jack saw was a folded sheet of paper on the chest of drawers with his name—or, at least, Jack King's name—inscribed on the outside in neat, slanting script.

'What's going on?' Kit appeared behind Jack, framed in the open doorway, his eyes narrowed in suspicion. 'I heard the commotion. Why are you in here in your undress?' He crossed the room in two swift strides and gripped Jack's shoulders. 'Tell me you have not—'

'No! Of course I haven't. Don't be a fool.' Jack shook open the sheet, scanning it quickly. It was brief and impersonal. He handed it to Kit without comment and gazed out of the window as his brother read it out loud.

'"*Dear Jack. I am exceedingly sorry to have caused such discord between you and your brother. I am aware Percy is here and, as we are now so close to London and because I have no wish to cause either you or Kit further concerns, I have decided it is for the best if I go on alone. This way, there is no risk we might be seen together. I am most grateful for your assistance and for your support. Your friend, Beatrice Fothergill.*"'

'Well! The chit has shown a modicum of sense after all.'

Jack rounded on Kit. 'Is that all you have to say? You

as good as drove her away with your suspicions and now you have absolutely no concerns about her safety?'

Kit shrugged. 'No. Why should I? She is a grown woman. I presume she had a plan of sorts when she left here. I shall not trouble myself any further about her now I know *you* are safe from her machinations.'

'*Machinations?* Will you listen to yourself, Kit? When did you become so cynical and so careless of others' feelings?'

Kit's face hardened. 'Am I not allowed to be concerned about my brother when I see him sleepwalking into a trap?'

Jack stepped closer, bringing them face to face. 'I am a grown man, Kit, just as Beatrice Fothergill is a grown woman. I have fought battles and I have been looking after myself for the past eight years. I am grateful for your help while I was convalescing, but I am no longer in need of a nursemaid and I'd appreciate it if you would stop predicting calamity for me at every turn.'

'But look at her actions, Jack! Leaving like that—what does that say about her character? What decent woman would sneak away in the middle of the night without even a maid to protect her reputation? She has shown herself in her true colours. She is no lady.'

Jack held his temper in check, contenting himself with pushing past Kit, out of the bedchamber, saying, 'I am going to dress now. I shall see you at breakfast.'

An hour later, Jack and Kit—barely speaking and tempers still simmering after a tense breakfast in which they once again clashed over Beatrice—emerged from the inn to wait for the carriages to be brought around from the stable yard. The earlier rain had cleared, but the low, threatening clouds promised further showers.

'Yoo-hoo!' A female voice hailed from across the street.

Jack's gaze snapped up from his contemplation of his boots, but it wasn't Beatrice and his heart sank back down into his chest as he recognised the tall figure of Lady Fothergill.

'Goodness gracious,' she puffed, after crossing the street to join them. 'Good day, my lords. What a coincidence, meeting you here of all places.'

Kit raised an arrogant brow. 'Why "here of all places", madam? Where, precisely, should you expect to meet us?'

'Oh.' She reddened. 'It was merely a figure of speech—words to convey my surprise. And my delight, of course.'

'Is Sir Percy with you, ma'am?' Jack jumped in to bring her attention to him, after sending Kit a look of warning. The mood his twin was in, he wouldn't put it past him to reveal that Beatrice had been with them until last night, but that she was now missing.

Missing! His stomach roiled again, making him sick with fear. *Where is she? How could she do this to me? Is she all right? Will she reach London safely?*

He was champing at the bit to get to London now, all of his fears of facing society subsumed by fear for Beatrice's safety.

'He is. Look! There he is now!' She waved frantically to attract her husband's attention, causing Kit to grimace. 'My brother, Sir Walter Belling, you will recall, travels with us, too. We are on our way to London, as are you, I presume. For the Season, of course.'

A little devil inside Jack prompted him to say, as Fothergill joined them, 'And your sister-in-law, ma'am? Does she not also travel to London?'

Fothergill scowled. 'She does. And she is likely to bring scandal upon us all.'

'Sir Percy...take care.' Lady Fothergill laid her hand

upon his arm. 'You must excuse my husband, my lords. He is a touch aggrieved—'

'Aggrieved? I should say so. Ungrateful little baggage.' Fothergill's jaw snapped shut and he visibly pulled himself together. 'I beg your pardon.' He bowed stiffly. 'I am a trifle overset.' He breathed heavily, then burst out, 'I have housed, clothed and fed that girl ever since my father died, all with not one word of thanks.' The man's sense of ill usage was so strong he was clearly unable to keep his outrage inside for long. 'And now, at great inconvenience to myself, not to mention Sir Walter—m'wife's brother, don't you know—I arrange an exceedingly advantageous marriage for her, but the silly wench takes some missish notion into her head and runs off before he even arrives at the Grange. A baronet! A chit like her, to be Lady Belling! I ask you...' He shook his head. 'Women! I'll never understand 'em. Apart from you, my cherub...' He simpered at his wife. 'That goes without saying.'

Jack frowned at his lack of concern for Beatrice's welfare. A spike of pain chose that moment to stab his arm and he winced, massaging his stump until the agony subsided to the dull throb that always followed. He read the pity in both Fothergills' expressions as their gazes latched on to his arm and anger roiled. He didn't *want* their damned pity.

'So...let me understand this...' he growled. 'You have abandoned the Grange without even knowing your sister's whereabouts and without a care for if she is safe?'

'Hah! She is bound for London, trust me on that.' Fothergill appeared oblivious to Jack's fury. 'And she's safe, right enough, for I saw her this morning with my own eyes, driving past in a post-chaise, cool as you please and without a care for the trouble she has caused.'

'And you did not think to go after her?'

Fothergill's top lip curled. 'Those yellow bounders don't hang about, sir, by Gad they don't. By the time my carriage was put to they'd be five miles ahead. Might catch her with a chaise and four, but not with my carriage and those miserable rips the posting inns fob off on decent travelling folk. But I shall catch her in town. You see if I don't. I'm still her brother. Head of the family.' His chins jutted, the flesh beneath wobbling in his indignation. 'She still has to answer to me. She *owes* me.'

His words confirmed to Jack that Fothergill had no idea Beatrice was not his half-sister. If, of course, what she had told him when they first met was the truth.

Now I'm as bad as Kit, doubting her. His scepticism must be infectious.

But Beatrice had not told him the whole of what she had learned at that meeting in Bristol, and her running away as she had—even with Kit's provocation—did prompt questions as to what she was hiding. Had she always intended to ditch her escorts when they got close to London? *Was* there a man involved somewhere? Although, as he had thought before, the man himself would surely have rescued her from Fothergill's house. She had mentioned her house in South Street and that friends would be there. It all sounded pretty havey-cavey—how could he be certain any of it was true?

Am I naive that, even with so many unanswered questions, I am still worried for her safety?

Kit was right in one respect. Jack had seen no proof of any of the details of Beatrice's story. The only tangible evidence was the pouch of coins she had in her possession when they first met. And twenty guineas was scant proof of anything.

The revival of his doubts had given Jack time to control his anger with the Fothergills, however, and he set out to discover more. 'You are positive London is your sister's destination?'

'Absolutely! She has to be in residence in Tregowan House by Eastertide…some sort of condition attached to her inheri— Well! You don't want to hear all about our troubles.'

Inheri—? Inheritance? That, at least, tallies with what she told me. But… Tregowan House? What the…?

Jack saw his surprise mirrored in Kit's eyes.

'Oh, I don't know,' he murmured. 'They do appear somewhat convoluted, but fascinating, none the less.'

Fothergill darted a suspicious look at Jack, which he returned with an innocent lift of his brows. To his relief, Murray drove their carriage into view at that moment, followed by Rodwell driving the second vehicle. The urgency to be on their way to London still simmered beneath all his uncertainties. Whatever the truth, he still cared enough about Beatrice to fear for her safety.

'We must bid you farewell now, for here are our carriages and, if I'm not mistaken, that is Sir Walter Belling over there waiting for you.'

He would recognise Belling's dandified form anywhere. He was quite the figure of ridicule in the *ton*, with his starched shirt points, skintight pantaloons and the multiple fobs adorning his vast collection of garish waistcoats.

'I owe you an apology,' Kit said as the carriage headed up the hill towards Slough, leaving Salt Hill behind. 'It appears I may have been mistaken in Miss Fothergill, unless Fothergill is playing a very deep game.'

'Good of you to admit it, Kit. But only *"may have been"*?'

Kit shrugged, his smile lopsided. 'Don't push it, Brother. All I admit is she doesn't appear to be in league with Fothergill. I still have doubts about her, and even so trusting a fellow as you must admit there are more questions than answers about her story. Who are these friends she will stay with, in a house in which she evidently owns a one-third share—which would now appear to be no less than Tregowan House? From what we've both seen, the girl was utterly isolated by that obnoxious pair, so where did she meet these friends? How do they communicate? And where does Tregowan fit in?'

Kit's questions were too close to Jack's own doubts for comfort, but he felt honour-bound to defend her.

'At least we know she told the truth about an inheritance and about their plot to marry her off to Belling.'

'That part might well be true, but she *is* hiding something. I can feel it in my bones. My guess is there is a man in it somewhere. A lover. Maybe Tregowan himself. He could very well be the friend little Miss Butter-Wouldn't-Melt-in-Her-Mouth Fothergill is so eager to join. And she used your infatuation—'

'I am *not* infatuated with her! I felt sorry for her. I wanted to help.'

Kit raised his brows in his inimitable way, making Jack itch to land him a facer. He clenched his fist and Kit laughed mockingly.

'She used you, Jack. Everything points to it. Or else why did she leave in that clandestine manner?'

'She saw Fothergill and panicked.'

'Why not come to you? She must have known you would protect her.'

And he would have protected her. And that hurt, more than he cared to admit. She hadn't trusted him enough to come to him, but had packed her bags and run away.

Or she didn't believe me capable *of defending her. And who can blame her? What use is a one-armed man to anyone?*

Jack gazed out of the window, his feelings in chaos.

He liked Beatrice too much for a man who could not contemplate marriage. He'd been attracted to her from the moment they met even though, on occasions, he'd found her timidity an uncomfortable reminder of his own diffidence as a boy. Her odd flashes of spirit had intrigued him, though, setting him to wonder how she might blossom if her spirit was no longer repressed by Fothergill… just as he had flourished once he escaped his own father's rule. And she had impressed him by standing up to Kit, even though she'd clearly been racked with nerves. She might be shy, but she did not lack courage.

'She must have planned it all,' Kit went on relentlessly. 'Fothergill saw her in a post-chaise, early, so she must have worked out where to hire one and got up early, knowing we had scheduled a late start and knowing she'd be long gone before any of us were awake. She's proved herself sly, and ungrateful, and cares only about getting her own way, Jack. You are better off forgetting all about her.'

Jack couldn't face yet another argument with his twin. Kit's accusations against Beatrice were pure guesswork, but Jack had no counterargument, as he did not know the whole truth either. And he still could not fathom where Tregowan House fit into all this. He'd suspected a man might be involved… Could it be Lord Tregowan, as Kit said? Tregowan House had belonged to Lady Tregowan, who had died a few months ago, so Tregowan had possibly inherited it, but then where did Beatrice and her one-third share fit in?

He rubbed his forehead and gave up trying to puzzle it out, but he resolved upon one thing. As soon as they reached London, he would track Beatrice down and demand the answers to his questions. He needed to draw a line under this whole episode for his own peace of mind and, to do that, he needed to understand everything.

He would miss Beatrice, though, even after so short a time on the road together. Despite Kit's suspicions casting a shadow over their meal that first night, Jack had enjoyed her company, recalling her enthusiasm for his invented charity for disabled veterans and her disappointment when she discovered it had been a fabrication. Her conviction he was the right man for the job still resonated, and now he wondered if she had been right. Maybe he *could* make a difference to those men's lives, despite having only one arm, and maybe he should think seriously about setting up a charitable foundation. The thought of having some purpose in his future stirred a long-dormant fervour deep inside him.

As soon as he'd confronted Beatrice, he would start to make plans and explore possibilities.

Beatrice.

His heart ached that she had gone and his blood quickened at the memory of their kiss, but he resolutely quashed those feelings, for their friendship could not lead anywhere. Nothing had changed. Beatrice's inheritance made Jack's position even more untenable—he could not afford to support a wife and family and he baulked at the idea of living off his wife, even though he was aware many gentlemen on their uppers would not share such scruples. And, anyway, why on earth would an heiress ever consider saddling herself with half a man?

He switched his thoughts to his brother. Kit's stubbornness in believing the worst of Beatrice's motives still troubled Jack, for he suspected there was a deeper reason for his twin's distrust. And that thought gave Jack the perfect way to stop Kit's gripes.

'One day,' he said, 'you will tell me why you are so

ready to attribute such selfish and hateful motives to a woman you barely know.'

Kit's jaw tightened and he turned his head, very deliberately, to stare once again out of the window.

Chapter Thirteen

Beatrice was shaking with cold and with fear by the time the post-chaise turned into South Street. Despite Bailey's confident reassurances, she'd spent the entire journey in fear of Percy overtaking the post-chaise and hauling her from it. Bailey leapt from his horse to pound on the door of Tregowan House, then hurried back to the post-chaise to open the door, lower the step and take Spartacus's basket from Beatrice before handing her down. She stared around her at the unfamiliar street, missing Jack with a visceral ache that had only deepened as the distance between them increased. Bailey's voice jerked her from her misery.

'You go on, miss. I'll bring your bag and the cat.'

The front door opened on Beatrice's approach and a large-nosed man dressed in black scrutinised her, his gaze somehow condemnatory.

He frowned. 'Yes?'

'I am Beatrice Fothergill.' Her teeth wouldn't stop chattering. 'Is...is either Miss Croome or Miss Thame at home? Or Mrs Butterby?'

The man's frown smoothed away and he bowed before stepping aside.

'Good morning, Miss Fothergill. I am Vardy, your butler. Does the postilion require payment?'

'No. I paid at the inn, but…' Beatrice faced Bailey, who
had brought her luggage to the door. 'Dear Mr Bailey…
thank you for looking after me so well.'

She fumbled with stiff, cold fingers in her reticule,
and in her gratitude to him for delivering her safely to
Tregowan House, she pressed a guinea into his hand as
a tip.

'Lor'! Thanks, miss. It's been an honour.' He passed
the cloak bag and basket to Vardy and tipped his hat to
Beatrice. 'I wish you well.'

Beatrice watched him run to remount his horse before facing Vardy, whose expression gave away nothing
of his thoughts.

'Come inside, Miss Fothergill. The fire is already lit
in the morning parlour, but none of the other ladies is
downstairs as yet. I shall, however, advise them of your
arrival. Gareth!' A footman appeared from the back of
the entrance hall. 'Take Miss Fothergill's luggage up to
her room.'

'Not the basket. I shall keep it with me.' Her cheeks
heated under Vardy's questioning look. 'It is my cat. I
had to bring him.'

'Very well.' Vardy inclined his head. 'Allow me to take
your cloak, miss, and then *I* will carry your cat to the parlour while Gareth carries your bag to your bedchamber.'

Beatrice followed Vardy along the hall to a door at the
rear of the property.

'The morning parlour, miss.'

Beatrice gazed around her at the cosy room, with its
floral wallpaper, a table set for breakfast and a fire crack-
ling in the grate. It felt like a fairy tale. Was this house
really hers? Or, at least, one-third hers. The heat drew

her like a magnet and she sank on to a chair next to the fire, shivers racking her. Vardy placed Spartacus's basket by her feet.

'I shall instruct the housekeeper, Mrs Burnham, to bring you a hot drink to tide you over until breakfast is served.'

'Thank you. Could I...might I ask for some scraps for Spartacus, please?'

Vardy's eyebrows shot up. 'Spartacus? Is that your cat's name?'

'Yes.'

The butler's startled expression faded and, to Beatrice's surprise, he smiled. 'Of course, miss. He must be hungry.'

He bowed and retreated, leaving Beatrice to hold out her chilled hands to the flames in an effort to warm them as she wondered what Jack had thought when he read her letter.

Spartacus meowed and she bent over the basket.

'Be patient a little longer, Spartacus. I dare not let you out yet. But I promise you shall have your breakfast very soon. I... Oh!'

Footsteps alerted her to someone's presence and her head snapped up. Joy erupted through her as she recognised the tall, slender figure, a long red braid draped over one shoulder. She leapt to her feet and hurried towards Leah, who was still clad in her nightgown, with a blue-and-gold paisley shawl wrapped around her. Beatrice recollected herself just in time to stop herself embarrassing them both by enveloping Leah in a huge hug, such was her relief at seeing her. She halted a few feet away.

'Leah! I cannot tell you how happy I am to see you again.'

She stretched her lips in a smile that, annoyingly, she felt tremble. She so longed for her sisters to see her and treat her as an equal, but all she wanted to do at this pre-cise moment was to weep like a baby. But Leah's smile was warm and welcoming as she enveloped Beatrice in a hug, kissing her cheek.

'And I am delighted you have joined us at last. Come, sit by the fire again. You are shivering.'

Leah drew another chair close to Beatrice's and, as she did so, Spartacus let out an indignant yowl and scrabbled around in the basket, causing it to rock.

'What on earth is in there, Beatrice?'

'Oh, dear. I hope it is all right. It is Spartacus. My cat. I *could* not leave him behind.'

'Of course you could not. Is it time to let him out of there, do you think?'

'He is hungry. I—I asked Vardy to bring something for him from the kitchen. Is that all right?'

'Beatrice…my dear…this is your home. Yours and mine and Aurelia's. If you wish to bring your cat and to give an order to the butler, you are perfectly entitled to do so.'

'I am sorry. I worry… I—I do not wish to take advan-tage, or to upset anyone.'

'Trust me. You will not upset any of us. Everyone will just be happy you have arrived, I promise.'

Spartacus uttered yet another frantic yowl from inside his basket as the housekeeper entered, carrying a tray.

'Thank you, Mrs Burnham. Place it here, if you please.'

Leah moved a small table next to Beatrice and the housekeeper poured two cups of chocolate from the pot on the tray. Beatrice's stomach rumbled as the scent of freshly baked rolls reached her nostrils. Mrs Burnham then removed two dishes from the tray—one containing meat scraps, the other water—and put them on the floor at the side of the room.

'For the cat.'

Rather than the censorious look Beatrice anticipated—all of Percy's servants had loathed Spartacus—the housekeeper's scrutiny was kindly.

'Thank you.' Beatrice knelt down to unbuckle the straps. Spartacus, sensing freedom, rammed his nose against the lid, pushed it up and squirmed through the crack. He hissed loudly, ears flat to his head, before streaking across the room and scrambling on to the windowsill where he glared at the three women. 'Oh, dear.'

Her heart sank as she viewed him through the other women's eyes. He was a difficult cat to love... He was neither pretty nor cuddly, nor friendly to anyone other than Beatrice. But he had been with her for nine years now and she adored him, whatever his appearance.

'Thank you, Mrs Burnham. And would you arrange for water to be heated for a bath for Miss Fothergill, please?' Leah smiled at Beatrice. 'A bath will warm you up and we can eat a proper breakfast afterwards with Aurelia and Mrs Butterby, if you are still hungry.'

Beatrice smiled her thanks as she wrapped her hands around the cup Leah handed to her and sipped the chocolate, grateful that neither Leah nor Mrs Burnham had commented on Spartacus's behaviour.

'I presume by your early arrival you travelled up on the mail coach, Beatrice? You must be exhausted. I...'

Leah hesitated and Beatrice opened her eyes. Ought she to confess the full story about her journey? Not yet, she decided—she could not yet face talking about Jack and the trouble she had caused.

'I am surprised your brother allowed you to travel all this way unescorted.'

Beatrice leaned back and closed her eyes again, rubbing

her forehead and swallowing past her pain as she tried to order her thoughts and her words.

'He did not know. I—I had to run away, you see. Percy…he's my brother…he found the will and he insisted he would bring me to London himself. Well, he and his wife, Fenella, and *her* b-brother…but, oh, Leah… I could not bear them to taint my new life and so I *had* to leave when I got the chance but, the whole way, I was so scared he would catch me and spoil everything.'

Merely thinking about Percy brought all her fears surging to the surface again.

'At least you are here now and you are safe from him, Beatrice.'

'You do not know my brother. He will not give up so easily.'

She bit her lip, mentally scrambling for a measure of the steel both Leah and Aurelia had displayed in Mr Henshaw's office. She straightened, searching Leah's face, reading nothing but compassion and…and *love*…in her expression. And her courage rallied.

'He is not my brother, though, is he? I ought not to feel guilty for running away. And I have another family now. He can no longer tell me what to do.' Doubt surged again, but not as fierce as before. 'Can he?'

Leah squeezed her hand, reassuringly. 'No, Beatrice. He cannot. You are a wealthy young lady now and we—Aurelia and I—are your family.'

Beatrice, unable to resist the rolls any longer, selected one and took a bite, her thoughts ricocheting around inside her head.

'But he knows this address, Leah. He will follow me here, I know it.'

'Let him come, then. You need never be alone with him—I, or Aurelia, will be with you.'

'Thank you.'

'There is no need to thank me. We are sisters. We will all look after one another. And look…even Spartacus has made himself at home.' She pointed at Spartacus, who was wolfing down the meat scraps Mrs Burnham had provided for him. 'All will be well.'

After bathing—with the help of her new maid, Maria, who had been appointed by Mrs Butterby—Beatrice went downstairs with Leah to meet their chaperon and to be reacquainted with Aurelia. But she was distracted by her cat's absence immediately when she entered the morning parlour.

'Leah! Spartacus—where is he?'

An upright, elegant lady with grey hair turned from gazing out of the window. 'He was a little too interested in our breakfast, so Gareth took him out to the garden— just in case, you understand—before shutting him in the drawing room.'

'Oh, dear. I am sorry. He is well behaved as a rule.' Beatrice surreptitiously crossed her fingers at her white lie.

'You must remember this is your home, Beatrice,' Leah said, 'and you are entitled to keep a pet. I am certain he will be made welcome downstairs as well—Cook is forever doing battle with mice.'

'She is indeed,' said the other lady as she crossed the room to Beatrice, her hands outstretched, her eyes smiling. 'I am Mrs Butterby, your chaperon, and I am delighted to meet you, Miss Fothergill.'

'Oh! I…um… Would you call me Beatrice, please?'

'Of course. I call both your sisters by their forenames. I did not like to presume, however.'

'Beatrice!' A whirl of scent and Beatrice found herself enveloped in a hug. 'I am so happy to see you. We were worried about you.' Aurelia released her and stood back, clasping Beatrice's shoulders, as she studied her. She laughed. 'I have gained weight since we met and you have lost it. Now we are more alike than ever.' She moved so they stood shoulder to shoulder, facing the others. 'Do you not see the family resemblance?'

Beatrice's face flamed. She was nothing like this glowing, beautiful creature with her golden hair and her bright blue eyes. Next to Aurelia she felt dowdy and countrified, dressed as she was in one of Fenella's hand-me-down gowns, albeit with Leah's beautiful blue-and-gold paisley shawl covering much of it, the shawl having been lent to her instead of her own threadbare one. No wonder Jack had regretted kissing her.

Aurelia had changed since Beatrice had last seen her… Not only had she gained weight, but her skin was now bright and her hair shone with health.

'I do see the likeness and I predict you will both take the town by storm,' said Leah.

'Come,' said Mrs Butterby. 'Let us eat and you can tell us all about your journey, Beatrice.'

As it happened, the questions Beatrice dreaded—because she would have to lie about Jack—turned out to be easy because, after only one or two perfunctory enquiries about her journey, Aurelia was more interested in damning Percy's iniquities, while Mrs Butterby wasted no time in preparing Beatrice for her new life in the *haut ton*, interspersing her warnings with the reasons why Lady Tregowan had left her entire estate between the half-sisters. Leah was quiet—in fact, she looked somewhat preoccupied—for which Beatrice was grateful as she tried to answer Aurelia and absorb all Mrs Butterby's warnings. By the time they finished eating, however, her fear of Percy's arrival was as great as ever. She had always felt safe with Jack, but would they—four women—really be able to fend Percy off? And now she had worries about surviving the myriad pitfalls of society to add to her dread.

Then there was Jack himself. Her yearning to see him again was tempered by yet more worries about when they met again. What would he say about her running away? Would he even speak to her? Whatever happened, however, she vowed to hold her head up and show him a brave front, for never again would she give him cause to think of her as a burden—a weak female in need of his protection.

Her head felt ready to explode with so many unanswerable problems and weariness dragged at her as she walked with Mrs Butterby to the drawing room—a pleasant room with gold-and-green wallpaper and lit by high windows—where Spartacus had already made himself at home on the seat nearest the fire, one hind leg poking to the ceiling as he groomed his fur. Beatrice went immediately to stroke him, escaping from Mrs Butterby's litany of warnings. He paused, his tongue half-out, eyes half-shut as he lapped up the attention. As Beatrice went to sit on the sofa next to Mrs Butterby, his green eyes widened, switching to the doorway as Leah and Aurelia entered the room.

'As do I,' Leah was saying, 'but I can also understand why Mrs Butterby advises caution.'

'Caution? About what did I advise caution?'

'Whether or not to openly acknowledge the three of us are half-sisters.' Leah sat on a vacant chair and smiled at Beatrice. 'We agreed to wait until your arrival, as the decision will affect you, too.'

Beatrice frowned. 'Why should we not admit to our relationship?' *Are they ashamed of me?* 'I am *proud* to have you as sisters and I care not who knows it.'

'There.' Aurelia sent Beatrice a warm smile of reassurance. 'Beatrice agrees with me.'

'But…you do not understand, Beatrice,' said Mrs Butterby. 'By openly admitting you are the offspring of the late Lord Tregowan, you are exposing your mothers' morals to the censure of society.'

'Speculation is already rife,' said Leah.

'Ah, but speculation is merely that. Once you acknowledge the truth, there will be no going back. And there will be suitors, and families, who will not even consider an alliance if there is a hint of a taint in your bloodlines.'

But if we do not admit to being sisters, Percy will still be my brother.

'If I am not good enough for a man to marry based upon my own merit, then *he* is not good enough for me to consider,' said Aurelia.

'And I, too, am proud to call you both my sisters,' said Leah. 'So I agree we should acknowledge our relationship, for, as Aurelia pointed out, to keep it secret would mean a lifetime of lies, and surely there can be nothing worse than starting out married life upon a lie.'

Beatrice found herself nodding in agreement, happy their relationship would be openly acknowledged.

'Well. If you are all determined…' Mrs Butterby paused. 'May I say… I applaud your courage and your integrity. And I am also slightly envious you have one another. I hope you continue to support each other and that you become lifelong friends as well as sisters.' Her voice quivered and she dabbed at her eyes with her handkerchief. 'There! I have turned all maudlin! Beatrice, my dear, you must be exhausted… Why do you not go upstairs to rest now? And—' She shot to her feet. 'Leah! In all the furore of Beatrice's arrival, I quite forgot! Lord Dolphinstone arrives shortly. Oh, my goodness.'

'Lord Dolphinstone?' Beatrice asked.

Leah blushed. 'I will tell you all about it later. Mrs

Butterby is right... You do look exhausted. Go and get some rest.'

All Beatrice's fears rushed to the surface. 'Oh, no. I couldn't possibly... What if Percy comes here?'

'What if he does?' Aurelia hauled Beatrice to her feet. 'We are here to support you and he no longer has any authority over you.' She hugged her, hard. 'You are safe, Beatrice. Come along, up the stairs with you. And perhaps you'd better take that monster with you.'

She pointed at Spartacus and Beatrice rushed to pick him up, ignoring his flattened ears and growl of warning. 'Oh. Of course. I'm sorry.'

Thankfully, Spartacus made no attempt to escape her arms as they went upstairs to Beatrice's bedchamber, which overlooked the back of the house, as did Mrs Butterby's room next door. There was an internal door between the two, which Leah had earlier told Beatrice was kept locked.

Maria—a slightly built Londoner of around thirty years of age—leapt up from the chair by the fire, saying, 'I waited here for you, miss, thinking you'd soon return for a rest.'

Beatrice put Spartacus down on the bed and the maid started, staring. 'What is that?'

Aurelia gave Maria a hard look. 'Spartacus is Miss Fothergill's cat. Do you have an objection?'

'N-no, Miss Croome.'

'Good. Because he is here to stay. Could you find no mending to be done while Miss Fothergill was downstairs, Maria?'

The maid stared at her feet. Beatrice touched Aurelia's arm. 'Please do not scold, Aurelia. This is all new for both me and Maria.' She smiled at the maid. 'That will be all, thank you. I will ring when I have further need of you.'

'You should take care, Beatrice,' Aurelia warned after Maria left, having slid a warming pan out from between the sheets. 'That one is the type to take advantage of a kind heart, according to my Bet. She's only been here a few weeks and has already ruffled feathers downstairs. You can always appoint another lady's maid if you find she does not suit. It's your decision.'

Beatrice thought fleetingly of Mabel and wished *she* were her maid, even though she was inexperienced. She had felt uncomfortable with Maria when she had assisted with Beatrice's bath in a way she never had with Mabel. But Mabel worked for Kit and probably hated Beatrice now for leaving without even saying goodbye. She hoped the maid had not got into trouble for not hearing Beatrice leave.

'I would not like to be the cause of Maria losing her job.'

Aurelia unbuttoned Beatrice's gown, and she stripped down to her shift and climbed into bed.

'Oh, this is blissful.' She snuggled down into the warm sheets.

Spartacus immediately moved on to her stomach and began to knead the eiderdown. Beatrice reached to stroke him, comforted by his presence as always. Laughter glimmered in Aurelia's eyes as she watched.

'Is he not heavy?'

'Yes, but he will not stay there long. It is his way of showing his love.'

'Ah. Then he is worth his weight in gold, is he not?'

'He is.' Beatrice felt her eyelids droop. 'Aurelia, who is Lord Dolphinstone?'

'Leah was working for him as governess before she came to London and, unless I am very much mistaken, he will soon be her husband and, hence, our brother-in-law.' She bent and kissed Beatrice's forehead, smoothing her hair back with a gentle hand. 'Sleep tight, my dear.'

Chapter Fourteen

Jack gazed up at the Kingswood town house in fashionable Mayfair. He had rarely stayed here, having joined the army at eighteen, but Kit had been a frequent visitor to London for the Season until he had suddenly stopped.

'Tell me again why you haven't visited London for the past two years, Kit,' he said as they entered the hall.

Kit shrugged. 'I merely decided country living was more to my liking.'

Jack caught Taylor's sideways glance at his master as the valet followed Kit upstairs and vowed to grill him when he got the chance. He wandered into the front reception room, his thoughts occupied by Kit and why his habits had altered. Funny he hadn't thought of questioning Taylor before, but he supposed he had been too caught up in his own change of circumstances and in coming to terms with his missing arm. He wrapped his right hand around his left elbow. If he didn't look, it felt complete. But running his hand along his forearm soon shattered that illusion as he met the neatly pinned up sleeve.

His stomach dipped, but increasingly over the last few days, he had found himself questioning his attitude to his amputation. Was his life really of no merit because of one impaired limb? There was much he could still do. Clumsily, maybe, but he would get better and he ought to count his blessings, not his woes. He still had a brain. Two legs. His sight. Hell, he even had his right hand... He was so much better off than those poor souls who had returned home to nothing, men from poor families who would struggle to support them. Men that Jack could surely help if only he put his mind to it. Beatrice had been right to be disappointed in him when he'd admitted his charity had simply been a ruse to call upon Fothergill.

I shall stop thinking about what I cannot do and begin to concentrate on what I can still achieve.

He crossed over to gaze out of the window. He did not take in the view, however, as his thoughts were consumed once again by Beatrice—hoping she had reached London without mishap. Praying she was now safe. Remembering his vow to confront her and to demand answers to the many questions still prowling inside his head.

A sense of urgency erupted. He spun on his heel and took the stairs two at a time.

'I'm going out,' he said to Carrick in his bedchamber. 'If Lord Quantock enquires, I do not anticipate being gone for more than an hour. Two at the most. I shall walk, so no need to message the stables.'

Half an hour later, Jack—having washed and changed his linen with Carrick's assistance—strode into South Street, asking a passing gentleman for directions to Tregowan House. Three minutes' walk brought him to the front door and, giving himself no time for second thoughts, he knocked. The door opened shortly to reveal a butler.

'Good day, sir.'

'Good day. Lord Jack Kingswood for Miss Beatrice Fothergill.'

Jack handed his card to the butler, who scrutinised it before turning his attention back to Jack.

'Miss Fothergill is resting, my lord. I shall inform her you called.' He stepped back and began to close the door.

'No!' Before he realised his intent, Jack leapt forward and placed his foot in the gap, preventing the door from fully closing. The butler opened it again, his expression a picture of astonishment.

'I wish to see Miss Fothergill for myself.' *I have to see her.* Jack stepped forward, so he was fully inside the entrance. 'If she is resting, I will wait until she is awake.'

'My lord!'

The butler blocked Jack with his body, but movement further along the hall caught Jack's eye and there was Beatrice. All his fears, from the moment he awoke to find Beatrice gone, disintegrated to leave him awash with fury. He pushed past the butler and strode towards her, taking in her pallor, her huge smoky blue eyes and the tremble of her lips. Without warning, the memory of their kiss exploded into his brain and the urge to grab her and kiss her now, ruthlessly, seized him, shocking him with its intensity. He wrestled that impulse under control, conscious of the still-remonstrating butler behind him. He stopped short of actually touching her, although he was so close by the time he halted, he could smell her scent, hear her ragged breathing and, he fancied, even feel the heat of her skin.

'Why did you run away?'

His voice sounded rough with emotion. He cleared his throat, but before he could say any more, the wretched butler grabbed his arm, dragging him back. Jack, aware he was at fault, did not resist, but his eyes clung to hers.

Beatrice frowned and hurried after them to step between them and tug at the butler's hand.

'Vardy...no...it is all right. Jack is my friend. I wish to speak to him.'

Astonished, Jack watched as the butler, after the briefest of hesitations, bent a benign smile upon her—she had won over Vardy as swiftly as she had won over Rodwell, Carrick, Taylor and Mabel. In fact, Kit was the only one who she had not managed to befriend, and that was only because he thought he was protecting Jack. And because he appeared to distrust women in general. Jack struggled to keep a lid on the simmering stew of his emotions as they threatened to erupt. He wanted to grab her and shake her, and demand answers to all those answers that pounded in his head.

And kiss her. Above all, I want to kiss her.

'Where are my sisters and Mrs Butterby, Vardy?'

'*Sisters?* You did not say you had sisters.'

She smiled at him—*beamed* at him. Who *was* this self-assured young woman? And what had she done with that little country mouse he had met on the road all those weeks ago?

'I did not know if I *ought* to say anything about them before, but we have all agreed it is not to remain a secret. Is it not wonderful? I have lost a half-brother and gained two half-sisters.' She took his arm. His left arm. She never even seemed to notice his impairment...either that, or it simply didn't matter to her. Jack found that hard to understand when he found it impossible to forget. 'Come up to the drawing room and I shall tell you all about it.'

'Miss Fothergill... I beg your pardon, but I do not believe that would be wise with none of the other ladies at home. Miss Thame has gone out with Lord Dolphinstone, and Mrs Butterby and Miss Croome have gone shopping.

They did not wish to disturb you but, in view of Miss Thame's sudden betrothal, there is rather a lot to achieve before the wedding on Friday.'

'A wedding!' Beatrice's eyes sparkled. 'Oh, Aurelia suspected that would be the case. I am so happy for Leah. And I cannot wait to meet Lord Dolphinstone. I am sure if Leah loves him, I shall, too. And you have no need to worry about me, Vardy, I promise. I trust Jack utterly. But you may send Maria up to sit with us if you think it best.'

'Dolphinstone?' Jack's head whirled as he tried to make sense of the tangled threads of Beatrice's life. '*Dolphinstone* is to marry your sister?'

'So it seems! Is it not wonderful? Although I have not met him yet. Leah was his governess, you know.'

Jack didn't know, although he was aware the Earl was a widower with children. Mechanically, he removed his hat and handed it to Vardy before following Beatrice upstairs, his mind and his feelings in chaos as the familiar scent of lemons wafted in her wake. He inhaled, his eyes on the enticing roll of the rounded cheeks of her buttocks as she climbed. Desire coiled and his mouth watered, the memory of her taste strong within him. Beatrice led the way into a room and Jack elbowed the door shut as he reached for her hand, tugging her round to face him.

'Why did you run away?' he growled. He pulled her closer. She did not resist, but tilted her face to meet his gaze, her bluey-grey eyes misty and, somehow, wistful. He stroked her full bottom lip with the pad of his thumb. 'Do you know how worried I was? Do you even care?'

'Of course I care. I wrote you a note with my reason. I am sorry if you were worried but, as you see, there was no need.' She brushed his cheek and then, gently, pulled away from him. 'Why are you here, Jack? Did you not warn me that we must avoid raising suspicions about how we know one another?'

Yes. I did. We must.

But was that what he still wanted? Jack pushed his fingers through his hair. Her eyes followed his gesture, creasing into a tender smile. He knew without recourse to a mirror his hair would be sticking up on end. 'I needed to know you are safe.'

'Vardy told you that. You could have walked away with a clear conscience.'

'I needed to be sure you are happy. That you aren't angry with me... Bea—' her name burst from his lips '—*why* did you run away? Why did you not come to me? Did you not trust me? I would have protected you from Fothergill.'

Her eyebrows twitched into a frown and her lips firmed. 'I do trust you, Jack, but I could no longer bear to come between you and Kit.' She gave a helpless shrug before crossing to the fireplace, where Spartacus was curled up on a chair. '*There* you are, you naughty boy.' She scooped her pet up and kissed the top of his head. 'I wondered where you had disappeared to.' She threw a smile in Jack's direction. 'Shall we sit?'

Beatrice settled on the chair opposite Jack's and the cat jumped from her knee to the floor. Jack cast about for what to say, scrambling to resurrect his anger. But it was impossible. Just being with her calmed him, and although he was still hurt by the way she had disappeared, he already had some of the answers to his questions. But he still needed to fully understand. Spartacus strutted across to Jack, leapt up on to his knee, circled twice and then began kneading. Jack winced at the needle-sharp catch of his claws, and fearing for his breeches, he gently but firmly returned the cat to the floor.

'He likes you, Jack.' Beatrice's smile was back, her dimples peeping out. 'He does not usually like other people, and yet, since we got here, he has made friends with Vardy and with Mrs Burnham, and even on the journey, he liked Mabel and Carrick *and* Taylor.'

'Might that be because you like those people and he senses that? You did not have many friends at the Grange, from what I recall.'

'That is true. Maybe you are right. Which is good, because it means he will be happy to stay here until my own marriage.'

'Marriage?' It was like a punch to his gut and a wave of possessiveness and, yes, of jealousy swept over him, even though he had no right to feel that way. 'Is that why you came to London? To get wed?'

'Why, yes.'

Pain stabbed him. Kit was right. She had been using him all along. That anger—and pain—erupted all over again and Jack shot to his feet. 'I wish you well.' His words ground out. 'Who is the lucky man? Tregowan?'

She stared up at him, her forehead wrinkling in puzzlement. 'Jack?'

'Now I understand why you ran off the way you did. It would not do for your betrothed to get wind of you travelling with two men you are unrelated to.'

Her brow cleared. 'Oh, dear. I am not betrothed, Jack. And I have never met Lord Tregowan. Indeed, I have no idea who I shall marry, although I *must* marry someone.' She caught her lower lip between her teeth, sending the heat of lust through Jack. He looked away. 'I have not explained myself very well, have I?'

She had changed, even in the short time she had been here in London. A matter of hours, that was all, and yet already her self-assurance had grown. Respect for her bloomed inside him—admiration for her strength of character in fighting against the subservience that life with Fothergill had instilled into her. He knew from his own experience the effort it took to break free.

'Jack. Please sit down again and allow me to explain.' When he hesitated, she added, 'The reason I left is truly as I wrote in my note—I could no longer bear to be the cause of arguments between you and Kit.' Her cheeks grew pink, but her chin rose. 'But I do not deny I was also angry. Kit believed me a manipulative Jezebel and *you* saw me as a burden. A helpless female in need of your protection. I needed to prove I *can* be strong and that I am *not* a charity case.'

A burden and a charity case? Jack recalled telling Kit he felt sorry for Beatrice and wanted to help her, and accusing his twin of being uncharitable. Ashamed, he could see why she might believe that was the sum of what he thought of her.

He sat down again as a maid came into the room and sat discreetly at the far end.

'Very well. Explain away…for I am sure I do not understand any of this. Why Tregowan House? Who are your sisters? And why *must* you marry?'

Jack listened as Beatrice told him all about Lady Tregowan's will. She was an heiress, with an income he could only dream of, and a one-third share in both this house and in Falconfield Hall in Somerset.

'But why did Lady Tregowan leave everything between you and your half-sisters if she had never even met you?'

'It is quite complicated. It seems our father told her about us before he died because he wanted to clear his conscience. Lady Tregowan felt guilty and blamed herself because she could not give him children—soon after they wed, she fell ill at Tregowan, in Cornwall. She re-

mained a semi-invalid for years. When she discovered
Aurelia had fallen on hard times after her mother's death,
she made enquiries about Leah and me and discovered
we were both also in difficult circumstances, and so she
changed her will.'

Jack frowned, trying hard to follow the story. 'And if
you do not marry within a year, you will lose your share
of the inheritance?'

Although he should be happy for her, his heart ached
at the thought of her married to some other man.

'Yes.' Beatrice's cheeks bloomed even pinker. 'She
wanted to be sure we would not follow in our mothers'
footsteps. And *that* is why I spoke of my marriage. Although...' and her brow puckered '... I do worry the only
men who will be interested in me will be men like Walter
Belling, whose only concern will be my fortune. I am re-
signed to a marriage of convenience—I would never expect a love match—but I wish to be certain my husband
is a good and kind man.'

A good and kind man was no less than she deserved
after her life so far, but he didn't understand why she believed she could not expect a love match. Who could fail
to love her?

'Well,' he said, 'you are free of Fothergill now and of
Belling. How did you know they were in Salt Hill, by the
way? Did you see them?'

'No. I overheard Kit tell you he had seen them.'

Jack tried to recall what else they had said. No doubt
the usual argument, with Kit warning Jack not to trust
Beatrice—no wonder she felt driven to run away.

'And they must be in London by now. I fear they will
not give up easily.'

For the first time, Jack glimpsed the old vulnerable
Beatrice. 'Surely they cannot harm you now?'

Beatrice straightened, but her smile lacked conviction. And dimples. 'Of course they cannot. I have my family here. I have nothing to fear.'

There was nothing more to say. He had much to mull over and he took comfort from the fact they were both here, in London, and would no doubt be moving in the same circles. It was not as if he would never see her again and at least they were friends again.

'I am certain all will be well, Bea. And...' he lowered his voice, conscious of the maid's presence, so she could not hear his words '...to set your mind at rest with regard to our acquaintance, do not forget we met legitimately at Pilcombe Grange. Nobody needs to know about the journey, unless you choose to confide in your sisters, of course. Now, I must go. Kit will wonder where I am.' He rose to his feet and bowed. 'Good day, Beatrice. I have no doubt we will meet again soon.'

Beatrice stood up as Jack left the room, a war of emotions raging inside her. Pride that she had presented Jack with the calm, collected lady she longed to be. Guilt that she had not been entirely truthful about her fears, not only about Percy and Walter, but also about the ordeal of the society marriage mart awaiting her. Worry that her longing to confide in him was...well... Was it unnatural? She had Leah and Aurelia now. Jack was no longer her only friend. Confusion over her feelings for him, especially after their kiss and his reaction afterwards. Anger—diminished, but still there, deep inside—that he had seen her as a burden.

Sorrow. Oh, yes. A deep, gut-wrenching sadness that he was leaving now, and when they next met it would be in the public eye, and they must behave as society expected. As Mrs Butterby had warned her.

He was at the door when she opened her mouth to call him back, but a cough from the far end of the room reminded her of Maria's presence. She met the maid's gaze, her cool appraisal making Beatrice feel stupid for even thinking about stopping him, for what on earth did she think she could say to him? She wasn't even sure what she did want, not really. But she did know she would miss him.

Miserably, she trailed after him.

As she reached the door, however, she heard voices. Raised voices. Aurelia's. And…oh, dear God, no! That was Percy. Jack had paused on the landing, peering down over the balustrade.

'That's Fothergill,' he whispered. 'Shall I send him away?'

Yes, she screamed silently.

'No,' she said out loud.

If she meant to take control of her own life—*and I must, for if I do not, then who will?*—she must not shy away from facing her erstwhile brother. The cacophony of voices in the entrance hall below continued unabated.

'*I* will go to him and send him away. It will be better if you keep out of sight, I think. He has a violent temper at times.'

A flicker of something like pain crossed Jack's face, but Beatrice, for all her usual sensitivity in recognising others' moods, could not immediately understand the meaning of it and she forgot it as she headed for the staircase. Maria accompanied her, while Jack waited out of sight.

Chapter Fifteen

Beatrice took in the scene in the hall. Aurelia, Mrs Butterby and Vardy were blocking the staircase from a red-faced Percy, standing wide-legged, chin thrust forward, fists propped on his ample hips. Sir Walter Belling—tall, slim and dandyish, his expression supercilious—stood to one side, looking on.

'Percy!'

The arguments ceased and five faces looked up as Beatrice descended the stairs, her insides churning and her legs a-tremble, but determined to conceal her nerves.

Two steps from the bottom she paused.

'Have you told him yet, Aurelia?'

Aurelia shook her head, her golden ringlets bouncing, her blue eyes bright with the delight of confrontation.

'Told me what?' Percy was forced to look up to address Beatrice. 'You're to come home with me, Beatrice. I am your brother—'

Beatrice raised her chin and gave him a cold look. 'No. You are not my brother. You never were.'

Percy's already small eyes narrowed further.

'My father was Lord Tregowan,' Beatrice continued. 'Miss Croome here is my half-sister and I also have another—Miss Thame. You and I share no blood, Percy, and I count my blessings that is the case.'

'But…that is a lie! Father was married to your mother when you were born. I remember it. My father raised you and I have cared for you. You *owe* me.'

'It is no lie and I owe you nothing. Your father raised me as an unpaid servant and you continued to treat me the same. Now, please leave our house. I do not wish to see you or speak to you again.'

Percy started forward, but Sir Walter put a restraining hand on his arm. 'And our betrothal, Miss Fothergill?'

'There is no betrothal, Sir Walter, as well you know.'

The look in his pale eyes sent shivers down her spine, but all he said was, 'Come, Fothergill. There is nothing we can do here. For now.'

As they left, Percy still blustering, Aurelia whispered, 'Bravo, Sister. I am proud of you', and Beatrice heard Maria say to Vardy that she would arrange for a tea tray to be sent up before she trotted down the hall towards the back of the house. Vardy forgot himself so far as to smile approvingly at Beatrice before he, too, disappeared into the nether regions. The three women climbed the stairs together.

'Well! This *has* been an eventful day,' said Mrs Butterby. 'I trust not every day with you will be quite so exciting, Beatrice, for I am quite exhaust— Oh!'

Beatrice followed her gaze. 'Ah.'

She had forgotten Jack was still here. As they reached the landing, she took in his tall, powerful physique, his shock of dark blond hair, his blue eyes and the smile that always seemed to hover on his lips, on the verge of breaking out. She tried to see him through the others' eyes, especially Aurelia's, although she doubted any of them would see further than the false bonhomie he presented to the world. She found herself praying her sister would like him even as she realised it hardly mattered, as they would rarely, if ever, see him once Beatrice married.

'Lord Jack Kingswood, this is Mrs Butterby, my chaperon, and Miss Aurelia Croome, one of my half-sisters.'

Jack bowed. 'Delighted to meet you both.' His gaze sought Beatrice's and she did not mistake his brief nod of approval as his lips now twitched into that half-smile of his that never failed to send a tingle down her spine. 'I enjoyed watching you rout those pompous asses, Bea.'

A glow of pleasure spread through her body at his praise—proof that he recognised the effort it had cost for her to stand up to Percy.

'Bea?' Mrs Butterby glared at Jack. 'Would you care to explain how, *precisely*, you come to be acquainted with my charge, my lord?'

Beatrice flinched as Mrs Butterby speared her with a sharp look and her stomach roiled as she appreciated for the first time the danger. Jack's brow furrowed—and he might well look worried after all his warnings about the consequences if they were seen together on the journey. If Mrs Butterby were to accuse him of compromising her charge...oh, heavens! A forced marriage would be utter disaster. She could just imagine Kit's fury... He would never believe she hadn't deliberately contrived this, even though it was Jack who had called on her.

'I... I am sorry. This is my fault. I meant to tell you the truth about my journey to London, but there hasn't been time.'

Aurelia put her arm around Beatrice's waist, standing with her as she faced Mrs Butterby. 'There is no need to look so anxious, Beatrice. Mrs Butterby is not an ogre... She only wants the best for you. As do we all. Come into the drawing room. We shall sit down and you can tell us what happened. It need not go further than the four of us, if that is what worries you. Need it, Mrs Butterby?'

'No.' The chaperon looked stricken. 'Beatrice…no, of course it need not. I was taken aback, that is all. And, of course, concerned for you…your reputation.' She shot a questioning look at Jack.

'You need have no qualms on that score,' he said. 'The only reason I became involved was because Beatrice needed someone to help her. To protect her. You have seen for yourself what her brother is like. He planned to force her into marriage with that weasel Belling.'

They were doing it again. People always did that—dismissing her presence, talking about her and over her. Because, she realised with a flash of insight, that was what she had always allowed them to do and that was how Percy and Fenella had schooled her to behave. Even now, it would be so easy to sit back and allow them to sort it all out, but that was not the Beatrice she intended to be from now on. Part of taking control of her own life was surely to face up to her responsibilities and not to give up as soon as a problem arose.

'He is *not* my brother.' Beatrice set her shoulders back and lifted her chin. 'Shall we all sit and *I* will explain what happened.'

She did not wait for a reply, but marched into the drawing room and sat on the sofa beside Spartacus, who was sleeping peacefully at one end, curled in a ball. Aurelia joined her, and when the other two were also seated, Beatrice told them all that had happened and how Jack and Kit had escorted her to London.

'Lord Quantock also brought along Mabel, one of his maids, who travelled with me in the carriage and slept on a truckle bed in my room the first night and in an antechamber the second night, so it was all perfectly respectable.'

'And you sneaked off in the dead of night to complete the journey on your own?' Aurelia squeezed Beatrice's hand. 'That was brave, but I do not understand why you felt compelled to do so.'

'That was my fault,' Jack said. 'Well, mine and my brother's. He suspected Beatrice of feeding me a cock-and-bull story about her inheritance and that she and her brother intended to entrap me into marriage. Beatrice left because she could no longer bear to be the cause of arguments between us.'

'I see. And you are here with Miss Fothergill now because…?' Mrs Butterby's eyebrows rose.

'I needed to be certain she had arrived safely.'

'Vardy could have told you that.'

'*I* invited Jack in. I wanted to explain everything to him properly—about the will and our inheritance and my sisters.' She smiled shyly at Aurelia. 'And I needed to apologise for running away like that. I knew Jack would worry, despite the note I left.'

'I did. And I am relieved to find you safe and well.' Jack stood. 'It is time I left, as I am sure you will have a lot to organise.' He bowed. 'Good day.'

As he straightened, he captured Beatrice's gaze and heat rushed through her, gathering at her core, as she tried to interpret the meaning in his look. She recalled the tender brush of his thumb over her lip… Would he have done that if he did not have feelings for her? That was not like taking advantage of a conveniently available woman by kissing her. Was it?

He did not linger, but turned on his heel and left, leaving Beatrice feeling horribly flat as she wondered when she would see him again.

'Well,' said Mrs Butterby. 'I cannot say I approve of such goings-on, Beatrice, and you need not think you will get away with such lax behaviour in future. It is my job to protect your reputation in order that you can make a suitable match. And an heiress of your stature should look much higher than a younger son with one arm.'

Beatrice felt numb all over again. She wanted to feel angry at Mrs Butterby's verdict on Jack, but she could not summon the energy.

'Yes, Mrs Butterby.'

Mrs Butterby rose to her feet and headed for the door, saying, 'I am going for a lie-down. All that shopping has quite worn me down, and although we do not go out tonight, I anticipate a busy day tomorrow preparing for the wedding. I shall see you both at dinner.'

'I will say this for you, Beatrice,' said Aurelia after Mrs Butterby left the room. 'You have a keen eye for a handsome, well-set-up gentleman, even if he has only got one arm.'

'Aurelia! As if his arm would make any difference to me! But Jack and I are nothing more than friends.'

Aurelia tilted her head, her golden eyebrows arched. 'Well, darling…if you are certain,' she drawled. 'So you will have no objection if I happen to flirt with Lord Jack Kingswood the next time our paths cross?'

Was she teasing, or was she serious? Beatrice hesitated, stroking Spartacus to give herself time to think. Teasing, surely. 'Why should I object?'

'I thought so.' Aurelia laughed, put her arm around Beatrice's shoulders and hugged her. 'You are priceless, my dear, and as transparent as that window over there.' She grew serious then. 'A word of warning, though. I've come across men like him before. Stiff-necked with pride. It's an oddity… For most younger sons, an heiress is eminently desirable because their eldest brother will inherit the bulk of the family wealth and property. Some, though—men like your Jack—are too damned proud to marry wealth. He'll be a hard one to break down, but I have every faith you will succeed.'

'*Break down?* I… That is a horrid expression. I have no wish to break Jack, or any man, down.'

'Not even if it is what you both patently want? Beatrice… my dear…we do not know one another well as yet. But a man like your Jack is worth a hundred of most of the aristocrats you will encounter, most of them panting after your money rather than your person. And, trust me, I recognised that glint in his eye whenever he looked at you. I shall not plague you, I swear, but my advice is to find a way to overcome that pride of his or you will both end up lonely and dissatisfied. And do not forget those pesky conditions attached to our inheritance. You must marry someone within the next year, so why not your Jack?'

That was so close to what Beatrice had imagined after Jack kissed her it was almost painful. But Aurelia's words reminded Beatrice that, although Mrs Butterby had told her why Lady Tregowan had left her estate to the three half-sisters, Beatrice still did not know the reason for those conditions.

'Do you know why Lady Tregowan stipulated we must spend the Season in London? And the reason for the other conditions?'

'Evidently dear Sarah… Oh! That is what Prudence called Lady Tregowan, and Prudence, before you ask, is Mrs Butterby.' Aurelia smiled mischievously. 'Although, of course, I do not call her that to her face. Anyway, Sarah was convinced a London Season would give us the best chance of snaring a *good* husband.' She snorted. 'Good! You wait until you meet some of these fine specimens of manhood, the so-called cream of society. Men who care for nothing but their own pleasure, running up debts willy-nilly, yet still fervently convinced of their superiority. Although…' she paused for breath '… I *will* concede that Dolph has grown on me since we first met.'

She tucked her lips between her teeth, then took Beatrice's hand and gave her a rueful smile. 'Take no notice of me, my dear. Leah and Prudence are both constantly telling me not all aristocrats are the same, but I have yet to meet an available one who would even halfway tempt me. I should much prefer a self-made man.'

Beatrice bit back the temptation to leap to Jack's defence. She did not wish to give Aurelia yet more reasons to tease her, but she did wonder what in her sister's past had given her such contempt for aristocratic men. She suspected it might be the man who had raised Aurelia, but Beatrice did not wish to provoke a further outburst by mentioning him.

'What about the other two conditions?' she asked instead.

'Ah. They are both linked to Sarah's love for Falconfield, which was her childhood home. The condition that if any of us wish to sell it we must first offer it to the other two is because she hoped one of us would want to live there permanently. She worked hard to prevent the sale of Falconfield to raise funds to invest in Tregowan, even though our father didn't need her permission. Then, after his death, she learned of the current Lord Tregowan's substantial gambling debts and she feared that, given the chance, he would sell Falconfield to fund the Tregowan estate, which is evidently close to ruin. That is why she changed her will, leaving everything to us on the condition we do not marry the man. As if that is likely!'

'I see.' Beatrice hoped never to meet Lord Tregowan. 'He must be very bitter about that if she left everything to him in the first place. That is what Mr Henshaw said, isn't it?'

'It is.' Aurelia shrugged. 'But what should he expect if he's run up so much debt? I have no sympathy for the man.'

The sound of an arrival filtered up the stairs from the hall.

'That sounds like Leah has returned,' Aurelia went on. 'She went to Lord Dolphinstone's house to visit the children, as she hadn't seen them since she came to London. *She* was in denial about her feelings, just like you, until Dolph turned up this morning and proposed. Oh!' Aurelia leapt to her feet. 'We must go to the modiste— the wedding is the day after tomorrow and none of your gowns are complete.'

'Well, I shall be happy to go there,' said Beatrice, grateful for the change of subject and with a girlish thrill at the thought of new gowns and accessories, even though she was nervous about the Season ahead, 'but Mrs Butterby is resting. I am sure she will not care to go out again today.'

'That is true. Tomorrow will be soon enough, I dare say, for we took the liberty of ordering several gowns in advance for you, as you and I are of similar stature. They will need final adjustments, of course, but that won't take long. I do hope you will approve of them, my dear… Leah and I had a marvellous time imagining what would suit you best.'

'Thank you.'

'You will need several ball gowns plus all the fripperies if you and I are to cast all those society misses in the shade.'

Beatrice knew she must present her best appearance if she was to attract a proposal from a suitable gentleman, but she could not help a shiver of dismay at the thought of parading herself in front of a throng of strangers.

'There is no need to be nervous,' said Aurelia. 'You will have me and Mrs Butterby, and Leah, too, for she and Dolph are to remain in London for the Season. And, of course, you will have every opportunity to show your Jack what he is missing and to make him jealous.'

Beatrice was saved from the need to respond to that sly dig about Jack by Leah entering the room, hand in hand with a tall, dark, ruggedly handsome gentleman who was carrying a young child. Two young boys and a massive dog with a thick, black-tipped tawny coat followed them.

'Here she is. My love…this is my half-sister Beatrice Fothergill. Beatrice, I should like you to meet Lord Dolphinstone. My husband-to-be.' Leah's smile transformed her face into a beacon of joy.

Beatrice stood and curtsied. The Earl's initially rather sombre expression disappeared as a smile creased his face. He bowed, carefully supporting the child's back as he did so.

'It is a pleasure to meet you, Miss… Well, as we are to be related, might I call you Beatrice?'

'Of course.'

'And you must call me Dolph. All my friends do.' He winked at her and Beatrice's nervousness at meeting him eased. 'This is my daughter, Tilly…' he indicated the child in his arms '…and these scamps are Stevie and Nicky.'

The two boys, clearly on their best behaviour, bowed, so Beatrice curtsied again, just for them.

'This is Wolf,' announced the smaller of the two lads— Nicky—as he pulled the huge animal over to Beatrice and Aurelia.

'Wolf?' Beatrice stroked the dog's tawny head. 'That

is a good name for him, as he does look rather like a shaggy wolf.'

'These ladies are to be your aunts, boys,' Leah said, as the dog set off to explore the room. 'Aunt Beatrice you have met. And this is Aunt Aurelia.'

'Well, how lovely to have two nephews and a niece,' said Aurelia, her eyes suspiciously shiny. 'Such a difference to all our lives in so few months. From being alone to having a ready-made family.'

Hiiiisssssss.

'Oh, dear,' said Beatrice, as she took in Spartacus, in the middle of the sofa, his back arched, green eyes almost starting from his head and his fur standing on end while Wolf, with a small yelp, leapt back, a trickle of blood on his black nose. 'I am so sorry. I forgot Spartacus was even there.'

Wolf licked the blood from his nose and stood, his head cocked to one side, tail slowly wagging, as he and Spartacus locked eyes. Slowly, the cat relaxed his posture until, with a final disdainful look at the dog, he circled and settled back down on the sofa.

Beatrice glanced at Dolph. His eyes were creased and a smile tugged at his mouth. 'That,' he said, 'could have been a disaster. However, it seems the victor was agreed with very little bloodshed and peace will now reign. But I am rather relieved the two of them won't be sharing their home in the future.'

Chapter Sixteen

Late the following morning—the day before Leah and Dolph's wedding—Beatrice, Leah, Aurelia and Mrs Butterby travelled by carriage along Oxford Street to Miss Fleury's establishment, which was situated in a side street off the main thoroughfare. Beatrice had never seen so many shops, their wares enticingly displayed in their windows, and she was glued to the sights throughout the journey. But the shops were not her only interest. She also perused every gentleman they passed, hoping against hope to catch sight of Jack, but to no avail.

'It is quite magnificent, is it not? If not a little overwhelming when experienced for the first time,' said Leah, who sat opposite Beatrice. 'I still have not become accustomed to all of London's glitter and glamour... This is my first visit to the city, too, you know.'

Beatrice wrenched her attention from the shops and the people. 'It is? I thought...you seem so...'

Leah laughed. 'I promise, deep inside I am as openmouthed as you, Bea. I have learned to hide it, that is all.'

Beatrice loved how both her sisters, and even Mrs Butterby, had already slipped into calling her Bea at times.

It made her feel…accepted. Not just tolerated, but part of a family. *Her* family.

'And, tomorrow, you will become a countess, and you will be an intrinsic part of all that glamour that us mere mortals may only goggle at,' teased Aurelia.

Leah blushed and laughed. 'It is hard to imagine myself in that role. To me, Dolph is just Dolph. The title is by the bye. Oh, look!' She leaned forward. 'We're here. I cannot wait to see which of your new gowns you will choose for my wedding tomorrow, Bea. I am so happy you arrived in time to be a part of it—I so longed for you to be my attendant, together with Aurelia.'

Miss Fleury had several gowns almost ready for Beatrice. The one she chose to wear for the wedding would have the final adjustments completed today, along with further gowns she would require immediately. The remaining gowns would be finished off over the next few days, in time for their first evening engagements next week.

A short while later, Beatrice stood in a back room, before a cheval glass, clad in a beautiful celestial-blue evening gown, its bodice cut into a deep V both front and back, and very low over the shoulders, with short sleeves. The skirt had a deeply vandyked hem and it flowed and swished beautifully when she moved. Never had she worn such a gorgeous gown. What would Jack think, if he could only see her in it?

Maybe he will. I shall wear it to other events, not only to the wedding…a ball, maybe, and he might even ask me to dance with him.

But the thought of balls and dancing unnerved her because she had no idea how to dance. She had never had the opportunity, apart from dancing with Mama when she was a child. Her heart ached at the memory.

'Well? Are you happy with it?' Aurelia came to stand by Beatrice's side, gazing at her reflection. 'I am pleased you chose this gown, for I have one in a similar style and with the same shade of blue, but striped. I can wear that tomorrow and we shall look more like sisters than ever.'

Leah joined them, standing behind them, her arms around each of them as her smiling face appeared between theirs. 'And my gown is a lovely deep shade of cream, so we will all blend beautifully.'

'It's perfect.' Beatrice quashed her longing to see Jack and tried not to worry about her lack of dancing experience.

'Then why the long face, sweet Bea?' Aurelia captured Beatrice's gaze in the mirror. 'What is it?'

'I cannot dance,' she blurted out. 'I never learned.'

'Then we shall teach you,' declared Aurelia. 'As soon as we finish here. We have all afternoon and several days until your first ball next week. You will soon learn.'

'Do not forget we must be ready for callers later, Aurelia,' said Mrs Butterby. 'Lord Sampford—'

'Oh, *pfft* to Sampford and his ilk,' Aurelia retorted. 'Beatrice is *far* more important.'

'Aurelia!'

Mrs Butterby signalled a warning, flicking her eyes towards Miss Fleury and her assistant, who were bringing out further fabrics for Beatrice to choose from, so they could make yet more gowns. She could barely believe the number and variety of outfits that were considered essential for a Season—when would she get time to wear them all?

'Well...' Aurelia hunched her shoulder '... I am sorry, but I believe helping my new sister to find her feet here in town *is* more important than any number of gentleman callers.' She raised her eyebrows at their chaperon. 'Do you not agree?'

Mrs Butterby shook her head. 'When you put it like that, I cannot *dis*agree, can I? But do not lose sight of what this Season means for you, Aurelia. I am afraid gentleman callers are a necessity if you wish to meet the conditions of your inheritance.'

'Come now, ladies,' said Leah. 'I am sure there will be time for both practising dances *and* greeting callers. Besides...who knows, Aurelia? You might not be the only one to receive callers later.'

Beatrice's cheeks heated. *Would* Jack call? Anticipation quivered deep inside as she hoped he would.

The following evening, after dinner, Aurelia was again helping Beatrice to practise her dancing while Mrs Butterby played for them on the pianoforte. The lessons were not going well and, finally, Beatrice asked if they might leave any further practice until tomorrow.

'I do not know why, but I simply cannot concentrate.'

Aurelia smiled and hugged her. 'It's understandable, for today has been long and tiring, has it not?'

'It has. But exciting and happy as well.'

Happy in one respect, anyway.

The wedding, at St George's, Hanover Square, had been beautiful and emotional. Beatrice and Aurelia had attended Leah as she married Dolph, and Beatrice could still see the look of joy and pride on his face as his bride joined him. Stupidly...pathetically... Beatrice had found herself imagining it was Jack standing there, waiting for her, wearing that same expression. Stupidly and pathetically because he had not called on her yesterday, despite her hopes, and neither had he called on her this afternoon, when she and Aurelia had been home to callers after the wedding breakfast. Later, she, Aurelia and Mrs Butterby had walked with the happy couple—and Dolph's children, who were an absolute delight—in Hyde Park and, although Beatrice's silly heart had leapt at every gentleman who came into view, there had been no sign of Jack.

After the tea tray was brought in, Aurelia said goodnight and went upstairs, leaving Beatrice and Mrs Butterby, who pushed a disgruntled Spartacus off the sofa so she could sit next to Beatrice. She took her hand between both of hers.

'Do not worry about the dancing, my dear. It will come to you in time and you will find most gentlemen will be understanding about your lack of experience.'

'Do you think so?'

'I do,' Mrs Butterby said firmly. 'And I can also see—even after such short acquaintance—that you are kind and thoughtful as well as beautiful. I predict you will not want for gentleman callers once they have had a chance to meet you. And I will make certain you do not end up with anyone who will treat you badly. I promise you that.'

Her kindness was too much on top of Beatrice's disappointment about Jack. Mrs Butterby's face blurred and, through a haze of tears, Beatrice saw her expression change.

'Oh, my dear… I did not mean to upset you.'

She put her arms around Beatrice and pulled her close. Beatrice laid her head on Mrs Butterby's shoulder and, just for a minute, allowed herself to succumb to her tears, and to the pain of missing Jack, as well as to the sheer pleasure of a loving hug. After a few minutes, however, she pulled away.

'I am sorry. I did not mean to be such a ninny.'

'Beatrice. You have been through a stressful time, with

many changes to your life…changes that would challenge anyone, much less a sensitive soul like you. Just remember that all of us are on your side and wish you nothing but happiness.'

Beatrice felt her smile falter, but her heart brimmed full. She hadn't felt this loved since Mama died. Resolutely, she pushed Jack from her thoughts. She had so much to be grateful for, and when they did meet again, she would continue to strive to become the sort of strong, confident woman he could admire.

'I hear Dolphinstone got shackled on Friday,' said Kit, as he and Jack entered Stanton House in Cavendish Square for a supper party hosted by Lord and Lady Stanton five days after their arrival in London.

'He did,' said Jack, glad of the distraction from the nerves that tangled his stomach. He felt awkward and conspicuous with his left sleeve pinned up—a signal to every casual observer that here was a man who was not whole. Less of a man. 'It was to one of Miss Fothergill's half-sisters.'

Kit gave a low whistle. 'Was it, indeed? Where did you hear that?'

'When I called at Tregowan House the other day to make sure Miss Fothergill had arrived safely.'

Jack hadn't told Kit he'd called on Beatrice. He'd avoided any mention of her since their arrival, wary of causing yet more arguments. He had also deliberately avoided places where he might see her, both to give her time to settle into her new life and also to give himself time to try to banish her from his thoughts instead of worrying about her all of the time—wondering if she was happy, and if she was safe from Fothergill and Belling or from the countless other fortune hunters that prowled around the edges of society like a pack of slavering wolves. To distract himself, he had instead made a conscious effort to focus his thoughts on ways in which he might help disabled veterans if he succeeded on raising funds on their behalf.

'So…are these rumours I have heard true?' Kit went on. 'Did Lady Tregowan really leave her entire estate to three strangers, including Beatrice Fothergill?'

'She did. The three of them are half-sisters. Tregowan's by-blows.'

'By-blows?' Kit sucked air in through his teeth. 'You had a fortunate escape, then, Brother.'

'As if that would make any difference to me!'

The minute the words left his mouth, Jack regretted them.

'Oh-ho. And so what *does* make a difference to you, Jack? I know you like the girl—I am not blind. And if she is indeed an heiress, your money worries could be in the past.'

Jack clenched his jaw.

'Ah. Of course. That stiff stubborn neck of yours. You can't unbend enough to stomach a wife wealthier than you, is that it?'

'Let us not forget you owe her a grovelling apology, Kit. Everything she said—everything you doubted—was true.'

Kit merely grunted as they handed their coats, hats and gloves to the footmen on duty in the marble-floored entrance hall and made their way up the stairs, the ebb and flow of chatter getting louder. They paused on the galleried landing, and a passing footman carrying a tray stopped to offer them drinks.

'Where can we find Lady Stanton?' asked Kit.

'In the salon, my lord.'

'Best go and pay our respects first,' he said to Jack.

As they entered the room, a slight, brown-haired lady detached from the group she had been with and crossed the room.

'Quantock! How lovely to see you again. I was delighted when Avon told me you were in London… You have been missed!'

Dominic, Lord Avon, was an old schoolfriend of both Jack and Kit's and he also happened to be Lady Stanton's cousin.

'It's a pleasure to see you again, ma'am.' Kit bowed. 'Might I present my brother, Lord Jack Kingswood?'

Lady Stanton turned her clear amber gaze on to Jack. 'You are most welcome, sir.'

Jack bowed. 'Thank you for your last-minute invitation, Lady Stanton.'

'The pleasure is all ours, I assure you. It is but a small gathering of family and friends to celebrate our arrival in London for the Season, so two more guests are very welcome. Especially those from Somersetshire.' Her amber eyes crinkled. 'I am Baverstock's sister, so I also hail from that county.' Her gaze moved from Jack to Kit and back again. 'Avon told me you were twins, but I had not anticipated you were so alike. You must have had fun when you were young, taking one another's place and confusing everyone.'

'We did enjoy playing such pranks,' Jack replied. They had also been soundly punished for such behaviour. He indicated his left arm. 'There is little chance of us being mixed up nowadays, though.'

Better to make a joke of it than for anyone to realise how exposed he felt, out here in the public view. But Her Ladyship's gentle smile was somehow rebuking and that prompted him to question his true feelings around the loss of his hand and forearm. Could it be *shame* he felt? That had never occurred to him before.

'That may be so, sir, but you can view your loss as a badge of courage and hold yourself tall—you have the gratitude of the entire nation.'

'Thank you, ma'am.'

Her praise made him uncomfortable, as though he didn't deserve it. Not while he was so…yes, it was true… *ashamed* by his loss now he was among people again and viewed himself through their eyes. That insight unnerved him.

'Avon tells me you intend to set up a charity to raise money for your injured comrades.'

He tore his attention from his inner thoughts to attend to Lady Stanton. He had discussed the idea with Avon, knowing the Marquess supported an asylum and school for orphans, and now he recalled Avon mentioning his Cousin Felicity—Lady Stanton—was also involved with it. 'It is as yet just a vague idea, ma'am.'

'Ah, I see. Well, if you do decide to go ahead, I have been involved in raising charitable donations for several years and would be happy to help. Also, my good friend Lady Poole—who is here somewhere—has experience of starting a charity on her own from small beginnings. I am sure she will be delighted to advise you.'

'Thank you. That is most generous, ma'am.'

'I hope you know what you're letting yourself in for with this charity,' Kit said when Lady Stanton had moved on.

'Not really. But I am sure I will learn. Come on, let us go and see what entertainments are on offer in the other rooms, unless you have acquaintances in here you wish to greet?'

Kit cast a look around the room. 'No. There's no one

here I care to talk to. I'm surprised you are so eager to mingle, though, Jack. I thought you were dreading this sort of event and being out in the public eye?'

That was too close to the truth. Jack had lurked on the fringes of fashionable events since their arrival in town, telling himself he was giving Beatrice space to become accustomed to her new role even while pandering to his own fears. But, he realised, Kit had been doing the same and had also avoided society events until this evening, by spending much of his time at his club.

'Have you never heard of facing your fears, Kit? Are we both not doing that here, tonight?'

Kit scowled. 'What have I to fear? Come,' he growled, before stalking across the room to a pair of double doors beyond which music played.

With an inner shrug, Jack followed him into a room where a lady sat at a pianoforte. The furniture had been stripped from the room to allow for dancing. A sweeping glance around the room revealed no Beatrice and he was conscious of a well of disappointment.

'So, do you intend to grace the dance floor?' he said to Kit.

Kit, who had been scanning the dancers, shot him a scathing look. 'No. I prefer not to indulge.'

'The Kit I remember enjoyed dancing. What happened?'

'I grew up.' Kit gazed around restlessly. 'Shall we find the card room?'

About to agree, because he had no intention of dancing either, Jack paused as a flash of movement by another door caught his attention. Beatrice—enchanting in a primrose gown trimmed with lace, with her honey-coloured hair caught up on her head, curls tumbling around her face and neck—entered with Miss Croome and Mrs Butterby.

They were followed by the tall, dark figure of the Earl of Dolphinstone with an elegant, vibrant redhead on his arm, presumably the new Lady Dolphinstone and the third half-sister, although she bore no resemblance to the other two.

Jack watched the group, noting Miss Croome's confidence compared to Beatrice, who looked nervous and for all the world as though she wished she could fade into the wallpaper where no one would notice her. The urge to talk to her, to boost her confidence, engulfed him.

'Not yet.' He nodded at the group. 'You, my dear brother, have an apology to make.'

He thought Kit might stalk off again, but after a tense pause, he sighed.

'You are right. I must. Come along, then. Let me get it over with.'

Jack bit back his triumphant smile. Two birds. One stone. A satisfactory revenge on Kit for causing such trouble with his groundless suspicions and the perfect excuse to join Beatrice and her family without it appearing in any way particular.

He strolled in Kit's wake.

Chapter Seventeen

Beatrice stayed close to her new family as they moved through the crowded rooms at Lady Stanton's supper party. Dolph had assured her this would be a small, informal gathering, hosted by the wife of his old friend Lord Stanton. If this was small and informal, what on earth would the Smethwicks' ball—her first ball—later this week be like? How would she cope when even this—a simple supper party—seemed so daunting? She had never experienced anything like it before and she felt inadequate, insignificant, intimidated. The heat of so many bodies made it hard to breathe. The noise—voices, laughter, music—made it impossible to hear. All these people. Faces and names that came and went. She would never remember them all and they would think her rude, hopelessly unsophisticated and stupid when she forgot they had even been introduced, let alone remembered their names. She longed to crawl away and hide somewhere quiet and safe.

She hauled in a deep breath, craving fresh air to cool her down, and for somewhere to sit to make herself less noticeable. Her confidence had been high when she'd first seen herself in her new primrose, high-waisted gown with its lace-trimmed, scalloped hem. She looked better than she ever had before, and—despite her determination to keep her silly hopes under control—she couldn't help hoping Jack would be here tonight and that he would see her with new eyes. Her confidence had dived almost as soon as they arrived as she realised her appearance was only part of what would matter if she was to fit in with these society people. A lady's accomplishments—her ability to flirt, to converse, to dance—were also key and Beatrice lacked all those gifts.

More than ever, she prayed Jack would be here—no longer because she wanted to impress him with her appearance, but because she knew his presence would give her strength to face this ordeal. She had missed him so badly over the past five long days, missed him with a visceral ache that only intensified as the days passed.

'Beatrice. My dear. Are you all right? You have gone very pale.' Mrs Butterby eyed her anxiously. 'I know this all seems overwhelming, but I promise you will get used to it.'

I do not want to get used to it.

But her sisters were here. And Beatrice could not show herself up in front of them. She discreetly dabbed her upper lip, aware she was beginning to *glow*, as Aurelia put it. She inhaled again and bit her lower lip hard to distract herself from her silly, weak knees and her swimming head.

'I shall be all right. It is a touch warm for me. And noisy.'

She gave Mrs Butterby a shy smile. She had been so kind to Beatrice since her arrival. Leah had quite rightly been engrossed in her new husband and family, and Aurelia—lovely, teasing, lively Aurelia—could also be disturbingly fierce at times. She clashed regularly with Mrs Butterby, and Beatrice, who hated confrontation, was therefore a little wary of her new sister, even though

Aurelia was only ever kind and protective towards her. Mrs Butterby, in the meantime, had been Beatrice's anchor now she had finally stopped throwing reams of rules and advice at her.

'Good evening, Miss Fothergill.'

Beatrice's head snapped up. Kit—Lord Quantock, as she must remember to call him—was bowing before her. Her gaze drifted past him and there was Jack. Her heart flipped in her chest—he looked so handsome. So serious, his dark blond hair combed ruthlessly flat. She frowned and then spied the quiver at the corner of his mouth, and she immediately felt better. Stronger. He was the same Jack—her friend—even though they now met in such different circumstances.

'Good evening, my lords.' Beatrice curtsied. She introduced Kit to the rest of her family, and then Jack to Dolph and Leah, whom he hadn't yet met.

Jack's easy smile was fully in place as he spoke with Dolph, who was quizzing him about the war and who revealed he had also been over on the Continent, but in a diplomatic capacity rather than a military one. Jack's blue eyes, however, were wary, and Beatrice sensed that—like her—he would rather be anywhere than here in the public eye. Her courage rallied.

'Miss Fothergill.' Beatrice's attention snapped back to Kit. 'Might I beg a moment of your time?' He indicated with his head and she followed him a little way from the others. 'I owe you a most humble apology, it seems.'

This man had caused Beatrice much upset, and so she thrust down her instinct to immediately forgive him. She pictured Aurelia's likely reaction to such unjust treatment and arched her brows.

'You do, my lord?'

Kit's eyebrows bunched and his mouth firmed. It was

like facing a darker version of Jack but, recalling Mabel's revelation about Lady Newcombe's betrayal in his past and that he had avoided London ever since, Beatrice realised that Kit, too, felt uncomfortable at being here, despite his high rank and wealth. Her heart softened, but she remained silent, awaiting his response.

'I do. I am sorry for doubting your story of your inheritance and for my suspicions. I was wrong and I beg your forgiveness.'

'Thank you. I am happy to forgive you.'

Kit smiled, and at that moment, Jack joined them. Beatrice's insides fluttered, as though a thousand butterflies invaded her stomach. How could she be so calm when talking to Kit, but so utterly discomposed as soon as Jack appeared?

'All friends again?' Jack cocked his head to one side.

'Indeed. Miss Fothergill has most generously forgiven me. I hope we may begin again and put the past behind us?'

'With pleasure, sir,' she said.

'Thank you, and before you even think of offering to pay anything towards that journey, please do not, for I shall not accept.' For the first time, Beatrice was treated to a genuine smile from Kit, making the resemblance between him and Jack even more remarkable. 'Now, Jack, how about that card game?'

'You go ahead. I fear I should slow play too much without two hands.'

Kit's lips pursed, but he did not try to persuade Jack further. He nodded at Beatrice and strolled away, but she could see his tension in the set of his shoulders. Jack stared frowningly after his twin.

'I wish I knew what was bothering him,' he muttered. Then he started. 'Sorry. I did not mean to speak aloud.'

'You are worried about him?'

He shrugged and gave her a lopsided grin that made her heart flutter. 'Of course. He's my brother. As you have found out, we worry about each other.'

Beatrice bit her lip. She could not betray Mabel, but she wanted to help Jack. And Kit, because Jack cared about him.

'Do you think he might have been betrayed by a woman in the past?'

'What makes you say that?'

'There had to be another reason for his suspicions of me than just a fear I would try to trap you into marriage. It seemed possible he views all females as untrustworthy.'

'I confess I have wondered the same thing. I wish he would confide in me…but…' Again, he shrugged. 'Anyway, enough of Kit. Tell me what you have been up to. Are you enjoying being in London?'

'Oh, yes, although I am already exhausted. And that is despite this being our first *proper* evening engagement.'

'As opposed to *improper*?' His mouth curved and his eyes teased.

'Oh! You *know* what I mean!' She tipped her head to one side. 'What about you? Are you enjoying being in London?'

'Oh, you know…' He shrugged vaguely. 'So, why the exhaustion if you haven't been out dancing till dawn every night?'

'There has been so much to do and so much to take in. We had all the preparations for Leah and Dolph's wedding on Friday, and there have been fittings with the modiste, and shopping, and walks in the Park. Not to mention dancing lessons.'

'Dancing lessons? Can you not…? But no. I don't suppose you have ever had the opportunity to attend dances.'

Make light of it. If Jack can joke about his missing arm, and hide his discomfort from others, then I can do the same about my lack of dancing skills.

'No. I have not. And, unfortunately, I have little aptitude for the activity.' She laughed. 'Aurelia is horrified at my clumsiness and my seeming inability to remember the sequence of moves.'

'I am sure you exaggerate. Does that mean you are hoping no gentleman will ask you to dance tonight?'

'It does. Although I cannot put it off for long—we attend the Smethwicks' ball on Wednesday, so I shall have to dance there, although two days hardly seems enough time to prepare. I just hope…' She allowed her words to tail into silence.

'You hope?'

She made herself smile as she gave a little shrug. 'I am determined to do my best. Leah and Aurelia are so beautiful and elegant, and accomplished, and they are both so kind to me… I hope I won't let them down by making a fool of myself and getting the steps wrong.'

Her words reached deep inside Jack and tugged at his heartstrings. Beatrice still had no idea of her own worth. No idea how people were drawn to her warmth and her kindness and her modesty.

'Your sisters are kind to you because they *like* you, Bea. Do you imagine they will change towards you if you make a mistake?'

'Well… I suppose if you put it like that…no. At least I hope not.'

'They won't.'

'Anyway—' her smile looked gay enough, but there was an absence of dimples '—do not allow my abstention this evening to stop you asking another lady to dance if you wish, Jack. You do not have to stay here to keep me company.'

'I have no intention of standing up with anyone.'

'Why not, when there is already a lack of gentlemen in comparison with the numbers of ladies? *You*, I am sure, are able to dance?'

'Of course!' Jack pushed his fingers across his scalp, ruffling his hair. 'But even you must admit I would not be much of a partner these days.'

He indicated his left arm and grinned at her. She frowned back at him.

'I am certain you will overcome any difficulties with ease.'

He stared at her curiously. 'You do not think these fine ladies will shy away from dancing with a one-armed man?'

She shook her head. 'Why should they? One or two idiots may be hesitant, I suppose, but are they worth bothering about? If you enjoy dancing, you should just do it.'

Jack studied the floor, frowning as he pondered her words. She was right. He must start somewhere. He looked up. She was watching him, her brows slightly arched, her bluey-grey gaze confident. On his behalf, he realised. She had confidence in him, if not in herself.

'Let us make a pact, Bea. The Smethwicks' ball. You and I...we will dance together and the devil take any critics. As long as we enjoy ourselves, what is it to anyone else?'

Although he read the doubt in her eyes, Beatrice gave him a smile. 'It is a deal.'

'Have you experienced any more trouble from Fothergill or Belling?'

'No. I have not seen them since that first day.'

'Good. With any luck, they will see it is hopeless to

pursue their plan. You made your position abundantly clear and you have your half-sisters now to help keep you safe. And Dolphinstone's protection will shield you from unacceptable suitors far more effectively than your chaperon is able to.'

'I do feel more secure than I did to start with. I am very fortunate to have my new family.'

Beatrice chewed her lower lip a moment, while she stared up at Jack, her cheeks turning pink. He stifled the urge to reach out and to stroke his fingers across her silky, blushing skin. To touch her lips. To kiss her. He wrenched his gaze from her to stare at the dancers.

'Have you thought any more about starting a charitable foundation, Jack?'

His unwelcome urges back under control, he looked at her again. She was so pretty…so earnest…her huge, trusting eyes, her delicate nose, her soft, kissable lips. But what he admired most was her kind, generous heart. The thought of her even dancing with another man, let alone *marrying* another, dismayed him…and yet, Kit was right. His pride baulked at the idea of marrying a woman far wealthier than he. Besides, Beatrice knew so little about this life… She would surely blossom once she found her feet and would have no further need of his help or support. She deserved time to discover what…*who*…she truly wanted.

'I have,' he replied, 'but it is hard to know where to start, although Lady Stanton did mention both she and her friend Lady Poole have experience of raising funds and will be happy to offer advice.'

Beatrice beamed. 'I am so pleased. Just think how rewarding it will be to help those poor men. Have you thought yet what use you could put any funds to, other than just to hand it out to people?'

Jack laughed. 'I'm afraid I have not got that far.'

'Only…well… I saw a man begging on the street a few days ago and he had no legs, and I did so worry about him. I gave him some money but, afterwards, I thought surely there must be jobs he can still do? If he cannot move easily, could he not learn to make something useful? Or to repair things? But how can a man in his dire straits learn? Who would teach him? Could you not use any money you raise to teach such men new skills and give them a chance to earn their own living?'

Jack stared at her, his gut stirring with excitement. 'Bea, you are brilliant! That's it. I can raise funds, lease a house and then take in veterans and help them to learn new skills.'

Beatrice beamed at him again and he could see his own enthusiasm mirrored in her expression.

'Lord Jack Kingswood?'

The soft, well-modulated voice belonged to a beautiful blonde lady, her voluptuous curves draped in blue satin. A stranger.

Jack exchanged a puzzled look with Beatrice. 'That is me.'

'Please forgive the interruption, but Felicity—Lady Stanton, that is—told me you mentioned starting a charity for injured soldiers and that I might be able to advise you. My husband…' she indicated a tall, auburn-haired gentleman by the door '…and I are about to leave, so I wished to introduce myself while I had the opportunity. I am Lady Poole.'

Jack bowed. 'There is nothing to forgive, my lady. I am delighted to meet you. May I present Miss Beatrice Fothergill?'

'Fothergill? One of the Tregowan heiresses?'

Beatrice blushed. 'Yes, my lady.'

'Well, I am impressed by your ideas for helping those poor veterans, Miss Fothergill. I'm afraid I overheard you. You have some excellent ideas.'

Jack would swear Beatrice grew two inches at Lady Poole's praise.

Her Ladyship smiled at Jack, and he noticed for the first time her extraordinary violet eyes.

'This is neither the time nor the place to go into great detail,' she said, 'but, if you feel you would benefit from my experience, I shall be delighted to meet with you one day. If you wish, I can show you the house in Cheapside where the charity I founded is based. It is a refuge for those unfortunate servant girls who are seduced—often by force—by their employers and then cast out when they get with child.'

A tiny gasp escaped Beatrice. 'That is similar to what happened to my mama. She was Lady Tregowan's companion before…before…'

Lady Poole patted Beatrice's hand. 'I have heard the story, my dear. Perhaps you would like to visit my charity as well.' Her violet eyes twinkled. 'After all, you are an heiress and we are always in need of funds.'

'I would like that very much, my lady.'

Lady Poole's smile gleamed. 'And that, Lord Jack Kingswood, is how it is done.'

'You made it appear effortless.' Jack shook his head, laughing.

A wry smile stretched Her Ladyship's lips. 'It is not always easy to persuade people to sympathise with girls such as the ones in our care, so I have learned to be bold— some might say brazen—in my requests for donations, and I have also become something of an expert at raising funds by holding charity dinners as well as balls and, in the summer, garden parties at our estate in Kent.'

'Unfortunately, as a younger son with no property of my own, I would be in no position to host dinners or balls,' Jack said.

'Ah, but what you do, you see, is you cultivate the people who *do* have such property and you persuade them to donate that property on one night, or one day, for the fundraising event, whatever it might be.' She smiled, her violet eyes again twinkling. 'I have a feeling you can be most persuasive when you wish to be, Lord Jack Kingswood. Is that not so, Miss Fothergill?'

'Oh.' Beatrice reddened. 'I do not—'

'Hush, my dear. I am teasing. Probably most inappropriately. I apologise. Ah, here is my husband to hurry me along. Sir Benedict Poole, might I present Lord Jack Kingswood and Miss Beatrice Fothergill?'

'Kingswood. Miss Fothergill.' Sir Benedict bowed. 'My dear. I thought we agreed twenty minutes ago that you need your rest?'

'I am coming, Ben. Please do not fuss.' Lady Poole eyed her spouse lovingly, belying her words. Then she smiled at Jack. 'I saw you with Quantock earlier—you are so alike. Benedict and I have twins, you know. They are three years old now, but a boy and a girl, so they differ in both looks and character. Now, I shall give your fundraising some thought, and I shall drop you a note soon and arrange a meeting, if that is acceptable? I am sure we will come up with many useful ideas.'

'Harriet…' Sir Benedict's reproach was close to a growl.

Harriet laughed. 'Yes, yes. Here I come. It was a pleasure to meet you both—we are holding a soirée on Thursday evening; I do hope you will both honour us with your attendance? Your family have already been invited, Miss

Fothergill, but I shall be sure to send you an invitation to-morrow, sir.' Her smile radiated forth again. 'Goodnight.'

'I am most grateful, my lady,' said Jack.

'Oh, Harriet, please. We do not stand on ceremony in our circle of friends, and I feel sure you will fit right in.'

'Such a beautiful lady… I wonder if she will have twins again,' whispered Beatrice as the Pooles walked away.

'I beg your pardon?' Jack stared after the couple. 'Is she…?'

'With child? Yes.'

There was a note of envy in Beatrice's voice that prompted Jack to give her a sidelong glance. Then she coloured and her gaze flew to his.

'Oh, dear. I spoke without thinking. I should not have said that out loud, should I?'

'Bea. You can say anything to me. I hope you know that.'

Her dimples appeared for the first time that evening. How he adored them.

'I do. Thank you, Jack.'

Chapter Eighteen

Two nights after the Stantons' supper party, Jack headed towards Lord and Lady Smethwick's Portman Square mansion in a mood of some trepidation. It was one of the first major balls of the Season, thrown every year on the twenty-seventh of March—according to Kit—by Her Ladyship to celebrate His Lordship's birthday. Kit had declined Lady Smethwick's invitation, but Jack, although he'd as soon accompany Kit to his club as attend the ball, could not break his promise to Beatrice to dance with her tonight.

He'd been unable to put her out of his thoughts—the way she'd appeared to fade into herself next to her more flamboyant sisters; her fear of making a fool of herself by getting the steps wrong in a dance; her determination to face her fears in order to prove herself worthy of her sisters. He would not let her down even though the thought of all those strangers' eyes on him made him break out in a sweat.

Beatrice.

The sheer need to see her again had ridden him relentlessly since the Stantons' supper party, but he had resisted it. That need, however, sparked nerves of an entirely different kind as he debated what it meant for him and for Beatrice, and where they might be heading.

Marriage? He barely knew her. She barely knew him.

Many successful marriages begin with less.

He was still an impoverished younger son. And she was still an heiress.

Think with your head. Not with your pride. Kit's right. A wealthy wife will solve all your worries in one fell swoop.

But she'd lived such a secluded life. She should not be tied down. Not yet. She might meet the man of her dreams.

There is no hurry. You can give her time to be sure of her own mind.

She deserved a whole man.

Silence.

A man who could protect her.

Still more silence.

By fleeing Jack's protection at Salt Hill, as well as by shielding him from Fothergill and Belling last week when they called at South Street, Beatrice had made clear her doubts about his ability to physically protect her. And she was right to doubt him… She deserved better.

Jack sighed as he paused at the corner of Orchard Street and Portman Square, eyeing the queue of vehicles that lined up around the square. He estimated it would take a good half-hour for the one at the tail end to disgorge its occupants. It was normal protocol for guests to arrive at balls in carriages, but to Kit's disapproval, Jack had elected to walk this evening, despite the weather threatening rain, as it seemed to do ceaselessly these days.

Stuff protocol.

He set off again, tucking his hefty umbrella more firmly beneath his arm, and striding out with grim resolution, still attempting to untangle his thoughts and emotions, but determined to support Beatrice at her first ball.

After that…who could tell? He liked her. Very much. He felt protective towards her although, God knew, she deserved better than a one-armed man with no direction in his life.

What about the charity? Surely that must be my direction now—an ideal opportunity to move on with my life. I will ignore my disability as much as possible—the people who matter will accept me for who I am, not what I am. At least no one else knows how I feel. And if I can continue to fool others into thinking it doesn't matter, maybe in time I shall learn to fool myself and it will become the truth.

'Kit! Darling…it's been an age. *Where* have you been?'

The voice that dragged him from his inner monologue belonged to a black-haired beauty who had lowered her carriage window. She eagerly beckoned and, with a sigh, Jack returned to her vehicle. He noticed the lady's smile falter as she took in the pinned sleeve of Jack's coat.

'Oh!' She drew back. 'My dear Kit…what on earth…?'

Jack deployed his easy smile and bowed with a flourish, cocooning his brittle ego deep inside. So much for his resolve to move on with his life and ignore his disability. One careless reaction and his defences were instantly raised, his fragile self-confidence bruised yet again.

'Allow me to enlighten you, ma'am. Lord Jack Kingswood at your service. Kit, thankfully, still has both appendages.'

'Oh!' The lady fanned her face. '*What* a relief! Although, of course, I am exceedingly sorry for your own misfortune, my lord. You were a Dragoon, I believe? Kit used to speak of you, often. He was enormously proud of you.' She extended one elegant hand from the window. 'I am Henrietta, Lady Newcombe. I am an old friend of your brother's… Dare I hope he has mentioned me?'

'Of course,' Jack lied. He bowed again. 'I am pleased to meet you, Lady Newcombe.'

'Henrietta, please.' She sent him a flirtatious look. 'Is Kit here? In town?'

'He is.'

'Are you heading for the Smethwicks'? Will Kit be there?'

'I am, but Kit had a prior engagement. Now, if you will excuse me…?'

'Oh, but…' She opened the carriage door. 'Would you care to arrive with us? I am certain Mr Hastings can have no objection.'

Jack peered past Lady Newcombe to the handsome young gentleman by her side, who made no attempt to hide his scowl.

'No.' Jack bit back his smile. Silly young cub. He didn't look much older than twenty…several years Lady Newcombe's junior, that was for certain. 'You are most kind, but I prefer to walk. I shall no doubt see you later.' He tipped his hat and continued on his way.

After greeting his host and hostess, Jack entered the ballroom at the rear of the house. The music was already playing and the dancing had begun, with only half a dozen couples on the floor. The first person Jack saw was Beatrice, partnered by Lord Dolphinstone in a country dance. As he watched, she missed several steps and a couple of turns, and her face flamed even though Dolphinstone quickly corrected her and there were few people to notice. Scanning the remaining guests, Jack saw both her half-sisters and Mrs Butterby watching from the entrance to an alcove flanked by two tall plinths supporting massive floral arrangements. Their concern for Beatrice was clear and, as the dance ended and Dolphinstone and Beatrice—mouth drooping—joined them, they closed ranks around her. Content she was protected for now, Jack found a chair and settled down to watch a while, reluctant to add to Beatrice's embarrassment by revealing he had witnessed her mistakes.

As both her sisters took to the floor, Beatrice retreated into the alcove, no doubt in the hope she would not be noticed and that no one would ask her to dance. But Jack, of course, had already made a pact to dance with her and he was reluctant to renege on their deal even though he, too, hated the thought of putting himself out there on display. Now, though, an idea occurred to him. He rose from his seat and wandered out of the ballroom. More guests were constantly arriving and he took advantage of the confusion to carry out a reconnoitre of the house. Within a very few minutes, he found what he was looking for—an unlit conservatory, reached via a short passageway at the rear of the house. The room was dim, but not pitch-black, courtesy of light from the tall ballroom windows—which were visible from the conservatory—as well as from the well-lit entrance hall, which illuminated that passageway and filtered through the glazed conservatory door. The stone-flagged floor—although not ideal for dancing—would be adequate for what he had in mind.

Brimming with satisfaction, Jack headed back to the ballroom. Now, he had only to work out how to separate Beatrice from her chaperon and her half-sisters. But Beatrice was neither in the alcove, nor among the dancers. After questioning a footman, Jack headed upstairs to a room that had been set aside for guests to sit and rest with a quiet drink if needs be.

On the landing, a small knot of people at the far end caught his eye and he recognised the bulky form of Sir Percy Fothergill. His lady was next to him, as well as the elegant figure of Sir Walter Belling, and several interested onlookers had gathered at the drawing room door. With a deep sense of foreboding, Jack strode towards the group.

'Good evening,' he said loudly.

The Fothergills and Belling split ranks, revealing Beatrice, glowering, with her arms folded across her chest, and Mrs Butterby, in the process of wagging an admonishing finger at the three of them.

Fothergill spun around and his scowl relaxed. 'Kingswood! Good to see you again. See…here is the silly chit. You recall we told you about her foolishness in running away? Well, if you please, she is now resisting our understandable desire to bring her back into the bosom of her family. You, sir, made her acquaintance at Pilcombe Grange—the only home she has ever known. You *know* where she belongs. You, I am convinced, will vouch for my authority in matters concerning her. This…this *female* here…' he flung an accusatory finger in Mrs Butterby's direction '…has *no right* to keep her from us.'

If only the floor could open up and swallow her. Beatrice concentrated on breathing in and out while her skin crawled as though a thousand ants were marching across it. Her vision blurred. It was bad enough Percy, Fenella and Walter cornering her here, at a ball, while she was with her new family, but that *Jack* had to witness it rendered her humiliation complete. She gripped her hands together to stop them shaking. She had stood up to Percy the other day, earning her Jack's praise, but it was more difficult in public. She hated to make a spectacle of herself, but…she had no choice now. Not if she was ever to persuade Jack she was capable of change and becoming the strong sort of woman he could admire.

'Percy!'

He faced her, his plump face puce.

'Please do not make me repeat myself. You are no brother of mine. You have no authority over me.'

'You *owe* it to me,' Percy growled.

Then Jack moved past Percy and pivoted to stand by her side, facing the others. She felt his hand settle at the small of her back, comforting and supportive.

'You are mistaken, Fothergill.'

His voice dripped with icy scorn, adding steel to Beatrice's backbone. Mrs Butterby had been wonderful in standing up to Percy, but he had been dismissive of her standing as a mere chaperon. But he would *have* to listen to a gentleman of Jack's standing. Wouldn't he?

'As I understand it, Miss Fothergill has no wish to continue under your authority, as you put it, and has made her choice abundantly clear.'

'What do *you* know about any of this?' Belling sneered. 'On the catch for a wealthy heiress, are you? D'you hope riches will help compensate for *that*?'

He gestured dismissively at Jack's missing arm and Beatrice felt the hand at her back tense. A peep at Jack's face showed a muscle leap at the side of his jaw as he clenched it. Intuition kept Beatrice silent, although she longed to leap to his defence. She'd noticed his flash of pain when she'd stopped him confronting Percy that first afternoon at South Street and she'd afterwards wondered if he had interpreted her determination to stand up for herself as a lack of belief in his ability to protect her. It had not been... but she understood how he might see it like that because she was aware that *he* held the belief—wrongly, in her opinion—that the loss of a part of one arm had somehow rendered him less of a man.

'I believe I can claim to know a sight more than you, Belling.'

Jack held the other man's gaze with look of contempt and Beatrice was delighted when a clearly discomposed Walter dropped his eyes.

'Miss Fothergill has already stated she will not marry you and that must be an end to it. As for you, Fothergill, it is time you accepted the truth. The details in Lady Tregowan's will have been verified. Lady Dolphinstone and Miss Croome are Miss Fothergill's half-sisters and she is therefore now under the protection of Lord Dolphinstone, as her brother-in-law.'

Fenella's eyes had narrowed in suspicion. 'You appear to be surprisingly *au fait* with our family concerns, sir, for a neighbour who visited our home just the once.'

'I have eyes in my head, madam,' Jack responded coldly. 'I recognise intimidation and coercion when I see it. I applaud Miss Fothergill for her courage in freeing herself from your control. Now, I think enough has been said.'

He stepped forward, his hand at her back, urging Beatrice to move with him, and Percy and Fenella stepped aside. Beatrice groped with her right hand for Mrs Butterby, and gripped it, so all three could walk away together.

Jack halted, though, once they had moved beyond the others and spoke over his shoulder. 'You'd be wise to heed my warning about Lord Dolphinstone, you know, Fothergill. *I* might have no authority, but you can be certain *he* will not take kindly to anyone treating his new sister with less than the respect and the kindness she deserves.'

As they approached the drawing room, the little knot of observers dispersed in a flurry of curious looks and Beatrice caught a muttered, 'Well done, sir!' from one gentleman. There were few occupants in the room, but as they paused on the threshold, an elderly lady sporting a purple turban and with her feet propped up on a footstool hailed Mrs Butterby.

'Prudence! My dear! I heard you were in town with those Tregowan heiresses.' She raised her pince-nez and studied Beatrice from head to foot, making her blush. 'Is this one of 'em? Fetching little thing, ain't she?' She examined Jack then. 'Hmph.' Then switched her attention back to Mrs Butterby. 'I was exceedingly sorry to hear about Sarah's death, by the bye. Come, sit by me, and tell me all about it. You look in need of a stiff drink. You!' This last directed at a footman on duty in the room. 'Drinks all round and be quick about it.'

'Oh, heavens,' murmured Mrs Butterby. 'Lady Deal! She was an old friend of Lady Tregowan's. I shall have to go and talk to her, but there's no need for you two to be trapped if you would rather not?'

'Speaking for myself, I should prefer *not*, I think,' said Jack.

'Nor me, but I do not wish to appear impolite.'

Mrs Butterby smiled. 'Leave that to me. Come.' She raised her voice. 'Good evening, Lady Deal. Might I present Lord Jack Kingswood and Miss Beatrice Fothergill?'

Jack bowed and Beatrice curtsied. Her Ladyship nodded regally.

'I shall be delighted to tell you about poor Sarah, but I am afraid Miss Fothergill is engaged for the next dance, so she cannot linger. Lord Jack...would you oblige me by escorting Beatrice to her sisters and Lord Dolphinstone?'

Jack bowed again. 'With pleasure, ma'am.'

He crooked his left arm, and Beatrice laid her hand on it. Lady Deal's eyes narrowed and she gestured at Jack's arm.

'Waterloo? Or earlier?'

'Waterloo, ma'am.'

'Hmmm. Grand job you lads did over there. Lost m'grandson there. Tragic.' She gestured again at Jack's arm. 'It's early days yet, lad. You'll get used to it, y'know. Learn to live with it. You're alive. That's the important thing. Live your life to the full, for the ones that didn't make it.'

Her voice quavered on her last words and Beatrice's heart went out to her. 'I am sorry for your loss, my lady.'

'Yes. Well. That's life. Death comes to us all, sooner or later. It's harder when the young go first. You go on and enjoy yourselves while you may.' She waved them away.

On their way downstairs, Beatrice studied Jack's strong, handsome profile. It was so good to see him again... How would she ever get accustomed to only ever seeing him in public? It was not enough...it would never be enough for her, yet how could she ever hope for more? For all her vows to prove herself a strong, capable woman, she had needed rescuing yet again.

He looked somewhat sombre now and she said, 'You're quiet, Jack. Did Lady Deal upset you?'

'No. Well, a little, maybe, in that she reminded me of all those who died.'

She squeezed his arm in sympathy. 'I am so pleased to see you here tonight. I did wonder if you would attend, even after that deal we struck at the supper party.'

'I wouldn't let you down, Bea. I know how nervous you are about dancing in public and I wanted to support you.'

'I am fortunate you appeared at just the right time to rescue me from Percy,' she said. 'I thought he would not risk confronting me in public, but I was wrong.'

'I hope he's learned his lesson. I shall warn Dolphinstone to stay alert, although I fail to see what they can do, other than try something outlandish like an attempt to kidnap you.'

'Surely he wouldn't go that far? Not even Percy can imagine he would get away with that.'

She said the words, but could not shake off the feeling that he just might. After all, if Walter compromised her, what other man would look at her? She'd be ostracised... Mrs Butterby had been clear about the repercussions should she be compromised, in among all the other warnings she had dished out since Beatrice's arrival in London.

'Hopefully not,' said Jack.

How she wished she had not come here tonight. Not only had she made a fool of herself on the dance floor, but now the gossip about the argument with Percy would be spreading from mouth to mouth, and everyone would stare at her all the more. As they neared the ballroom, Beatrice pulled Jack to a halt.

'I made an utter fool of myself dancing with Dolph earlier,' she confessed. 'I kept forgetting the steps and turning the wrong way. I don't know if I can face it again, even though we made that pact.'

Jack laid his hand over hers. 'Then we need not return. There's no need for you to feel uncomfortable. Bea... I've had an idea.' He captured her gaze then, his blue eyes sparkling with mischief, his lips curving. 'I found the conservatory. There will be no audience. We can make as many mistakes as we like. Can you waltz?'

'Well...' Honesty compelled her to admit, 'I have only had one lesson. I trod on Leah's toes.'

Jack laughed and her heart lightened. 'I am sure my toes will survive it...but they have just started to play a waltz and I have a fancy to dance. Just you and me. Come.'

Just you and me...

Her silly heart pitter-pattered at his words even though she knew he was just being kind. The hall happened to be deserted at that moment, and Jack grabbed Beatrice's hand and whisked her along a short corridor to a glazed door beyond which she glimpsed the shadowy forms of plants. The conservatory boasted a square of stone flags in the centre, and it was here that Jack halted and turned to her. And froze. In the dim light illuminating his features she could see his smile drop as his shoulders slumped. He did rally, but his smile was strained.

'A waltz may have been overly ambitious.' He raised his left arm and gave a false laugh. 'I cannot...'

Beatrice moved closer. 'But *I* can.'

She held his arm where it ended, folding her fingers gently around it, and placed her left hand on his right shoulder. After a beat of hesitation, she felt Jack's right arm encircle her waist, pulling her tight into his hard body. She felt wrapped in an invisible warmth, making her feel so safe, so secure, so *loved*...even though she knew that last was ridiculous, and merely her own wishful thinking.

'Thank you.' His lips were close to her ear. 'Now... don't think. Relax. Listen to the music and *trust* me.'

Her eyelids drifted shut and she put her trust in Jack as they started to move. At first, she clutched both his shoulder and his arm, but she soon loosened her grip as they pirouetted around the conservatory. There were stumbles but, somehow, they didn't matter. At the first, their eyes met and the smile they shared turned to laughter. After a time, though, their laughter faded and their movements slowed as their eyes still clung. Their lips moved closer.

'I know we shouldn't,' Jack murmured, his soft, warm breath caressing her skin. 'This is unfair...'

'Hush.'

Beatrice's arm snaked around his neck, urging his lips still closer. His musky, spicy scent filled her as his mouth covered hers. His tongue touched her lips, and she opened to him, tasting him. Desire rippled through her, pooling at that sweet spot between her thighs. Her nipples hardened and her breasts seemed to grow tighter, fuller. She pressed closer still to soothe their aching need, her fingers thrusting up through his hair, cradling his head.

Their bodies still swayed with the beat of the music as their kiss exploded with quiet groans and moans of approval, and although they had ceased to dance, Beatrice felt like she was floating on air. His lips left hers, feathering a path across her cheek to graze her earlobe before sucking it into his warm mouth and gently nipping. A shard of pleasure shot through her and her body arched into his without volition, her head tipping back as a warm tongue laved the pulse at the side of her neck.

Only when the music ended did reality return to bite. Beatrice straightened, pulling reluctantly away from Jack, ending their kiss, but remaining within his embrace.

Percy was still out there. She still faced the ordeal of finding a husband, not only to protect her from Percy and to secure her inheritance, but also to give her the family she dreamed of. She stared up at Jack, the fire smouldering in his eyes. He liked her; she knew that. He desired her, unmistakably. She could still feel the solid proof of that against her soft belly. Aurelia had warned her his pride would prove a fearsome barrier, but if she had to wait until he conquered it himself, might it be too late?

There was one solution. But could she summon the courage? Did she dare?

On the other hand, what if she did nothing and, somehow, Percy succeeded in forcing her to marry Walter after all? What was Percy capable of?

She sucked in a deep, deep breath.

Chapter Nineteen

Jack wished he knew what Beatrice was thinking as a myriad of emotions flickered across her expression. His lips throbbed from their kiss and the desire that had coursed through his body now lay thick and heavy in his groin, tangible proof of his arousal. Her lovely smoky eyes grew pensive then, and the urge to kiss away her doubts seized him. She sucked in a breath, expanding her chest, which had the effect of lifting her breasts in her enticingly low neckline. He craved a touch. Just one. But how would that be fair when—

'Jack.'

The intensity in that one word jerked him away from any thought of further dalliance. He tilted his head and raised his brows.

'Beatrice?'

'Might we sit?' She indicated a nearby bench.

Jack nodded and allowed her to lead him to it. She sat next to him and half turned to face him, taking his hand between both of hers. She nibbled at her lower lip, her eyes now anxious, and a sense of foreboding stirred deep in Jack's gut.

'I… I cannot help but worry that, somehow, Percy will still find a way to force me to marry Walter.'

He opened his mouth to reassure her, but she laid her finger to his lips.

'Please. Allow me to finish. It is just…' She paused. Then, with an expression of sheer determination, she rushed on. 'Jack… I know from your point of view it would not be ideal, but…well, I only ever expected a marriage of convenience anyway…so would you…do you think… Well, I know it is considered a bit of a joke, but it *is* Leap Year and I know I have missed Leap Year Day… but…would *you* marry me?'

'What?' Jack snatched his hand from hers and surged to his feet.

She winced. 'Would it be so dreadful? Jack…think of the advantages. You said yourself your income is not substantial, but that you wish to be independent of your brother. If you marry me, you will have that independence—'

That is not independence.

'—and…oh, just think. We could set up that foundation to help those veterans who cannot find work, just like we discussed with Lady Poole. We can help them train for new trades. We can use my money to help those men… Well, it is not even my money really, is it? My good fortune is but a fluke and I am happy to share it.'

Jack hauled in a deep breath and opened his mouth again, but Beatrice rushed on.

'And I would not *bother* you, I promise.'

Would not bother me? What does that mean?

'I would make no demands, although I *should* like to have a family,' she went on, her cheeks flaming. 'I have always wanted children but, other than that, I would expect nothing. You would not find me a needy wife always clinging to your arm, I promise. You could live your own life. I would not expect you to gain independence from Kit only to find yourself bound to a wife you did not love.'

Jack stared at her, dizzy with the speed of his spinning thoughts.

'Well?' Her lower lip caught between her teeth, her eyes worried. 'What do you say?'

'I… I am lost for words.'

It was true. The prize she dangled before him—marriage to a beautiful woman he desired; an end to his money worries; the ability to do so much more for the veterans; *children*…the family he could never, as things stood, afford.

Any sensible man—any *sane* man—would jump at the chance she offered. And yet…as much as his head urged him to snatch this opportunity with both hands, his heart felt…hollow.

Could he really bear to be married to a woman who viewed him as the solution to her immediate problems and whose only *real* need of him would be as a stud to sire the children she longed for? He already knew her opinion of his ability to physically protect her—she had run away rather than trust him at Salt Hill and the other day she had cautioned him to hide himself upstairs like a coward while *she* saw off Fothergill and Belling. How long would it be before she regretted tying herself to a one-armed man when she could have her pick of any number of able-bodied men? How long before she regretted her rash offer?

She surely had not thought this proposal through, but had blurted it out on impulse. The bribe of helping the veterans added to his discomfort. He shook his head as his pride reared up. What kind of man could agree to such a bleak, unequal union?

A fortune hunter, that's who.

He had long disdained such men, wondering how they managed to retain their self-esteem and also wondering how their wives could ever respect them. Not only would he bring nothing to such a marriage, he did not even have the satisfaction of making his own proposal. *She* had proposed to *him*. He shook his head again. Unheard of.

'Oh.' Beatrice leapt to her feet, her cheeks still bright red, and turned away, busying herself by brushing down her skirts. 'You are right, of course. It was a stupid idea— an impulse I did not think through. It would never work. Please…forget I ever mentioned it. I am foolish… It was a silly panic after meeting Percy. Of course I am safe here with my family. Nothing will happen to me.' She did not quite meet his eyes and her voice was strained. 'I trust we can still be friends, though, Jack. I should not like to lose our friendship over such a silly blunder.'

'Of course we are still friends.'

Jack knew he, too, sounded strained and, of a sudden, he could not wait to leave.

'Come, it is time we returned to the ballroom,' he said, 'or we shall find ourselves with little choice other than to wed.'

She said nothing but laid her hand on his arm as they left the conservatory.

'Beatrice…' he could not leave it like this '… I know you are worried about Fothergill and Belling but, as long as you take care never to go anywhere alone, they cannot harm you. Give yourself time and you will meet a man who can give you the happiness you deserve and you will breathe a sigh of relief not to be shackled to a one-armed man like me.'

Again she said nothing, but as they paused in the entrance to the ballroom, she removed her hand and faced him.

'I see you as a man with one arm, Jack. Not a one-armed man.' She raised her chin and looked him straight in the eyes, pain shimmering in her own. 'The difference is important and I hope in time you will come to think of yourself as the former, not the latter.'

She hurried away, skirting the dance floor, to join the Dolphinstones, who were sitting by one of the windows. Jack stared after her, pondering her words. Didn't they mean the same thing? Shrugging away the guilt that assailed him at that pain in her eyes, he turned to leave and came face to face with Lady Newcombe.

'Well, well. We meet again,' she purred.

Her young cicisbeo was nowhere to be seen, and only now, in the blazing light of the ballroom, did Jack fully appreciate her beauty and voluptuousness. And the sultry invitation in her dark eyes. He bowed.

'Lady Newcombe.'

'Do you dance, sir?' Her gaze dropped to his arm, then rose again, as did her brows.

'I do not.'

Except once. His heart faltered, but he hardened it. Beatrice deserved better than him. It would have been selfish to accept that impulsive proposal. She would have soon grown to regret it.

'Well...' and the lady tucked her hand around his left bicep, avoiding, he noted with sardonic amusement, any possibility of touching his stump, which was already beginning to itch with the heat from so many twirling bodies '...as you can see, neither do I at present, and neither do I have a partner for the next.' She smiled coyly. 'As that is the supper dance, might I suggest we two poor, partnerless souls keep one another company? You can tell me what your brother has been up to lately. I have missed his company.'

Something in the way she said that last stirred Jack's

suspicions, and he made a mental note to ask Kit about her when he next saw him.

'It will be my pleasure, ma'am,' he responded, with a gallant bow.

Numb. No physical feelings anywhere. But inside...oh, inside! Stupid. Embarrassed...no. *More* than embarrassed. *Humiliated.* Beatrice was still *drowning* in humiliation as she sat with Leah and Dolph at the side of the ballroom and watched Aurelia—graceful and elegant, but also dazzling and vivacious, all the things Beatrice was *not*—on the dance floor. She was partnered by Lord Sampford, a gentleman Aurelia claimed to despise, and yet no one would believe it to see her now. How did she put on such a convincing act? Beatrice might successfully conceal her current humiliation behind a serene smile, but there was no way she could sparkle as effortlessly as Aurelia.

Hopelessness added its weight to her despair. Did this simply prove Percy right, that she was indeed too stupid to be trusted to be in charge of her own life? She had acted on impulse and see what a disaster she had wrought. Utterly shamed herself and thoroughly embarrassed a fine gentleman like Jack. Her friend.

Her gaze moved to the doorway of its own volition, seeking him. Her heart dropped like a stone on seeing him deep in conversation with a stunning dark-haired lady who, even as Beatrice watched, took his arm, smiling up at him.

If only she'd not rushed into it. If only she'd thought about it from Jack's point of view, she would surely have realised he would never be happy saddled with a silly fool like her for a wife. She was good enough to kiss, when the opportunity presented itself, but how had she ever thought he'd accept marriage to a ninny like her? And as for using her fortune to try to entice him… She knew how proud he was. Knew how he'd chafed at the idea of being his twin brother's pensioner. *She* might view his lack of money as a positive reason for them to marry, but it was obvious *he* would see it as an insurmountable barrier to such a marriage and a mortal blow to his pride. And yet she had wafted it under his nose as though tempting a starving man with a feast.

She just thanked God Leah and Aurelia knew nothing about her crass, blundering idiocy.

'Are you quite well, Beatrice?'

Her head snapped round. Leah's beautiful blue-green eyes were sympathetic.

'I have sent Dolph to procure us a drink,' Leah said. 'It will give us the chance to talk… Forgive me, but you do not appear especially comfortable here. Is it the dancing? You will get better, I promise. I find it does help to imagine there is no one watching.'

Misery wound around Beatrice's throat at the memory of dancing with Jack. Of being held safe and secure in his arms. An illusion—something that existed only in her foolish mind. She shook her head and forced a smile.

'I am unused to such crowds,' she said, 'but I shall keep practising the steps. I know I shall improve.'

'And we will help you.' Leah frowned then. 'Where is Mrs Butterby?'

'She met an old acquaintance in the salon. Lord Jack escorted me back to the ballroom.'

Leah eyed the doorway, where Jack still stood with the dark-haired beauty. 'Ah.'

Beatrice cringed inside at Leah's knowing tone and another sympathetic look. The music ended then, and Beatrice drew Leah's attention to Aurelia, who was clearly determined to escape Lord Sampford's company for the next dance. Leah laughed, successfully distracted.

'She *is* naughty. Do you know, she scribbled a false name on her card for the next dance purely so she did not have to endure—her word, not mine—the company of any of her entourage over supper? She claims there is not one gentleman of her acquaintance whose company she would prefer to ours. I dare say we should be flattered.'

Jack had exited the ballroom while Leah was talking and Beatrice felt she could breathe again. She tried not to care that the dark-haired lady had gone with him.

'Aurelia has succeeded in escaping Lord Sampford, I see,' she said, keen to distract Leah from noticing her low mood, 'but who is that she is talking to now?'

Leah followed Beatrice's pointing finger and frowned. 'I have no idea. He is a stranger to me.'

They watched in silence for a few moments. Then Leah stirred. 'Ought we to go and rescue her, do you think?' The gentleman—very dark and haughty-looking—was facing them, standing rigidly as he glared down at Aurelia, who was growing visibly more agitated. 'People are beginning to notice.'

As Beatrice was about to agree, however, Aurelia pivoted away from the gentleman and marched across the ballroom to them, straight through the couples forming for the supper dance. Heads turned to watch her progress, then swivelled back to look at the gentleman who remained in the doorway, glowering at nothing in particular.

'Oh! Insufferable, rude man!' Aurelia flung herself down on to a vacant chair, snatched her fan from the table and plied it vigorously.

'Who is he, Aurelia? What did he say to upset you?'

Aurelia glared across the room at him. 'Tregowan,' she bit out through gritted teeth.

'Oh, heavens. How he must resent us,' said Beatrice, recalling what both Mr Henshaw and Mrs Butterby had revealed about the current Lord Tregowan and immediately sympathetic to his troubles. But she hoped never to meet him herself, for he looked so angry and extremely intimidating.

'What did he say?'

'He had the nerve to imply that, had that clause forbidding marriage to him not existed, he would have taken… *taken*, if you please…either me or Beatrice, as it would have been the easiest solution for all. *Easiest!* Arrogant, puffed-up swine! As if all he has to do is click his fingers!'

The rest of Aurelia's diatribe blew over Beatrice's head as her thoughts inexorably returned to Jack.

Did I ask him to marry me simply because it was the easiest solution for me?

Well, she couldn't deny that it *would* be easier for her, but she also couldn't deny her distress at his horrified reaction. She cared for him. Very much. In fact, given the frequency with which he occupied her thoughts— and the jealousy that had twisted inside her at the sight of him with that woman—she very much feared she loved him. The thought of never seeing him again…of marrying another man…squeezed her chest until she struggled to draw breath.

Both Dolph and Mrs Butterby had returned, and Beatrice gratefully gulped a mouthful of the cool, soothing lemonade Dolph handed to her, while Aurelia continued her bitter complaints about Lord Tregowan.

Love. I never thought…never realised…

Did you not? Truthfully, now?

Her every thought since her arrival in town had been of him. At the modiste's—would Jack like this gown? Would he think she looked pretty? In the Park, scanning every gentleman in the hope it was him. At home, her heart leaping at every knock on the door. Just because she had never consciously thought of love did not mean it was not true.

Her stomach was a lead weight. Her throat ached with the effort of holding her tears at bay. What an utter mess she had made of everything. Had she only been honest with herself about her feelings for Jack she would never have launched headlong into that stupid proposal. But she had and her self-recriminations near-crucified her, for she could see no way back now. In fact, she would not be surprised if Jack now avoided her, despite his agreement they would remain friends. He was being kind, that was all.

Leah's voice shook her from her thoughts. 'Dolph and I are going home straight after supper, my dear. Are you feeling better now?' She leaned closer and lowered her voice. 'We can take you home if you would prefer to leave?'

'I…thank you. Yes, I should prefer to leave early if Aurelia and Mrs Butterby do not object—I have a slight headache and am tired.' She smiled around at her family, which included Mrs Butterby, and she blessed her good fortune in finding them. 'I am not yet accustomed to these late nights and all the noise.'

Aurelia smiled ruefully. 'And I have not helped with my tirade about Tregowan, have I? I shall strive for more restraint in future. Well, at least in public. Mrs Butterby, I am sure, will be thankful.'

'I will, indeed, for no man desires a sharp-tongued scold for a wife. Really, Aurelia—if you do not take care, respectable young men like Sampford will drift away and leave you with only the truly hardened fortune hunters to choose from if you are to meet the conditions of the will.'

Aurelia merely laughed at that reprimand, shrugging her shoulders as she winked at Beatrice.

* * *

At supper, Beatrice sat with her back to Jack and the other woman, who were sitting at the far side of the room. She ate little, longing for it to be over, and refused to reveal her burning curiosity by enquiring as to the woman's identity.

Only later, as she lay in bed with Spartacus cuddled next to her, did she allow her mind to return to Jack and her disastrous decision to try to take charge of her own life with that pathetic proposal to a man who had only ever tried to be a kind friend to her.

Although...and a whisper of hope drifted through her... Jack *did* like her. She might be inexperienced, but she hadn't imagined the admiration in his eyes or the passion in his kiss. But he clearly did not care for her enough to marry her, even in a marriage of convenience such as she had proposed. Unless... For the first time since her proposal, she recalled Aurelia's warning. Could it be that he *did* care for her and it was pride alone that had spurred his refusal?

She searched deep inside her soul as she pondered where to go from here. Love, surely, was worth fighting for and, if it was possible that Jack's pride was the only reason for his refusal, she would be a fool to give up on him. So, for the moment, she would cling to the hope he would somehow manage to conquer that pride after all, and she...*she* must somehow find the courage to let him know her offer remained open.

Despite that hope, she still tossed and turned long into the night, reliving what had happened and fretting about seeing Jack again—what she could say; how she should act. It was Lady Poole's soirée the following night, and Jack would attend without doubt. Despite Beatrice's vow to stand up for herself and to be strong in this new life of hers, she finally concluded that—just this once—she would take the coward's way out and stay at home.

Once the decision was made, sleep claimed her.

Her dreams, though, were troubled and she had no need to fake a headache when she finally arose close to eleven o'clock in the morning—an unheard-of time to sleep to in her previous life with Percy and Fenella. As the day wore on—her hopes soaring at every knock on the door and diving when the caller proved not to be Jack—she grew more despondent and still could not find the words to tell Aurelia and Mrs Butterby that she would be staying home that evening.

Chapter Twenty

The day after Lord Smethwick's birthday ball Jack woke up to skies of unremitting grey, the weather uncannily mirroring his mood. Throughout that grim, rain-sodden day he battled the urge to go to Beatrice and try to explain himself. To smooth things over between them. To, maybe, even remind her that he had not *actually* refused her. Not in so many words. And all day long the same question nagged at him. If only he could relive last night... would he react differently? If time could be rewound and she asked him again, would he...*should* he...accept her?

But the arguments against him calling upon her were potent. Insurmountable, even.

Firstly, were he to call upon her, one or more members of her household would be present. He would be unable to speak freely but, instead, would be forced to sit there making polite conversation. He could just imagine how awkward that would be for both of them. Far, far better to speak to her in a public place where they would be more likely to get the chance to talk privately. Had the weather allowed, he would have gone to the Park in the hope of seeing her there but, no matter how often he stared out of the window, the rain kept falling.

More importantly, though, he could not work out what he would say to her. He struggled all day to resolve his internal tug of war between his pride and his…what? What was it that stopped him forgetting all about that offer of a marriage of convenience and getting on with his life? Obligation? No. It was more than a mere sense of responsibility towards her. Friendship? Desire? Undoubtedly… but were either of those sufficient to enter into a lifelong union? Love? His thoughts skittered away from that improbable idea before he could properly consider it.

After a great deal of soul-searching, he realised he was angry with Beatrice. Not for her actual proposal—he appreciated how much courage that must have taken—but for her readiness to settle for a marriage of convenience, as though she deserved no better. Such a marriage should not be enough for a kind, affectionate girl like her. That realisation led to another as he finally allowed himself to accept, with a jolt of self-awareness, that neither was such a marriage enough for him.

He wanted more. And only after yet more soul-searching did he admit his hurt that she had made no mention of love—either now or in the future—as an inducement for their marriage. Which made him an utter hypocrite. Did he really expect a shy girl like Beatrice to boldly speak of tender feelings, let alone love?

After dressing for dinner—and still torn—he went downstairs only to learn that Kit was dining at his club that night, reminding Jack that he had not seen his twin since breakfast, when Jack had happened to mention Lady Newcombe. Kit had growled she was no friend of his and promptly took himself out for the day, leaving Jack to suspect the lady had something to do with his brother's recent reclusive behaviour. Jack, therefore, dined in solitary splendour, tormented by the same repetitive internal arguments as he strove to reach a decision about his future.

Try as he might, his pride still stood in the way of what he now accepted as his heart's desire. His lack of income and his physical disability still rendered him, in his own eyes, a poor choice for an heiress like Beatrice, who deserved a far better man for a husband.

Her voice echoed in his head, chiding him. *I see you as a man with one arm, Jack. Not a one-armed man*, and he frowned at his braised beef. Last night he had not seen any difference, but now…*did* she see him as a man, first and foremost? A man capable of being loved for who he was, not for how he looked?

Beatrice deserved better than a marriage of convenience and she deserved happiness, but did he honestly believe himself incapable of making her happy?

And, suddenly, he was ready to see her. He *needed* to see her. In his mind's eye, he saw her again, standing up to Fothergill and Belling, and the urgent need to protect her gripped him—not only from them, but also from all the other fortune hunters out there who would take her for the wealth she brought and crush her emerging spirit without a second thought.

She had accepted Lady Poole's invitation to her soirée tonight. He would see her there. Jack thrust back his chair and strode for the door, calling for his hat, glove and umbrella.

After dinner that evening, Beatrice meekly went upstairs to change her gown for the soirée, still castigating herself for her utter spinelessness in not being honest with her family.

In her bedchamber, Maria—ever lackadaisical about

her duties—was nowhere to be seen, and Beatrice sank on to the bed, her thoughts still whirling.

Why am I scared to tell them what I want? They're not Percy and Fenella. They will understand, surely?

And she realised it was not fear that stopped her putting her own needs first. Nor even the wish to be liked, and accepted, although they were important to her. It was, rather, the desire not to upset anyone. Or to hurt their feelings. She cared enough about others—and not only her own family—to want them to be happy and it gave her pleasure to please other people. But, surely, there had to be times when she was justified in putting her own needs first? To be a touch selfish. And this was one of those times—to give her a little respite before having to face Jack again. It was ludicrous to imagine her absence tonight would prevent her family enjoying the evening when they had managed perfectly without her company up to now. She would be sorry not to see Jack tonight, but she was not ready to face him even though she was not yet ready to give up on him. She might have lost the battle, but not the war. She merely needed to replenish her energy.

Fortified by that realisation, she left her bedchamber and went to Mrs Butterby in the next room. The chaperon was seated at her dressing table when Beatrice entered, and twisted around on her stool. She took one look at Beatrice and sprang to her feet, coming to her with arms outstretched.

'Oh, my dear. You look dreadful. Is it your head again? I *thought* you looked peaky at dinner and you have been horribly quiet today.'

'I...' Beatrice swallowed down her emotions at Mrs Butterby's kindness. She hated to lie, but she could not admit the truth. 'Yes. I've had the headache on and off all day, but it is far worse now. I am so tired, too. I really cannot face the soirée. I am sorry.'

'Oh, you poor dear. You must go straight to bed. Is Maria in your room?'

Beatrice shook her head.

'Wait here while I find her. Really, she needs a good talking-to, that one.' Mrs Butterby was gone just a moment, and when she returned, she pushed Beatrice gently back to sit on the edge of her bed. 'Maria is arranging a bedwarmer for your bed and some warm milk. And I shall send a note over to Lady Poole to explain we are unable to attend her soirée.'

'No! Oh, please, do not miss it on my account. I know Aurelia is looking forward to it…' She couldn't help but smile at Mrs Butterby's sceptical look. 'Well,' she elaborated, 'I know she is eager to find a wealthy husband and *put an end to this charade*, as she puts it.'

Mrs Butterby laughed. 'That is true. And at least she makes some effort to attract a husband, unlike you, Beatrice.'

She perched next to Beatrice on the bed and put her arm around her. Beatrice fought the urge to put her head on the older woman's shoulder and succumb to the tears that crowded her throat. She swallowed past the painful lump that had lodged there, telling herself it was tiredness making her weepy.

'I do my best,' she said. 'But I do not care for the crowds… My tongue gets glued to the roof of my mouth and I am scared of saying something stupid. Please. You go to the soirée. All I wish to do is to sleep. I won't even know you and Aurelia aren't here.'

'Well. If you are sure, my dear…'

The door opened to admit Maria. 'The bed is warming, miss, and I shall bring your milk up as soon as I can.'

'Thank you, but can you delay the milk, please?' Beatrice smiled at Mrs Butterby. 'I should like to see Aurelia in her new bronze silk gown and I'd like to be there to greet Leah and Dolph when they call here for you both.'

Leah and her new husband had arranged to convey the ladies from Tregowan House to the Pooles' residence in Grosvenor Street to save their own carriage turning out.

'Very well, miss,' Maria said.

Beatrice was happy she had made the effort to stay up to see her sisters, despite the dull ache behind her eyes. Aurelia, as ever, glowed. No wonder the gentlemen were drawn to her like moths to a flame—she was irresistible, with her bright eyes and her glorious smile and her golden ringlets brushing her delicate shoulders. Beatrice kissed her cheek.

'You look gorgeous. I almost wish I were coming, too, just to see the gentlemen's expressions when they first set eyes on you.'

Aurelia laughed and pulled Beatrice into a fierce hug. 'I shall miss you, Bea. I hope your headache will be gone by morning, when I shall tell you all about our evening and you will regret staying away and being dull here all on your own.'

Leah was positively regal, her tall, slender figure set off to perfection in a gown the colour of sapphires. Her red hair piled on her head in soft waves added to, rather than detracted from, her height, and her astonishing blue-green eyes were serene, symbolising her deep contentment. Marriage to Lord Dolphinstone clearly suited her, and Beatrice could not help but feel a twinge of envy at their devotion to one another and to their ready-made family.

'Ladies... I hate to rush you, but it is time to go.'

Dolph's deep voice sounded from the front doorway, which framed his tall, broad form. His gaze, as ever, sought his wife, and his customary, somewhat sombre expression softened. He then stepped forward and took Mrs Butterby's mantle from Vardy, who was waiting to assist her. 'Allow me.' And Mrs Butterby smiled with delight as he added, 'You look absolutely charming, my dear ma'am.'

'You do indeed,' said Beatrice, and she kissed the chaperon's cheek, then hugged her. 'I hope you all enjoy the soirée.'

'I am sorry you do not feel up to it, Beatrice,' Leah said, 'but there will be plenty of other evenings out.' She hugged Beatrice and added in a whisper, 'I shall call tomorrow and we shall practise those dance steps again.' She turned for the door. 'Come along, then. Let us go and join the inevitable queue of carriages.'

After her family left, Beatrice breathed a quiet sigh of relief to be alone.

'Would you ask Maria to attend me upstairs, please, Vardy?'

'Of course, Miss Fothergill.'

Beatrice plodded up the stairs, her head still fragile, her eyes heavy. In her bedchamber the bedwarmer was already between the sheets and there, curled on top, was Spartacus. The bed looked so inviting, but she must wait for Maria to come and help her out of her gown, which buttoned down the back. She rounded the bed to the chair by the fire and sat down, staring into the flames, not at all sorry to miss the soirée, but haunted by the thought that the black-haired lady would be there, fluttering around Jack and making eyes at him. How could he resist such a beautiful woman? And why would he even try? She could surely have almost any man as her lover with a click of her fingers.

Her eyelids began to droop as she waited for Maria.

The sound of the door opening jerked Beatrice from her doze. Her eyes sprang open as the creak of a floorboard alerted her that something was amiss. Then her heart lurched as she saw Percy and Walter on the far side of her bed. As Walter closed the door, Beatrice leapt to her feet and ran to the bed, so it was solidly between herself and the men. Percy held up his hands in a placatory gesture, smiling ingratiatingly at her.

'Come now, Beatrice. Don't be a silly girl. We are not here to hurt you.'

Beatrice's chest rose and fell rapidly as she struggled to breathe. That old, familiar tremble began in her legs and her knees grew weak.

'Why *are* you here, then?'

Keep them talking. Maria must surely come soon.

'You must have realised we would not let you go that easily.'

Walter began to skirt the bed. Spartacus, having woken, stood up, his back arched, ears flat to his head, and hissed. Walter took no notice, but kept coming. Beatrice's legs seemed to turn to water as Percy began to follow Walter.

'Get out!'

Her voice was little more than a gasp, but it was enough to send Spartacus shooting underneath the bed. Beatrice dragged in a lungful of air, ready to scream, but Walter responded by speeding up, quickly narrowing the gap between them. Without conscious thought, Beatrice scrambled across the bed. Walter grabbed her ankle, but she kicked back, her heel connecting with something soft, and she heard a shout of pain, followed by a gasp. She tumbled off the far side of the bed, bruising her thigh on the bedwarmer's wooden handle that jutted out from beneath the covers at that point. She struggled to regain her feet.

Walter was doubled up, his face puce. Percy, however,

was already lumbering back around the bed towards her. There was no time to open the door and get out. Time only to take hold of that protruding handle.

Where she got the strength, she didn't know. She grabbed it with both hands and backed up, pulling the warming pan free from the bedcovers as she did so, and then swung it in an arc, all in one smooth motion. The copper pan hit the side of Percy's head with a satisfying clunk, whereupon the lid fell open and hot embers rained over his head and shoulders. He shrieked and a string of curses burst from his mouth.

Beatrice dropped the pan and fled the room. Her maid was on the landing, and Beatrice ran to her.

'Maria! Get help! Quick now!'

Too late, she registered the expression on the maid's face—not shock, but fierce determination as she grabbed Beatrice's arm. Beatrice raised both hands and shoved Maria away, but even as she thought she'd succeeded, an arm wrapped around her neck from behind and a balled-up cloth was forced into her mouth.

'You'll pay for this,' Percy growled in her ear as he began to drag her to the staircase.

The rain had finally ceased, and Jack, after that long, frustrating day alone with his thoughts, opted to walk to Sir Benedict and Lady Poole's house in Grosvenor Street. He tucked his cumbersome umbrella under his left arm— in case it rained again—and he set off.

The fresh air and exercise revived his spirits, as he'd hoped, and he was now eager to see Beatrice again, with the hope they could put what had happened last night behind them. As he strolled along South Audley Street, skirting the puddles, a carriage halted just ahead of him, at the corner of Grosvenor Square. The door opened and Dolph's head appeared.

'Are you heading for the Pooles' soirée, Kingswood? There's room inside if you care to join us?'

He longed to speak to Beatrice. To soothe her by explaining his hurtful reaction to her proposal, but he had no wish for their first meeting to take place while crammed into a carriage with her entire family.

'No. I thank you, but after being stuck indoors all day, I have need of the exercise.' Jack peered past Dolph into the interior of the carriage, hoping to catch Beatrice's eye. To smile at her and maybe convey a silent message. He frowned.

'Good evening, ladies. Is Miss Fothergill not with you? I was about to enquire whether she had recovered from her confrontation with Fothergill and Belling yesterday evening.'

'Confrontation?' Aurelia leaned forward, her gaze intense. 'This is the first I have heard of any confrontation.'

'Oh, heavens! I quite forgot to mention it last night,' said Mrs Butterby. 'It was before supper when Beatrice and I went to the salon for a respite. Those two scoundrels cornered us, and if Lord Jack hadn't appeared when he did— Well, I cannot tell you how relieved I was to see you, my lord. Fothergill in particular revealed a nasty, domineering streak and was worryingly persistent, but afterwards, what with meeting Lady Deal again and the excitement of Lord Tregowan turning up, and then Beatrice leaving early with Leah and Dolph... Well! I am afraid it went clean from my mind.'

'Beatrice is not feeling well, so she has stayed home this evening,' Leah said. She looked from Jack to Dolph and back again, her eyes troubled. 'I saw them earlier. Fothergill and Belling. They were at the bottom end of

South Street when the carriage turned in to call at the house for Aurelia and Mrs Butterby. They'd gone when we came out, though, so I thought no more of it. You don't think...?'

Jack didn't stay to hear any more. He turned on his heel and sprinted back to South Street, his legs pumping. He reached the corner and charged around it, racing on to Tregowan House. As he neared it, the front door opened. First, a woman carrying a valise emerged. She hurried away in the opposite direction to Jack. Then two men—one bulky, one lean—came out, with a struggling Beatrice held between them.

Jack's roar bounced between the houses, causing the horses hitched to the carriage waiting outside the neighbouring house to plunge with alarm. He had no time to think. No time to worry he might not be man enough, or how he would cope against two opponents. He reached for the handle of his umbrella and swiped it at the back of Belling's legs. Belling pitched forward, screaming as he landed hard on his knees. He had dragged Beatrice to the pavement with him, thereby unbalancing his accomplice, and Jack took full advantage by charging Fothergill with his shoulder, angling between him and Beatrice, forcing him to surrender his grip on her arm. Jack swung the umbrella again—for once grateful for the weight of it, with its whalebone frame and oilskin canopy—and connected with the small of Fothergill's back. He then spun around to face Belling, who was staggering to his feet, and cracked him over the head with the umbrella, following it up with a solid kick to his backside.

'Beatrice!' His chest heaved as he sucked air into his lungs.

Reinforcements, in the shape of Dolph, had arrived, and so Jack threw down the umbrella and bent to Beatrice, hooking his hand and his forearm beneath her arms to lift her to her feet. The energy still surging through his veins would not allow him to release her. Not now he had her in his arms. He manoeuvred his left arm behind her knees and swung her straight up into his arms as she pulled a length of cloth from her mouth.

'Jack!' she panted. 'Oh, thank God you came. But I am all right. I can stand up. I am unhurt.'

She wriggled, but Jack clasped her even more tightly to his chest. He gazed down into her beautiful eyes and her beloved face and gave her a crooked smile.

'Allow me to do this, Beatrice. Allow me to enjoy being the hero for once.'

She smiled, her dimples peeping out, and she wrapped her arms around his neck.

'You *are* my hero, Jack. You always were… It was only you who could not see it.'

Chapter Twenty-One

Something in Jack's chest shifted and unlocked, and he seized her lips with a heartfelt groan—a heady mix of pleasure and desire, and of pain and regret. Those last, though, were but fading echoes, for they had only been with him since last night. The pain of having to refuse a proposal from the woman he loved and the regret that in doing so he had hurt her. Now he just needed to convince her of his true feelings and to coax her to reveal hers.

He tore his lips from hers. 'Beatrice...'

But he was distracted by Dolph saying urgently, 'Shall I stop them, Kingswood? Have them arrested?'

Jack followed Dolph's pointing finger to where Fothergill was climbing into the waiting carriage.

'Oh, no. Please.' Beatrice wriggled again, and Jack, reluctantly, set her down on the ground. 'They did not succeed and I cannot bear to have everyone whispering about me. Well, any more than they already are.'

A carriage turned into the street from the Park Lane end, and Jack caught sight of Aurelia's golden head leaning out of the window.

'Here are the ladies,' said Dolph. 'They will soon have you back inside and settled, Beatrice. And then we shall discuss how we are to keep you safe from Fothergill. Although, after I have a chat with him in the morning—with your back-up, Kingswood—I hope to impress upon him the wisdom of him, his wife and his brother-in-law retiring to Somersetshire for the remainder of the Season.'

Jack faced Dolph, even as the Dolphinstone carriage drew to a halt beside them. He put his hand on Beatrice's back and noticed she was beginning to shiver, so he slid his arm around her waist and tucked her in close to his side to warm her.

'I believe I have the perfect solution to that particular dilemma, Dolph,' he said.

He went to touch Beatrice's chin and then remembered his only hand was already around her. His hesitation lasted only two beats of his heart. Beatrice already seemed to accept his disability. It was time he fully adjusted, too. So he continued the movement, using the end of his left forearm to gently turn Beatrice's face to him, so he could look into her eyes as he said this.

'If your offer still stands, Beatrice, then I should like to give you my answer now.'

Her eyes widened. 'You did answer me. You refused.'

He raised his brows, smiling. 'But I never actually said the word *No*, did I? I have been thinking about it—about *you*—all day and, if you are still of the same mind, I now say *Yes*. But only on certain terms.'

'Terms?' Leah was the first to emerge from the carriage. 'What is this? Beatrice…are you all right, my dear? Did those villains hurt you?' She gestured after Fothergill's carriage as it turned the corner on to Park Lane.

'Yes. I am all right.' Beatrice's eyes clung to Jack's even while she answered her sister. 'And, no, I am not hurt. You all should go on to the soirée.' A smile trembled around her lips. 'Jack will look after me.'

'Go to the soirée?' Aurelia had tumbled out of the carriage and now rushed to her sister, hugging her fiercely, nudging Jack aside so he had no choice but to release Beatrice. 'How can you think we can go and enjoy ourselves now? We want to know what happened.'

'And you shall.' Jack felt Beatrice grope for his hand and fold her fingers around it. 'But Jack and I have something important to discuss first. In private.'

'Oh!'

Jack saw Leah and Aurelia exchange a smile, and then he found himself under the scrutiny of four pairs of eyes.

'Well, that sounds…well…interesting,' said Mrs Butterby. 'I suggest, though, that we all go inside first, as we are presenting quite a spectacle on the doorstep and, besides, it is beginning to spit with rain again.'

'I will send our apologies to the Pooles,' said Dolph.

Once indoors, Beatrice—still clasping Jack's hand— said, 'Jack and I will talk in the morning parlour and then join the rest of you in the drawing room.'

Jack marvelled again at the rise in her confidence since her arrival in London, even if she did still dislike crowds and was reluctant to dance in public. Then her bravado cracked, just a little, as she added, 'If you do not object, that is? Only we do need—'

'Hush.' Mrs Butterby laid her palm against Beatrice's cheek. 'You have no need to gain permission, my dear. If that is what *you* need, that is all the explanation *we* need. Is that not so, ladies?'

Leah and Aurelia chorused their agreement. A blush stained Beatrice's cheeks as she beamed. 'Thank you.'

In the morning parlour her smile faded as she faced Jack. The anguish in her gentle eyes ripped at his heart and fired his rage at those bastards for putting her through such an ordeal. She had masked her distress in front of her family, but now, with him, the mask disappeared and he cherished that she trusted him enough to allow her true feelings to show.

'Bea...we will talk... I will explain myself...but first...' He opened his arms and she stepped into them without hesitation. He closed his eyes as he breathed in her lemony scent, resting his chin on the top of her head and holding her tight in his embrace.

'Thank you.' She heaved in a shuddering breath. 'Jack...what would have happened if you hadn't arrived when you did?' Her voice was muffled against his chest. 'I don't know... I keep thinking... I cannot imagine...' Her shoulders hitched as a sob erupted.

Jack cursed Fothergill and Belling—viciously and silently—as he swung Beatrice up into his arms again. He crossed to the sofa and sat down with her on his knee, her face now pressed into the angle between his neck and his shoulder, her warm tears dampening his neckcloth as her back lurched with her sobs.

'Shh. You mustn't think about it. You're safe now, sweetheart.'

It was several minutes before Beatrice pushed at Jack's arm and straightened. He handed her his handkerchief and she wiped her eyes and blew her nose.

'I am sorry. I did not mean to be so silly and weak.'

'Silly? Beatrice...my sweet, sweet Bea...you are not silly and weak. You've had a shock.' Jack tipped up her chin so he could see into her eyes. '*Did* they hurt you?'

Rage coursed through him at the very thought.

'No. I promise they did not. Although...' she gave a tearful chuckle '... I believe *I* might have hurt *them*.' Her smile was brave rather than humorous.

'Good!'

'I bashed Percy over the head with the warming pan

and the lid opened. You should have heard him scream when the hot embers showered over him.'

'You—?' Jack laughed at the image that formed in his head. 'That is wonderful! I hope they were exceedingly hot… It's no less than he deserves. And did Belling also suffer?'

'Ah.' Mischief glinted in her eyes. 'I had to scramble across the bed to get away from him. He grabbed my ankle and so I kicked back at him. My heel connected with him and, from his reaction, I believe I connected with a sensitive spot.'

Jack laughed harder. 'Priceless!' Then he sobered. 'They will never get the chance to harm you again, Bea. Not while I have breath in my body. That I swear to you.'

She stared into his eyes. 'How can you promise that? You cannot be with me every minute of every day and night.'

I want to be, though.

And it was true. He could not bear to think how close he had come to losing her. Of their own volition, his arms tightened around her, with the effect of moving her face closer to his, her lips within kissing distance. He searched her expression as he closed the gap slowly and brushed her lips with his. Immediately, she snuggled closer, her arms snaking around his neck, and she placed her mouth on his with a soft, velvety warmth that sent heady waves of longing crashing through him.

Their kiss was slow and dreamy…thoughtful and sweetly tender. But there was a shadow lurking in the corners of Jack's mind that meant he could not entirely lose himself in it. Before long, Beatrice ended the kiss herself.

'We must talk.'

'We must.'

He lifted her from his lap, feeling the chill…the absence of her warmth…as she moved away from him. He rose to his own feet and went to the fireplace, where he leaned his shoulder against the end of the mantelshelf. Beatrice had paced across the room and twitched the curtain aside to peer out before returning to face Jack, standing just out of arm's reach, her hands twisting together in front of her. He longed to touch her, to comfort her, but he did not. If he took her in his arms and told her he loved her right now, he might never discover her true thoughts. That same kind heart still beat within her breast no matter how far she had emerged from her long-ingrained habit of submission and she would naturally want to please him because she cared for him. So, he vowed to allow her to speak first and he would neither rush into comforting her nor try to coax her into agreeing with what he now knew he wanted with his whole heart.

'I want us to be honest with one another now, Bea. Do not be afraid to tell me what is in your heart.'

Her smoky eyes searched his as her hands stilled. 'My heart is easy to understand, but my head is filled with unanswered questions.'

'Questions about last night?' She nodded. 'Then ask them. Do not hold back… I shall answer honestly.' He smiled encouragingly. 'From *my* heart.'

She nibbled on her lower lip, sending Jack's pulse rocketing, and he forced his gaze to meet hers and not stray again, lest he break his own pledge not to touch her.

'Very well, then.' Her gaze slid past him to focus on the wall behind him. 'You might not have verbally refused my proposal last night, but your reaction was sufficiently clear. You were horrified. And yet now, all of a sudden, you wish to accept it.'

Jack opened his mouth to explain, but shut it again. He

would get his chance to speak. He had promised himself he would listen to her first.

'Go on,' he said.

'I feel I should be angry with you but, now we are here, I am simply confused.' She chewed her lip again, a crease forming between her brows before she sucked in a deep breath. 'I have so many questions, but what they all boil down to is this… What is the reason for your change of heart, Jack? Is it because of what happened this evening?'

The answer to her question was simple now he had finally acknowledged the love that had been growing in his heart almost since the day he'd met her. But doubts over what was in *her* heart still clawed him, even as he tried to convince himself he was being foolish. Surely, she would not respond with such honesty and passion to his kisses if she did not have feelings for him? But…what if he was mistaken? What if she merely felt sorry for him, and had grasped the opportunity to propose to him because it offered her the easiest protection against any further plots by Fothergill and Belling?

It was now he who must find his courage, with a giant step into the unknown.

Beatrice eyed Jack after asking her question. His expression had remained guarded while she spoke, but now something flickered in his blue eyes. Could it be…fear? No. Not as strong as fear, but he was undoubtedly uneasy, and she prayed that was not because he now regretted telling her he would accept her proposal.

She'd had more she wanted to say to him about the way she felt, but she'd held it inside because she was afraid Jack would be too kind to admit it if he'd accepted her proposal out of some misguided sense of obligation.

A frown creased Jack's brow. 'I will start at the end.

No, my change of heart is not because of what happened tonight. My decision was already made before I left home this evening. And the reason for it...' He pushed away from the mantelshelf and scrubbed his hand through his hair. 'I was taken completely by surprise last night, Beatrice. Your proposal came out of the blue... I never imagined...' He shook his head. 'I neither accepted nor refused. I hesitated because I was dumbfounded. Oh, I was tempted—never doubt that—but my damnable pride stopped me jumping at the chance even though my common sense told me I'd be a fool not to accept you. For all the sensible, unarguable reasons you listed.'

He paused then and Beatrice willed him to say more. He thrust his fingers through his hair again, a sure sign of his agitation. Doubts swirled in his eyes. With a muttered imprecation, he paced the room before returning to face her, his expression one of grim determination.

'But my heart... Beatrice...' His hand reached towards her, then dropped to his side again. He inhaled, his chest expanding. 'Today, I have realised nothing else matters. I have thought of nothing else but you, and my *heart* tells me to grab you and never let you go, even though my pride insists you deserve better than me.'

'*Better* than you? But...what do you mean? You are the son of a marquess...far higher in rank than me.'

Jack huffed a laugh and shook his head. 'This is not about status. There is my arm, and my income is insufficient to support a family.'

'Your *arm*? What has that to do with it?'

'How can I protect you, or our family, like this?'

'What do you call what you did tonight? You took on two able-bodied men and you vanquished them. I said it before and I'll say it again, Jack Kingswood. You. Are. My. Hero.'

Doubts still swirled in his bright eyes. His easy smile was nowhere in evidence. This was the real Jack, baring his soul. To her. Of a sudden, Beatrice could no longer face him without touching him. She needed him, his comfort and security, but first she would comfort and reassure him because she knew, from her own experience, how much strength it had taken him to speak with such honesty. She closed the space between them and laid her hand on his cheek. His hand came up and encircled her wrist, staying her.

'Not yet. There is something I must say first.' His blue gaze pinioned her, reaching deep inside, setting off a flurry of emotions. 'I love you, Beatrice Fothergill, with all my heart and soul. If your offer of marriage still stands, then I accept. If it does not…well then, I shall ask you… will you please do me the honour of being my wife?'

Beatrice breathed in his beloved scent. The words *I love you, too* hovered on her lips. But, first…

'My offer still stands,' she said. 'But you mentioned terms earlier… What are your terms?'

His lips tilted in that half-smile she adored. 'Ah, yes. My terms.'

Her heart sank momentarily at those ominous words, but leapt up again at the heat and the love in his eyes.

'Well, there is only one condition, as it happens,' he drawled. 'It is that I do not want that marriage of convenience you described. I want a marriage in every sense of the word. Can you find it in your heart to agree to that condition, Miss Fothergill?'

Beatrice smiled teasingly, tipping her head to one side. 'You drive a hard bargain, my lord—' she put her hands to his chest, feeling his muscles shift under her fingertips, and then slid them up to his shoulders and around his neck, threading her fingers through his hair as she moulded her soft curves to the contours of his body '—but I believe I can accept that particular condition.'

He smiled into her eyes as his fingers caressed her cheek. Then his eyes darkened, and his head lowered.

'Wait!'

He paused.

Beatrice tiptoed up and brushed her lips across his. 'I love you, Lord Jack Kingswood.'

'And I love you, my sweet Beatrice…she who brings happiness…bringer of joy… Never was anyone so aptly named.'

He crushed her to him, seizing her lips with a fierce hunger that shocked her with its intensity, banishing any lingering doubt as to the truth of his love.

A short while later they entered the drawing room, hand in hand. Four faces turned to them—only Spartacus, peacefully stretched out on the best chair by the fire, ignored their entrance—and four pairs of eyebrows lifted in expectation. Beatrice, although longing to stretch out the moment, could not hold her joy inside. She did not have to say anything… She simply smiled and the others' faces lit up with their own smiles as they stood as one. Leah and Aurelia rushed to Beatrice, exclaiming excitedly as they kissed and hugged her, while Dolph shook Jack's hand, clapped his back and added his congratulations to the general hubbub.

Mrs Butterby, however, crossed to the bell pull, then hovered at a discreet distance. Beatrice, still giddy with excitement, could see the chaperon's smile did not reach her eyes and, concerned, she went to her.

'Are you not happy for us, Mrs Butterby?'

'Yes! Of course I am. I did not wish to…well, to encroach on what is a family affair.'

Vardy entered at that moment and Mrs Butterby ordered a bottle of champagne to be brought to the drawing room to toast the happy couple. The butler bowed to Beatrice.

'May I offer my congratulations, Miss Fothergill? I am sure the rest of the staff will also be delighted, if I may be permitted to share your splendid news?'

'Of course, Vardy. Thank you. And, please, do open a bottle downstairs to share with the others—it would make me happy to know you are all joining in our celebration, too.'

Vardy bowed again and thanked Beatrice, but he did not immediately leave.

'If I might, Miss Fothergill… I should like to say how sorry I am for what happened tonight. It appears Maria was, somehow, complicit with those two…well, I shall not call them gentlemen. Bet said she saw Maria with a sum of money the other day and Mrs Burnham said she slipped out earlier this evening to run an urgent errand. We suspect it was to inform those scoundrels that you would be alone here this evening. It appears she opened the door for them, and she has, of course, now absconded, together with all her belongings. I can only apologise for my failing in not recognising the flaws in her character much sooner.'

'I do not hold you responsible, Vardy, I promise you. Maria made me feel uncomfortable from the start… If anyone is to blame, it is me. I should have dismissed her and found a replacement, but I kept giving her one more chance.'

'You are most generous, Miss Fothergill.'

He left the room, and Beatrice, seeing that Leah and Aurelia were excitedly chattering—no doubt happy to be organising another wedding—and that Jack was deep in conversation with Dolph, turned again to Mrs Butterby, whose comment about this being a family affair had shaken Beatrice.

'What is this nonsense about encroaching on a family affair, Mrs Butterby? Do you not know you are a part of our family? You are the linchpin that holds us steady... You are indispensable.'

To her alarm, Mrs Butterby's eyes sheened over and Beatrice realised she knew next to nothing about Mrs Butterby, other than that she had been Lady Tregowan's companion until her death, having taken the position after Beatrice's mother left.

'That is so kind, Beatrice...but I would expect no less from you. I shall miss you more than you know when you wed.'

Beatrice laughed. 'You would miss me keeping the peace between you and Aurelia, you mean. But, as it happens, Jack and I were hopeful we might live here, with you and Aurelia. The alternative is to live in his brother's house, and neither of us is keen to do so. What do you think?'

'Oh! That would be... Well, I should be delighted, and I am sure Aurelia will be as well.'

'Come.' Beatrice linked her arm through Mrs Butterby's and urged her towards the others. 'Let us ask her.'

'Did I hear my name mentioned?' Aurelia studied the pair of them. 'What are you two plotting? I warn you—I shall fight you every inch of the way if you are to gang up on me to force me, too, to wed in an obscenely short time.' She grinned, taking the sting out of her words. 'It was bad enough Leah arriving in London with her future all but sewn up, but now you have followed suit, Beatrice...' She shook her head, with an exaggerated expression of despair. 'I hope you feel suitably guilty that you'll be leaving me at the mercy of every one of those fortune-hunting nin-compoops. At least they were a shared problem before.'

Jack and Dolph had finished their conversation and they all laughed at Aurelia's words.

'Well, I hope you won't feel too abandoned, Aurelia,' Beatrice said, with a glance at Jack. He nodded, and she went on, 'We are hoping you will not object to us living here with you and Mrs Butterby?' She eyed her sister anxiously, praying she would agree, for Beatrice had no wish to move into Kit's house even though peace had now been declared between them.

'Of course I don't object, you goose.' Aurelia beamed. 'It will be fun. I really didn't want to lose you and Leah one after the other, so it will be ideal.'

'I have been thinking,' said Mrs Butterby. 'If I move into Leah's old bedchamber, then you and Jack can have the two back rooms, with their connecting door.'

'That sounds perfect, ma'am, if you are sure it will not inconvenience you too much?' Jack smiled at Beatrice. 'Dolph and I have been discussing Fothergill and Bell-ing, and we have come to the conclusion that, if you are agreeable, I will arrange a marriage licence tomorrow and we should be wed as soon as possible. Just in case they decide to try again.'

'And *that* sounds perfect to me,' said Beatrice, with a shiver of joy that soon she would be Jack's in every sense of the word.

Chapter Twenty-Two

His twin was slumped in a chair in the salon, drinking, when Jack arrived home later that evening.

'How was the soirée?' Kit leaned forward, refilled his glass and then waggled the decanter, which had an inch or so of spirit in the bottom. 'Want one?'

'Thanks. Yes, I will.' Jack fetched a clean glass from the cabinet between the windows. 'And I never actually got to the soirée.'

'Hmph. I know. I saw you not there.'

Kit frowned with concentration as he poured brandy into Jack's glass, his hand less than steady. Jack eyed him, certain that decanter had been three-quarters full after dinner that evening.

'How long have you been sitting here drinking alone?'

'Long enough. Waitin' for you. Got something to tell you.'

'Go on.'

'Lady Newcombe. Henrietta. You asked. Saw her today. Draped all over some young whippersnapper. I'm better off without her.'

'Ah.' Jack sat down. 'So she *is* the reason you stopped coming up to London.'

'Yep. She's the reason. Only now I see she was never the lady I thought I knew.' Kit drained his glass and set it down with a bump on the side table. 'God, what a damned fool I've been, brooding over a hussy like her. So…made up my mind…not goin' to brood any more. She ain't worth it.'

Jack listened as Kit told him how he had courted the young widow, how he'd planned to ask her to marry him, how he'd found her in bed with one of her footmen. How he'd hidden himself away at Wheatlands, convinced his heart was broken.

'But d'you know, Bro…when I saw her again? Nothing. That was what I felt. Absolutely nothing. No pain here…' he thumped his chest '…no ache here…' he grabbed at his crotch '…and no more regret or longing up here.' He tapped his head. 'But what I did feel was pity. For her. And pride in myself as I brushed her and her advances aside and caught up with my old friends.

'I feel better.' He grinned at Jack. 'And where have you been? I noticed the Tregowan heiresses were absent as well.'

'They were. I was with them. Fothergill and Belling tried to abduct Beatrice.'

'*Abduct?*' Kit straightened in his chair. 'Tell me what happened.'

Jack did, finishing his story with, 'And I asked Beatrice to marry me.' No one but he and Beatrice needed to know the full, muddled story. 'She accepted. I hope you will wish us well.'

'Bro…' Kit only ever called him Bro when he was drunk '… I wish you both happy. I wish I could start again with your Beatrice. I did apol'gise, didn' I?'

'You did. And she is a generous soul… She has probably already forgiven you.' Jack drained his glass and stood up. The sooner he slept, the sooner he would see Beatrice again. 'Come along, Kit, m'boy... Let's get you to bed. I need you with me in the morning.'

'Why?' Kit's brow furrowed.

'We're off to Doctors' Commons. I have a marriage licence to purchase and I'll need you as a secondary signatory on the bond they'll need to support the allegation for the licence.'

'You seem to know a lot about it. Have you done this before?'

Jack laughed. 'Of course not, you idiot. Dolph told me all about it, having been through it all so recently.'

He hauled his twin to his feet and pushed his shoulder under his armpit. With his arm around Kit's waist, Jack helped him up the stairs.

'There is one gesture you could make that would make Beatrice extremely happy,' he said as they entered Kit's bedchamber.

'Wass tha'?'

'If Mabel is agreeable, you could offer her services as lady's maid to Beatrice, after her last maid turned out a wrong 'un. I can confidently predict Beatrice will be forever grateful.'

'I'll ask her tomorrow. Now... I wanna sleep.'

Taylor was already in the room, waiting to help Kit undress. He exchanged a speaking look with Jack when he saw Kit's inebriated state and Jack remembered that he had never actually got around to questioning the valet about Kit's distrust of women as he'd intended. He'd been too preoccupied with his own woman to even think of it again. He was glad now he'd forgotten... It was so much better that Kit had worked out his own problems for himself and had confided voluntarily in Jack.

'Can you wake His Lordship around nine in the morning, Taylor? I need him to come with me. I have a marriage licence to arrange.'

Taylor's face split in a huge grin. 'Congratulations, my lord. Everyone here will be thrilled…especially Mabel. And I am sure she will jump at the chance to work for Miss Fothergill.'

Jack grinned back, still barely able to believe his good fortune. 'Thank you. And goodnight to you both.'

The only answer from Kit was a gentle snore from where he lay sprawled across the bed.

It was one o'clock the following afternoon by the time Jack rapped on the door of Tregowan House, a licence for his marriage to Beatrice—complete with the Archbishop of Canterbury's seal—tucked securely in his pocket. The licence, obtained from the Prerogative Court of Canterbury that morning, enabled them to marry without having to wait for the banns to be read, for which Jack was profoundly grateful—not only for the sake of Beatrice's safety, but also for the sake of his sanity, for he could not wait to claim her as his own. But that thought raised another spectre in his mind. It was all very well Beatrice talking of him as a man with one arm, but how would she react at the sight of his arm when she first saw the sewn-up stump halfway between his elbow and where his wrist had been. Plus, he also must learn how to make love to a woman with the use of only one hand.

Impatiently, he thrust his doubts aside as Vardy held the door wide for him.

'Miss Fothergill is in what will be your bedchamber, my lord, if you would care to join her?' Vardy said.

Jack stared at the butler, momentarily dumbfounded. Vardy permitted himself a small smile. 'She and Mrs But-

terby have been moving her belongings to Lady Dolphinstone's former bedchamber.'

'Ah. Yes. Of course. Thank you.'

Jack climbed the stairs and followed the sound of voices
to an open doorway from which Mrs Butterby—her arms
full of clothing and followed by a maid, her arms equally
loaded—emerged, speaking back over her shoulder.

'We shall stay in my new room now and get everything
tidied away, Beatrice, if you do not need any further help
in there,' the chaperon was saying. She saw Jack then.
'Good morning, Lord Jack.'

Jack bowed. 'And a very good morning to you, Mrs
Butterby.'

'Oh! Jack…'

He could hear Beatrice's smile in her voice, even before she came into view. When she did, his heart clenched
as love for her hit him anew. She looked adorable, wearing an apron over her gown and holding a feather duster,
her hair delightfully dishevelled and a faint smut on the
tip of her nose.

'You have arrived at precisely the right time! That is
the last of Prue's belongings—Mrs Butterby has asked us
all to call her Prue, by the way… Isn't that wonderful, for
now we are even more of a family? But I digress… The
problem is we are short-staffed now, which is why we are
all helping. Well, we were all helping, but Aurelia had to
go out urgently, with Bet, her maid. And…oh, but I must
look a mess.' She discarded the duster and tucked several
tumbling locks behind her ears. 'You are here just in time,
though—you need to decide if you wish for any of the furniture to be moved around before your belongings arrive.'

She stopped speaking abruptly and drew a visible
breath. 'I am sorry. I have attacked you with all this in-

formation before even greeting you.' Her speech was slower…less frantic… 'It is excitement.'

She put her hands on his shoulders and tilted her face to his, her gaze lowering to his mouth. Jack needed no further encouragement. He wrapped his arms around her waist and pulled her close as he claimed her lips, his tongue tracing their soft fullness. She opened to him and he plunged inside, passion rising up within him with an urgency he was helpless to resist. He walked her backwards into the bedchamber and kicked the door behind him shut as his fingers worked the bow securing her apron. His tongue still exploring her mouth, he eased her body from his and slipped the apron from her shoulders and down her arms. She gasped into his mouth as he pulled her body tight to his again, his hand carving through her hair, holding her head still as he continued to plunder her mouth.

That gasp penetrated the lust that had seized him. He tore his lips from hers although he did not…*could* not… release her. He wanted her close to him, under him, skin to skin…but she was untried. An innocent. And she would be his wife soon. He did not want to frighten her with his eagerness but, oh, how he wanted her. Now. He tipped his head until his forehead rested against hers, his breathing harsh in the quiet of the room. But just as he mustered the words to apologise, she arched against him, pressing her belly to his aroused manhood, reigniting the passion firing his blood.

'Not here,' she whispered. 'Come.' She grabbed his hand and snatched up the discarded apron, then tugged him through a door that led into another bedchamber. She locked the door and smiled up at him, a teasing glint in her eyes. 'This is *my* bedchamber and you now know I can lock you out if you misbehave.' She captured his gaze then, her eyes dark with longing. 'No one will come in here.'

She slid her palms beneath his coat and caressed his chest before tiptoeing up to kiss him again. Jack closed his eyes in slight desperation—the sole restraint on his lust had been that thought he was driving her too fast. If she took over the reins and began to set her own pace, would he...*could* he...keep control?

Yet...must I keep control if this is what we both want? We marry tomorrow...

Permission given, decision made, he hoisted her up in his arms and, lips still joined, he crossed to the bed, lowered her and followed her down, half covering her as he propped himself up on his left elbow. She felt so good to his touch, her skin soft and smooth and warm and scented... His lips traced a path across her delicate jaw, nibbling and caressing as she tilted her head to expose her neck. As he laved the sensitive skin behind her ear, she emitted small moans that further fired his blood. He tugged her fichu free and cast it aside before pushing her bodice off her shoulder and exposing her breast. He stopped feasting on her mouth to feast his eyes.

'You are perfect,' he murmured, taking in the generous mound tipped by a nipple the same blush pink as her lips.

His mouth watered as he gently squeezed her. She felt perfect, too—her pebbled nipple teasing his palm as he kneaded her soft flesh. He lowered his head, flicking her with his tongue, relishing her quiet gasp and the clutch of her fingers in his hair. He grazed her with his teeth and then sucked her deep into his mouth, his tongue swirling. She arched up against him, moaning her pleasure, and sheer masculine satisfaction ripped through him. When he released her nipple, he admired the glistening pink tip, then lifted his eyes to meet her heavy-lidded gaze.

Her hands slipped between them, splayed across his chest, and then she was pushing his coat from his shoulders. Jack reared back, blanking her murmur of displeasure. He scrubbed his hand through his hair before he grabbed his courage and met her questioning gaze. They were to marry. There would only be one time to endure this. He shrugged out of his coat himself and her lips curved. He began to tug his shirt from his breeches before pulling it off, but it wasn't the smooth motion it had been with two hands. The heat of embarrassment swarmed through him...but Beatrice sat up and then scrambled to her knees.

'I love you so very much, Jack,' she whispered. Her breath against his skin sent waves of gooseflesh rippling across his body. 'I want to undress you. I want to love you in every sense. I need you to show me. To teach me.'

Her words relaxed him as, between them, they pulled his shirt over his head. He watched her face, anxiety knotting his stomach. Her gaze roamed his chest and she wet her lips with the tip of her tongue as she stroked. Then her attention moved to his shoulders and his upper arms as she traced the shape of his muscles and then squeezed his biceps. Her eyes then dropped to his stump and every one of Jack's muscles tensed, waiting for her reaction.

'May I touch you? I do not want to hurt you.'

She raised her gaze to his. No disgust. No sympathy or pity such as he'd dreaded, but pure love with a touch of curiosity.

'It only really hurts if it gets knocked.'

She smiled. 'Then I promise I will be gentle.'

She stroked from his elbow to the still-healing scar at the end of his stump and cupped her hand around it. The she took his breath away as she gently urged it higher and she leaned down and caressed it with her lips.

'I imagined it far worse.'

And I imagined your reaction far worse.

He should have trusted her. He knew her... How had he imagined she would react with anything but kindness and acceptance?

She lifted her gaze and captured his, her smoky eyes widening and darkening. Her lips curved in a sexy, confident smile.

'Now, Lord Jack Kingswood.' Her voice was husky and lust roared through him. 'Where were we?'

Chapter Twenty-Three

The next day

The bridal gown was of striped French gauze over a white satin slip with a deep flounce of Brussels lace surmounted by a single tuck of bias white satin and a wreath of pale pink silk roses. The bodice was cut low at both back and front, exposing the shoulders and her décolletage, and with short melon sleeves trimmed with pink ribbon.

'You look beautiful, Bea,' breathed Leah as she fastened a pearl necklace around Beatrice's neck.

Beatrice blushed as she pulled on her elbow-length white kid gloves and held up her arms for Mabel to fasten the pair of pearl bracelets around her arms. She smiled her thanks at Mabel in the mirror, so happy the maid had agreed to come and work for her.

'You may go now. My sisters will help me to finish getting ready.'

The Tregowan House servants, as well as Kit's staff from his London house, were invited to attend the ceremony and they were to walk to Grosvenor Chapel, which was just around the corner in South Audley Street.

'Thank you,' she said now to Leah. 'And so do you and

Aurelia.' She twisted to look round at her sisters, Aurelia in pale pink and Leah in lilac, and they all shared smiles of delight. 'Never did a bride have such stunning attendants. I am so very fortunate.'

Leah stepped back and Aurelia took her place, tutting at Beatrice.

'Stop fidgeting,' she ordered, 'while I fit your tiara in place.'

She placed the diamond-and-pearl ornament—a wedding gift from Jack—on the crown of Beatrice's head and stepped back to view the result. 'Beautiful indeed,' she said, with a decisive nod. 'Absolutely gorgeous. Your Jack won't believe his luck when he sees you walking up the aisle towards him.'

At the mention of the ceremony to come, Beatrice's tummy teemed with butterflies.

But why am I nervous? It will only be my family there...and they all love me and I love them. And now— she hugged her secret close—*I don't even have to worry about the wedding night.*

She was a woman now in every sense of the word and she was looking forward to her wedding night with unbecoming eagerness. If her sisters could read her mind... Her cheeks burned at the very idea and at the memory of how she had seduced Jack yesterday in this very room. His sudden uncertainty had driven her to put aside her shyness and entice him into continuing his lovemaking. And she had learned the lesson that, although Jack was a man and strong in so many ways, there were times when *she* must be strong for *him*. And the awareness of the vulnerability he took such pains to hide beneath his confident humour only increased her love for him.

Mrs Butterby—*Prue!* Beatrice still wasn't accustomed to calling her that—rushed in, dressed in a deep blue gown and a turban with a plume of feathers pinned to the front.

'The carriage has arrived,' she gasped. 'Come along. You do not want to be late, Beatrice.'

'Yes, she does,' said Aurelia, pressing down on Beatrice's shoulders as she made to rise from her stool. 'It will not hurt Lord Jack to wait a few minutes for his bride. It will make him all the more eager and help him to appreciate her all the more.'

Beatrice gazed at her reflection in the mirror—her lips tucked between her teeth as she held her giggle at bay; her dimples, that Jack had told her he adored; her eyes, sparkling like the diamonds in her tiara. Jack had left her in no doubt exactly how much he appreciated her yesterday, after they had made love. And she had left him in no doubt exactly how much she loved him. Her man.

She counted to ten, very slowly, and then she rose to her feet.

'It is time.' She gazed at the other three women. Women she loved with a deep, abiding affection that she was certain would only grow stronger over the years ahead of them. 'Thank you all.'

The carriage ride was a matter of minutes, and it seemed almost before Beatrice could draw breath, she was walking up that aisle, her eyes glued to Jack, who turned to watch her, his smile, for once, not easy, but brilliant. His eyes not merely bright, but glowing. His strong body—the body she had learned could give her such pleasure, and which she had only just begun to learn how to pleasure in return. She now knew what lay beneath those impeccably tailored clothes and the memory made her mouth water.

Her husband-to-be. Her hero. Her beloved.

Not a marriage of convenience, but a union built from love.

Not a husband who would merely tolerate her, but a

husband who loved and cherished her for herself, not for her inheritance.

Not an unequal marriage, but a partnership in every sense of the word as they would work together to help others less fortunate than themselves.

And when Beatrice spoke the words *'I do'* they rang out loud and true and full of confidence, for she meant them with every fibre of her heart and her soul.

* * * * *

If you enjoyed this story, be sure to read the first book in Janice Preston's Lady Tregowan's Will miniseries

The Rags-to-Riches Governess

And whilst you're waiting for the next book, why not check out her other great reads

The Earl with the Secret Past
Lady Olivia and the Infamous Rake
Daring to Love the Duke's Heir
Christmas with His Wallflower Wife

And look out for the next book in the Lady Tregowan's Will miniseries, coming soon!